Acknowledgments

I send my sincere and heartfelt thanks to the following individuals who helped make Desert Jade a reality: to Ed Szeremet for his lovely cover photo. See more Ed's work at desertargonaut.com; to Lynne East Itkin (lmeastdesign.com/) and Ryn Shane-Armstrong (rynshanearmstrong.com) for very excellent cover design; to Steve Passiouras at Bookow for making everything easier; and to Diane C. Taylor (dianesfusedglass.com). When Diane isn't creating fused glass art, she is an amazingly skillful copyeditor and proofreader who made Desert Jade a much better book. Thanks, too, to those individuals who kindly helped me with cultural and language questions. Finally, my deep appreciation goes to those Indiegogo supporters who brought Letty Valdez to life.

Please sign up for my email newsletter on art, books and the natural world HERE>
https://www.cjshane.com/contactnewsletter.html

Letty Valdez Mysteries

Desert Jade 2017
Dragon's Revenge 2018
Daemon Waters 2019
Direct Evidence 2022

Cat Miranda Mysteries

Kissed 2020
Fair Play 2021
The Broken Pot 2022

DESERT JADE

C.J. SHANE

Rope's End Publishing

Published by Rope's End Publishing

ISBN:
978-0-9993874-0-5 hardcover
978-0-9993874-1-2 trade paperback
978-0-9993874-2-9 epub
978-0-9993874-3-6 mobi Kindle

Typesetting services by BOOKOW.COM

CONTENTS

CHAPTER ONE

Mɪᴅ-Dᴇᴄᴇᴍʙᴇʀ: Chukut Kuk District, Tohono O'odham Reservation, Pima County, Arizona

The girl watched the footprints fade away into nothingness in the sandy soil. Looking left and right, and then back from where she'd come, she searched carefully for any sign of human passage. There was always hope that she might pick up their trail again. It had been early morning since she'd actually seen the others. As she fell behind, she began following their footprints, thinking that she might catch up with them when they stopped for a rest.

Now she knew that would not happen. There was no sign of them. She knew now that she was lost – lost and alone in this strange desert place. Taking one step, then another, she continued walking slowly toward the north. She followed a low, wide area that looked like it might have once held a stream of water. Now the dirt was completely dry and very sandy. Scrubby sad-looking trees with thin green limbs and feathery leaves were scattered here and there across her field of vision. They were nothing like the tall, vine-covered trees with thick clouds of emerald green leaves in her faraway mountain home. And it was so quiet here. She could hear only a soft breeze and the occasional cry of a hawk.

The sun inched higher in the sky. Despite the fact that it was winter now, the low desert seemed warm to her, almost hot. The sun was intense and so much hotter than her mountain homeland so far to the south. She pulled her red-striped cotton rebozo, her shawl, around her head to shield her eyes from the intensity of the light. Soon it would be noon and time to eat again. She had a little food left in her bag, but she wasn't hungry. She was thirsty. Really thirsty.

Water. That was the problem. Her water bottles were empty. She drank the last ounce over an hour ago. She was thirsty again. Again? She'd never stopped being thirsty since she came into this godforsaken desert.

What she would give to be home again in the highlands, to step into one of the mountain streams and immerse herself in the cool water, to float lazily in the pools, to try to catch a fish in her hands, to play hide-and-seek with her little brothers among the rocks on the banks of the river.

She shook herself and mentally said no. She must not think of that cool, pleasing wetness in this unbearably dry, sun-drenched desert.

For the thousandth time, she thought instead of the one who brought her and the others across the border in the night. The coyote. That's what the smuggler called himself – a coyote. He told her and the others that the barbed wire was the border. He led them across a six-strand barbed wire fence about two in the morning. The coyote said the fence marked the place where Mexico became America.

What did migrants know? It could have been the back pasture of some Mexican farm for all she was concerned. In the faint light of a crescent moon, it all looked the same. The only thing pleasing in this dry desert country was the sky. She had never seen so many stars. There must have been a million or two million glittering in the inky black sky. There were more stars than all the saints in heaven. And it was cold. When the sun went down, the temperature dropped rapidly, and she struggled to stay warm.

She took more steps, slower now. Al norte. That's all she knew. She was going al norte.

There were fourteen of them in the group. They had all paid their hard-earned cash to the coyote to lead them away from La Migra, out of sight of those border agents in their green uniforms and white trucks. She paid him all that hard-earned money saved by her family to lead her to safety, to an American city, to a job and to riches beyond her wildest dreams.

She imagined filling an envelope full of money and sending it to her papa. He would know what to do. He would go to see a doctor and buy himself some medicine and perhaps then he could get well. Her mama would go to the market and buy food, lots of food. Masa harina for the tortillas, avocados, and frijoles, and chiles, and maybe even some cheese and some meat, too, to put in the soup. Everyone in her family would have enough to eat and then a second helping if they wanted it.

Her brothers and sisters would have shoes for the first time in their lives. Maybe they could buy books and pencils and notebooks and go to school down in the valley for the first time. Maybe they could have a toy or two. Yes, she would buy a doll for each of her sisters. That would make them very happy.

When she came home to visit from her job in the city, she would wear a beautiful pink dress. She would paint her nails pink and wear pink lipstick like the models in the magazine she saw once. She would invite her brothers and sisters and all her cousins, maybe even all the other children in the village. She would invite them to go with her to Sylvia's corner store for an ice cream, and she would pay for everyone.

She was the oldest. She would show her brothers and sisters and all the other children how brave and bold she was. She would tell in great detail the tale of her two-week journey north, of crossing the border in the night, of the long, long walk through the sunny desert, of finding a job in the city, and of sending money home. They would be very proud of her.

On the night that she first gathered together with the others in the little border town, when they met the coyote for the first time, he told them that it was only a two-hour walk to Tucson. She knew even then that he was lying. She could hear it in his voice and see it in his eyes. So she put in two extra plastic bottles of water and a little extra food. Her bag would weigh more, but she accepted that.

She knew she might need all that water. She was right. She needed that and a whole lot more.

Mentiras, mentiras, mentiras. Lies, lies, lies, she said to herself in time with her footsteps. Men-tir-as, men-tir-as. Uno-dos–tres. Men-tir-as. Uno-dos-tres. Men-tir-as. Two hours walking to Tucson, she laughed derisively.

She'd been walking now for three days in this great light-filled desert that was too dusty and dry in the day and too cold in the night.

May the Holy Mother curse him for his lies, she whispered to herself.

The coyote smuggler was long gone, of course. He had disappeared before the light of morning on the very first day.

They crossed over the border in the night and kept going well into the first day until they were too tired to take more steps. They rested in what shade they could find under the miserable thin little trees, then they moved on in the late afternoon and into evening until exhaustion overtook them. The evenings were the best. It was cool then, but not cold. The stars in the black sky seemed like tiny fishes swimming in a deep dark lake. So many more stars than in the misty mountains where she came from. But then the cold came seeping in, and she struggled to stay warm.

On the second day, the group began to fall apart. They stretched out over a mile, following the wide, low rocky wash that held water only in the most violent of summer monsoon rain storms. She'd been told about the monsoon storms, about their wild fury, about how there was no place to go to seek shelter. She'd been warned to get out of the washes quickly if there was any sign of rain upstream. The deluge could come upon her suddenly and wash her away to her death. She found it hard to believe that so much water could appear so suddenly in this desert. And yet that is what some in her group told her, the ones who had made crossings before this one.

The group broke into smaller and smaller groups on that second day. They began to trudge along either alone or in couples. One woman ahead of her was carrying an infant. To die in the desert with your child was a great tragedy, she thought. She was grateful that she at least was spared the agony of seeing a child go silent and shrivel from no water. She thought of her little brother Diego. He was twelve and thought himself old enough to go north. He'd begged her to take him with her. She was so glad now that she had refused. I will send for you, she promised him. If she died in this hellish place, at least her parents would lose only one child.

Ay ay ay, she whispered to herself. Just for one cold drink, no, not cold, just a drink of water. It need not be cold. The juice of the pineapple, licuado de piña, thick and wet, eating a peeled mango on a stick, the juice dripping down her chin. Yes. Pink wet melon in the summer evenings. Spitting out the seeds. Un cafécito in the morning, jugo de naranja at lunch, She asked for none of that. Just a simple cup of water from the stream above where the women washed their clothes on the rocks – that's all she wanted. The light shone on the water and butterflies skimmed over the surface even now. She could see it there just beyond her reach.

Ahead for miles and miles, she could see only more of the same. Now it was midday. The heat created shimmering waves of light on the horizon. It looked like a lake of water. There was no lake. The ones who had been here before told her about that, too – the mirages of water where there was no water at all. They told her that she could walk for miles seeking the mirage, but she would never find it.

She sighed again and wished that she'd never left her home, never left her mama and papa and little brothers and sisters. Would they know what had happened to her if she never returned? Perhaps she should be praying to the Virgin for deliverance or, better yet, Saint Jude, the patron saint of lost causes. Yes, Saint Jude, because she was certain now that she would die in this place. Only a miracle could deliver her.

No, I must not give up. I will not die in this place.

Her muscles were cramping. Yes, she needed a little rest in the shade. Just rest now beneath this skinny green tree with its skinny,

skinny leaves. Even the leaves try to hide from the sun. Almost no shade. Dios mio.

She began to sing an old folk song from the Revolution taught to her by her old great-grandfather. He knew. He knew the song and the Revolution. He knew Emiliano Zapata. He fought with the Zapatistas before Emiliano was gunned down.

"La cucaracha, la cucaracha. Ya no puede caminar." Her voice sounded thin and weak, even to her. She giggled. If she had a cucaracha right now, she would eat that little cockroach, six legs and all. Maybe the little cucaracha would be full of water. She giggled again at the idea of drinking water from a bug.

Far away to the east, she could see a range of purple mountains on the horizon. Clouds caught on the peaks and relieved themselves of their water burden. Rain. Rain. What would it be like to stand there in the rain clouds and feel the wet all around you? To open your mouth and let it fill with raindrops? Her throat hurt.

Would her mama know that the angels had carried her away from this hell into a heaven of lakes and rivers, to the mountaintop and into the rain cloud?

Dios mio! So thirsty. Although it took considerable effort, she again searched her woven bag. She removed the cap from the last water bottle and lifted the bottle it to her lips. One drop fell onto her tongue.

She sang again. "Ya no puede caminar. Por que no tiene. Por que le falta. Marijuana que fumar." Her voice floated away in the dry wind. She thought she heard someone giggling again at the amusing words. She tried to look around to see if someone was there, but she was too weak.

Time passed. The sun moved around to begin its descent toward the western horizon.

She leaned against the palo verde tree which gave her a patch of wispy shade. Her eyes closed after a while. She was so thirsty. She fell into unconsciousness.

* * *

The cool touch of a wet cloth on her face woke her. She opened her eyes.

He was here. The Angel had arrived. Come to take her away, away from the desert to the mountaintop rain cloud. Take her to heaven. He was watching her with his dark eyes and waiting for her to wake up and go with him.

She tried to smile and speak to him, but she was so weak and so thirsty.

The Angel was not what she expected. He did not look like the angels painted on the walls of the old church in the valley where she took her first communion. He looked like an *indio* with his black eyes and long black hair tied back with a strip of cloth. His skin was brown like the men in her village. He had no wings like the angels painted on the church wall. He wore blue jeans and a cotton shirt.

So what does that matter? So what if he wore a cowboy hat? Who was she to say what an angel should look like? Do angels ride horses now? Are angels young, dark-eyed and brown-skinned, and handsome, too?

She smiled at the thought of an angel galloping off to heaven on the back of a horse. In the native language of her childhood, she muttered a greeting to the dark Angel. Then she closed her eyes. Vague consciousness gave way to a soft sound of whirling wind as darkness enveloped her again, and her body slumped backwards against the tree.

* * *

Eduardo Ramone dismounted gracefully from his mare. He pulled his sunglasses from their precarious perch on his hat and slipped them into his shirt pocket. Removing his pack from the saddle, he retrieved a bottle of water, the last full one. All the while he never took his eyes from the girl lying beneath the palo verde tree. The water bottle, and two more just like it, had been much cooler when he started out from his grandmother's place. Now the water in the bottle was getting tepid and well on its way to becoming warm. Just right, he thought. Too cool would be bad for her.

Before he had approached her, he looked around to see if there were other migrants nearby. He could see no footprints other than hers. Not wanting to stir up rattlesnakes and get himself bitten, he carefully scanned the ground around her, and listened for a warning rattle. Snake-bitten meant he would be of no use to her at all. He saw and heard nothing. He stepped toward the girl.

A young one. He guessed mid- to late-teens, even younger than his nineteen years. He shook his head slightly. Seems like these border crossers are getting younger and younger, he thought to himself. More and more females, too. It used to be just the men that came north. Now it's the women, often with children. Sometimes he saw entire families driven by the desperation of poverty to leave life in their villages and go north.

The law said that he was supposed to report the illegals to the Border Patrol. Mostly he didn't. If they weren't in trouble from heat and lack of water, Eduardo figured that he'd leave them to their fate. He replenished their water, and he told them where to find the water stations that had been put up by Tucson humanitarian groups. He pointed them in the right direction to wherever they said they wanted to go.

But if the migrants were in trouble, too sick and too dehydrated to go on, then he called the reservation police or the Border Patrol. There was no other option. They would die if he left them out there in the desert. The Border Patrol deported them, of course, after they were full of water and on their feet again. The migrants would wait a day or two on the other side, and then they would try again to cross the border in the dark. Maybe the next time they'd have more luck, and make it to the cities and to the waiting jobs.

Eduardo squatted on his heels next to the girl and looked her over. He watched the rise and fall of her chest and saw that her breathing was rapid and shallow. His long brown fingers reached out and touched her cheek and brow. She was too warm. She looked very dehydrated.

Once, only once in the hottest month, the month of June, he found a man who was too far gone. Eduardo was still haunted by the experience. The man's skin felt like fire, a fever beyond belief, when Eduardo touched him. The man was middle-aged, small, dark-skinned, babbling in Spanish, out of his mind with delirium, his brain and organs cooking inside his body. The man had gone into convulsions and died before Eduardo could get him to medical aid. Eduardo frowned and shook his head to clear it of the specter.

This one, though, it looked like she wasn't so far gone. Maybe Eduardo could save her. Just maybe.

She was pretty, too. Long dark hair, dusky skin. Looked like a native, just like himself. Not O'odham. Not a desert Indian. Probably she was from one of those southern tribes in Mexico or even farther south, Guatemala maybe. Her simple cotton clothing told him little more than that she was a peasant. Full cotton print skirt, simple white blouse, red rebozo, a hand-woven bag with long shoulder strap, and some cheap canvas shoes.

She looked like what she was, a dirt-poor, uneducated, inexperienced, innocent peasant girl from some isolated village come north looking for a minimum wage job cleaning toilets. Instead she was led like a little chicken into the desert by a greedy people-smuggler. Now she's lying here dying a slow miserable death. Eduardo calculated that only one more day like this, and she'd be beyond his help.

She was lucky that he'd even seen her. Eduardo usually didn't come this way. It was rocky, and there were often snakes down close to the wash under the trees. He didn't want his horse getting spooked by the rattlers. But he was in a hurry today. He meant to leave his grandmother's house earlier in the day, but she asked him to help her with chopping some mesquite for her cook stove. He ended up staying for lunch, then lying down for a little siesta. He didn't leave his grandmother's place until the late afternoon.

Wanting to make it to his uncle's before dark, he took the shortcut across the wash. Just as he and his horse entered the wash, a wild coyote appeared suddenly on the bank, stared brazenly at Eduardo, then disappeared. That's when Eduardo saw a flutter of red. A little breeze had come up and caught the migrant girl's red rebozo. He saw the fluttering movement out of the corner of his eye, looked that way, and there was a young woman's body crumpled beneath a palo verde tree.

Looking at her lying there, Eduardo suddenly felt very sad for all the poor people in the world who died here just trying to find a way to make a better life for themselves and their families. He felt sad for this one here at his feet who was flirting so dangerously with death. A sudden firm determination came over him.

"Don't give up hope yet, chica. I'm not going to let you die," Eduardo said gently.

He bent forward and pulled the girl to a sitting position. She didn't regain consciousness so Eduardo leaned her back against the palo verde tree trunk. He pulled a red cotton bandana from his pocket and poured some water on it, then put the wet cloth to her throat and face.

For a brief moment, the girl's eyes opened, and then she fainted again. He continued pressing the wet cloth to her dry skin.

As he tried to revive the young woman, Eduardo contemplated the meaning of what was happening here. He was attempting to save a life, and he would save hers, God willing, or I'itoi willing, or whatever god or cosmic awareness might be listening to his wordless prayer as he worked to save the girl's life.

The movements of his hands and the intentions of his heart were deeply felt. It meant something to save a dying life, even if his own life had been so confused and without direction as of late. Eduardo didn't seem to fit in anywhere, not at school when he was younger and not at a job now. He didn't like studying, and he was profoundly relieved when he finally graduated from high school. He had no job that meant much to him. He worked just when he needed to at odd jobs or helping out on the reservation's ranches. Working with horses was enjoyable. They talked to him with their big eyes. Sometimes he went into Tucson and stayed at his big sister Letty's house for a few days to find temporary construction jobs. He didn't like the city, but the pay was better. Those jobs meant he could take back home a little money to his grandmother or to give a little to his aunt and uncle. He did the best he could.

All Eduardo really wanted to do was wander around on horseback on the vast Tohono O'odham reservation, nearly three million acres stretching across southern Arizona. Watching Hawk and Owl and Rabbit and Coyote, watching the rain clouds come over Baboquivari Peak, watching the thick white petals appear on the saguaro blossoms, watching the sun come and go in the sky, watching the changing of the seasons, remembering the old stories, and talking to the elders about the old ways – this was the center of his life. He didn't give a damn about television and driving into Tucson to see a movie or go to the mall. Sometimes he felt like he was born five centuries too late. He felt like an Indian only comfortable in an Indian world – a world that didn't exist anymore. He was lonely most of the time.

Eduardo wasn't like Elena, his twin sister. The stories that people told about the closeness of twins were true of Elena and Eduardo. They were inseparable growing up. Sometimes they could feel each other's feelings, and they seemed to be in psychic connection with each other, even at a distance.

Yet they were so different. Elena was daring in a way that Eduardo would never be. She put herself forward and sought out adventure. She fit into the *Milga:n* world without losing her O'odham self. She loved school and was very good at it. She won a scholarship and went off to the university. She was headed to a career and success. She found a young man who adored her. Eduardo was happy for Elena. He could feel her joy. At the same time, he missed her. And he wished again that he, too, could find something that worked for him.

Maybe Eduardo could do as well as his Uncle Armando who patched together a living from the land. Uncle Mando ran some cattle, had a small orchard of pecan trees for a cash crop, did odd jobs like Eduardo, patched up other people's old cars and refrigerators and swamp coolers and kept those machines working. It was whatever came Mando's way. Aunt Valerina helped out, too.

Mando did a good job of surviving in the *Milga:n* world, and still he maintained his indigenous identity. Maybe Eduardo would figure out how to do as well someday.

As Eduardo swabbed the young woman's cheeks and forehead with the cool, wet cloth, he wondered if maybe this was what his life was all about. He might not fit into the *Milga:n* world like Elena, but he could find a dying person in the desert and save a life. Or, at least, he could save *this* life, this one here and now.

Eduardo had to re-wet the bandana frequently because it dried so fast in the arid air. The girl's eyelids flickered. He continued for several minutes to wipe her throat, her face, her neck, and her arms. He felt a little tension in her arms and hands. That meant she was coming around. He worked patiently. Eventually the girl's dark eyes opened and focused. She looked into Eduardo's eyes.

"Angelito," the girl said weakly. She gazed into his face as he continued to gently bathe her throat and arms.

"Ya viene por mi, Angelito? Va portarme al cielo?" She spoke in Spanish, a heavily-accented, rural peasant Indian Spanish.

Eduardo grinned. "Well...you might say I've come for you. But I'm not taking you to heaven. I'll take you to my Uncle Mando's house instead. He and Valerina can help you.....And I'm no angel." The thought that she imagined him to be angel was very amusing. If she were here, his twin sister Elena would be laughing out loud.

He reached again for the water bottle and offered it to her. She was so weak that she couldn't take it from him so he put one arm around her neck and held her head as he used the other hand to hold the bottle to her lips. She drank greedily. Drops of water spilled down her chin as she gulped.

"Whoa, slow down, chica." He pulled the bottle away and then tilted it so that she could only sip a little at a time. "You'll make yourself sick if you drink too fast."

She began to drink in little sips only because he wouldn't let her do otherwise.

"What's your name?" he asked.

The girl looked up at him blankly. Her eyes were very big and dark brown, the lashes thick.

"Uh...como te llamas?" Eduardo asked again. He understood her when she spoke, but he realized that he had been speaking to her in English.

As a child, Eduardo had spoken Spanish often, especially when he went south across the border to visit Gonzolo who was a distant relative on his dad's side of the family. The old man spoke only Spanish and the O'odham language which the *Milga:n* used to call Papago. The relative was already an old man when Eduardo visited him. Gonzolo let Eduardo ride his horses. That was where Eduardo learned to love horses.

Besides riding the horses, the best part of visiting Gonzolo was hearing the stories that the old man told. The two of them sat in handmade rocking chairs in front of the old adobe house in the evenings and watched the sun set. Gonzolo told Eduardo about I'itoi and how he killed the old witch Ho'ok and about how Ban the Coyote got tricked by Rabbit and lots of other really good stories. Eduardo liked those old stories a lot. The old man told the stories in the O'odham language, but the rest of the time, he spoke to Eduardo in Spanish. Eduardo had been pretty good at understanding and speaking it. But when the old man died, Eduardo quit going down south, and his Spanish got rusty. Now he only spoke English and sometimes a little of his own O'odham tongue with the old timers and tribal elders and with his grandmother.

"Como te llamas?" Eduardo asked again with more confidence.

A little color was back in the girl's cheeks.

Maybe if he could get her somewhere safe so he could get more liquids in her, she would be okay. The muscles in his shoulders began to relax a little in relief.

"Esperanza Morales," she said shyly.

"Esperanza Morales," Eduardo repeated. "Esperanza? Hope? That's your name? I guess that's about all you have left is hope." He grinned at her and the girl smiled back weakly. She had dimples in her brown cheeks. Very pretty, Eduardo thought.

"Welcome to America, Hope," he said.

Eduardo rose to his feet, bringing her up with him. He carefully held her against him, and he half-guided, half-carried her to his mare. Mounting easily, Eduardo reached down to pull her up to sit behind him. He pulled Esperanza's slender arms around his waist and felt her muscles respond. She was holding on. As Eduardo guided his horse away from the wash and toward the northeast, he could feel Esperanza lean forward until her head rested against his shoulders.

"Angelito," he heard her murmur, and Eduardo laughed. He liked it a lot that she thought he was an angel.

CHAPTER 2

SOMETHING was wrong.

Jade Lopez opened her eyes, closed them, then opened them again. She forced herself to keep them open as she fought against the grogginess caused by her nap.

Something had awakened her, but she wasn't sure what it was.

It was a late afternoon in December not long before sunset. Jade was on the roof of her adobe house in midtown Tucson lying on a mat under the overhanging branches of an old and very large mesquite tree. The roof was her haven, her secret place where she went to relax and to think about things. An old ladder handmade of thick mesquite branches was propped up against the back of her house. The ladder was the entry to her sanctum. She went there nearly every afternoon after work when the weather was cool. Later in the year the days would be so hot that the roof would ripple with heat despite the shade from the overhanging branches. Winter afternoons were perfect though. From the flat roof, Jade could watch the setting sun casting late-afternoon light on the Santa Catalina Mountains to the north, turning their ridges and canyons into shimmering colors of copper and red and deep purple. The colors changed as the sun lowered in the December sky, and her appreciative eyes enjoyed every nuance of the changing light on the mountains and in the clear desert sky above her – gold, magenta, pink, silver, mauve. Jade loved the desert winter sky.

Earlier that afternoon, Jade said goodbye to her fellow teachers and a few straggling students at Moreno Elementary School.

"Merry Christmas! Feliz Navidad!" she called out to them cheer-fully. Tying her long unruly red hair back with a scarf, she put on her helmet and climbed onto her bike. She headed home happy but exhausted.

The children had been so excited all day that they spent most of their time jumping around and giggling. The prospect of two weeks of vacation, the fact that Christmas was coming. It was all too much for most of them. The sugar in all those Christmas cookies and candy at the school party didn't help. Jade tried her best to keep her third graders more or less under control without being too hard on them. Finally, after exchanging presents, singing Christmas carols in English and Spanish, and after an appearance by a Santa Claus that looked suspiciously like the school janitor Freddie Gonzalez wearing a fake white beard and a red Santa suit, the fall semester was over.

The children's excitement was infectious. Jade liked the excite-ment of Christmas, but it wasn't really her favorite holiday. She liked Halloween best because she loved dressing up in a costume. She was happy for the children to have their Christmas vacation but even happier for herself. She needed the time off and looked forward to a couple of weeks of quiet. She planned to spend most of her Christmas vacation listening to music, reading, riding her bicycle, and playing with clay.

Her friend Seri had asked Jade to accompany her on a trip to New York over the Christmas holiday, but Jade had said no. There had been a time that she was profoundly grateful to go with Seri on those wonderful trips. Jade couldn't bear being alone then. For a long time after Carlos disappeared, Jade found their home too silent and lonely. The idea of being there for a holiday vacation or worse, the long summer, was just unbearable. Seri was lifesaver then. But things were getting better now. Jade could breathe again, and the house was beginning to seem like home even though her husband would never be there again – *probably* would never be there again, she said to herself. That was the problem with disappeared people.

There was no way to know if they would return tomorrow or never return at all.

Half an hour after leaving the school grounds, Jade pulled her bicycle into the driveway on the side of her adobe house. She opened the wrought iron gate set into the adobe wall surrounding her property and entered the backyard. It was quiet and cool and shady there. The orange tree put out its wonderful fragrance as she brushed past it. She could hear the music of the small fountain she had installed when she landscaped the backyard, but she could not see the water for the wild tangle of trees and cacti and flowers planted in her garden.

Jade parked her bike, unlocked the backdoor, dumped her backpack in the living room, and changed quickly from her school dress into jeans and an old, loose long-sleeved t-shirt that had become thin from too many washings. She grabbed a cold bottle of Mexican cerveza from the fridge, went out the back door, and headed up the ladder to the roof. It was very warm on the roof in spite of the season. There, she found the one spot on the flat roof that had been shaded all afternoon on the west side of the house. She rolled out the mat that she kept there, sat down to drink her beer and watch the sun behind her cast its long rays on the Catalina Mountains to the north.

Jade thought about what else she would do on her vacation. Definitely she'd make some pottery in her garage studio. Yes. Pots. Playing with clay had been Jade's favorite pastime for as long as she could remember. The love of clay started in elementary school, and pottery had become a serious hobby into adulthood. After Jade and Carlos married, he remodeled the old garage behind their house into a studio for Jade. She had a wheel for throwing pots. The remodeling job had only been finished a few weeks when Carlos disappeared. For months after, Jade couldn't touch the clay at all. But now, a year later, she thought maybe she was ready to go back to it. She thought about the pots she planned to work on over the holiday. It would be fun to create some new glazes in new colors.

Jade knew she wouldn't be seeing her parents. They were off on yet another trip. But naturally Jade would go to visit Carlos's family and pass out gifts to all his nephews and nieces.

After she was on the roof for a few minutes, she was joined by her cat Zorro. The old cat seemed to enjoy climbing the ladder despite his age. He liked sitting on the roof with her and watching the sun set or whatever it is that cats do.

"Where's your friend?" Jade asked the big white cat with the black mask as she rubbed his ears. Jade's second cat, a big black fur ball named Don Diego, wasn't as enthusiastic about ladder climbing as Zorro. He preferred to sit near the fountain and snooze. If he became too hot in the sun, as black cats and black dogs quickly do, he would move to the shade. Then back to the sun. Today he was nowhere in sight.

Jade finished her beer, stretched out on the mat, and closed her eyes.

Yes, the roof had always been a place of serenity for her, and she felt the calm of the late afternoon come over her. She dozed off quickly with pleasant holiday thoughts on her mind.

Then Jade suddenly awakened. There was a sound. Yes, something was wrong.

Her eyes opened, fully awake now, Jade listened carefully. For a moment, she could hear nothing unusual – only the familiar soft whir of hummingbirds at their feeder, a car passing in the street out front; a neighbor's door closing, a dog barking half-heartedly at a passing bicyclist. Perhaps she had dreamed the sound, and the dream woke her up. Perhaps there had been no sound at all.

Jade stretched and sat up. She yawned and looked at her watch. Only 20 minutes before sundown. She told herself she'd better get off the roof while there was still light, and before the winter night's chill set in. Winter days might be warm on the desert, but the nights were cold. She thought about what to fix herself for dinner. Maybe thaw out some of that soup she'd made and frozen last week? Nah, too much trouble. She would settle for a sandwich….again.

It wasn't much fun cooking for just one person. Eating alone was …well…eating alone.

Jade started to pull herself to her feet, then froze. There it was again…a strange sound coming from below her. It wasn't a dream. It wasn't her imagination. There was someone moving around inside her house! She could hear bumping sounds, footsteps, the opening and closing of drawers in the kitchen. Whoever it was made no attempt to be quiet.

Fully alarmed now, Jade crept on her hands and knees to the edge of the roof. She flattened herself against the roof, and waited, barely breathing. Her heart pounded in her chest. She had never, ever had anyone break into her house. Yet she was sure someone was below her moving around – an uninvited someone – a potentially-dangerous someone. For a brief second, she tried to reassure herself that maybe the intruder was a friend, but she knew immediately that could not be. A friend would have called out to her.

Jade raised her head just enough to view the ceramic tile patio below her and the garden rich with citrus trees, bougainvillea, nopal cactus, and a profusion of flowers. In the dusky light, she could barely make out the adobe wall at the far end of the garden that enclosed her home, her studio, and the garden.

Suddenly, Jade saw movement in two places simultaneously: below her and toward the back wall of her garden. Directly below her a man was exiting her back door, coming from the kitchen. She could see the top of his head though the wooden slats of the ramada that extended over the back door and patio. He was slender, had very dark hair cut long, just long enough to touch his shoulders. He was dressed in a white suit. He moved quickly into the yard and began moving toward the garage and Jade's art studio.

At the same time the intruder left the house, Jade saw another man emerging from behind a large bougainvillea covered in magenta blossoms at the back of her yard. The second man also had dark hair but cut shorter. He was dressed casually in khaki pants with a long-sleeved cotton shirt. The second man moved forward steadily but very quietly, his body erect and alert. Unlike the intruder who seemed hurried, the second man's graceful movements made Jade think of a cat stalking prey.

For just a brief second, Jade imagined that she saw the second man glance up at her, but she wasn't sure. Then suddenly the first man who had been in the house saw the second intruder. They were now face to face only a few feet apart. They spoke no words to each other, but came together in a violent martial arts battle. The intruder attacked first by attempting a punch that the second man easily deflected. Kicks and more punches followed.

"BB movie," the words popped into Jade's head. Carlos loved those Chinese kung fu movies. Jet Li was his favorite star, but Li was just one of many. Carlos loved the old Jackie Chan films, and Chan's pals like Sammo Hung and Yuen Biao, any film by the Yuen Woo-ping, and, of course, Bruce Lee. When they were in high school and Carlos's friends were all agog at the martial arts in *The Matrix*, Carlos just laughed and said, "Hey, cabrones! It's all been done before. Yuen Woo-ping!"

Later, after Carlos and Jade married and had a home of their own, Jade would sit with him on the couch with a bucket of popcorn between them. They watched those Hong Kong kung fu films, fascinated by the "brutal ballet (BB)" in these films that Carlos so loved. The martial artists in the films were graceful, like in classical ballet, but violent to the point of brutality. Carlos was the sweetest, kindest person she had ever known, and yet he was addicted to these films. When she asked him why, he shrugged his shoulders, laughed, and filled his mouth with popcorn. She wondered how long these memories of him, unbidden and painful, would suddenly appear in her mind.

Jade's attention went back to the men below her. This wasn't an exhibition, and it wasn't a movie. The fight was real, very real and very serious. The only sounds were of fists and feet hitting flesh, accented by grunting and heavy breathing. They moved warily around each other in the small space of her garden. Punching and blocking punches, kicking and dodging, the two men were giving her a superb exhibition of classic martial arts. She could see now that both were Asian, and this just reinforced the feeling that she had woken up in the middle of a movie. She had never seen either of the men before, and she could not imagine why these strangers were silently battling each other in her backyard. The Hong Kong movie notion resurfaced. Were they Chinese? Japanese? Korean? Jade had no idea.

After about three minutes but what seemed much longer to Jade, the second man seemed to be getting the upper hand in the battle. His fist found its target more often and his kicks seemed stronger and swifter. Suddenly, the intruder who had been in her house a few minutes earlier began to back away from the fight. He muttered something angrily in an unfamiliar language, then turned and fled through the gate. The second man stared after him, then turned abruptly and entered Jade's back door.

What the hell? thought Jade. Who are these guys, and why do they both think they can just waltz into my house? She rose abruptly with the intention of descending the ladder and confronting the second man. But prudence stopped her. If this second intruder can beat up the first, he can certainly stop me, Jade thought. She lowered herself against the roof and waited.

A few minutes passed, and the second man left her kitchen door to stand briefly under the ramada. He paused, then walked around the right side of the house and exited through the iron gate. He did not look back.

Jade had been holding her breath and now released it slowly. Time to call her friend Letty. Letty would know what to do.

Jade swung her leg over the roof's edge and onto the ladder. She was about half way down when she heard a small noise. She swung quickly to the left and saw the second man, the victor in the kung fu contest and the last to leave Jade's backyard. He had returned silently and without warning.

CHAPTER 3

LETTY Valdez clicked the Send button on her computer screen. Then she pushed her rickety office chair back from her desk. She stretched her long legs out in front of her and sighed deeply. She was tired, but she felt really, really good. The departing email with attached file folder was the final report for her latest investigative case. Sending the report to the client was the last step in several weeks' worth of work. This case had been another skip job. Her task had been to find her client's former business partner who had disappeared one day about six months earlier, taking with him nearly a million dollars from the company's bank account. It took her a while, but Letty finally found the skip living the high life in Playa del Carmen on the Caribbean coast. The client would be pleased. Now it was time for his attorneys to take over.

The phone rang. Letty ignored it.

The phone rang again. This time she answered. It was a potential client, someone in the Foothills of the Catalina Mountains who identified herself as Mrs. Baird. She wanted to talk about a shooting that had occurred a few days earlier. Letty suggested calling the police. Mrs. Baird said the police had been there, and they hadn't done their job. She said the wrong person had been arrested. Letty frowned. Okay. She agreed to meet the potential client and set an appointment for the next day. She doubted much would come of it. The police were not as incompetent as many people seemed to believe. She hung up the phone and looked out of the window again.

Late afternoon merged into evening. It was Letty's favorite time of day on the desert...that half hour just before the sun set. The city of Tucson glowed with a gold-tinged light. Palm tree fronds rippled dark against a dusky mango and watermelon sky. As far as Letty was concerned, winter evenings like this one were the best. She could see a lot of the sky now. Her office was a nondescript, strip mall address, but her window had a million-dollar view of the Santa Catalina Mountains on the north side of the city. She swiveled her chair to look out and see the mountains turn a coppery gold as the sun journeyed downward into the Sonoran Desert's western horizon.

Once the light turned to a soft glow, Letty turned back toward her desk. The last light of the setting sun glinted on the glass of a framed certificate on the wall. It caught Letty's eye. The document proclaimed that she, Ms. Leticia Fernanda Antone Valdez, was a licensed private investigator in good standing and fully certified to work in the state of Arizona.

It had taken three years of hard work and a whole lot of help from Marv to make it, but now she could legitimately claim to be a self-employed, licensed private investigator. She started as Marv Iverson's assistant, and over time, she had become his business partner. Then when Marv retired, Letty took over the agency. As far as Letty was concerned, Marv had saved her. He gave her a job and a way to support herself and her family. The job turned into a career and a life, something she thought wasn't possible after the devastation she'd lived through in Iraq. She could still remember the words in the brief ad on Craigslist. "Private investigator seeks assistant. Will train. Veteran preferred." Letty could never repay Marv.

She sighed again, this time from satisfaction. She would go home now and make something for supper. Her baby brother Will had a job that kept him at the bike shop until seven p.m. Letty liked the idea of fixing her little brother some supper and eating with him. It seemed so normal – a family kind of thing after the lives that both of them had lived. She was trying hard to give him a stable home.

The cell phone on her desk buzzed for the second time. The first time that the phone had announced an incoming call, Letty ignored it in favor of finishing her report to the client. This time she decided to answer. She saw that the call was coming from Jade Lopez.

"Hey, Jade. What's up?" It was unusual for Jade to call Letty, and she wondered why.

"Oh, Letty. Thank God! I thought you'd never answer!"

Letty's eyebrows went up. That must have been Jade when the phone buzzed the first time.

"I'm here now."

"Letty, I don't know how to start. I came home from school. You know today's the last day of school, we had a Feliz Navidad fiesta, and I gave all my kids a send-off and wished them Merry Christmas, and I talked to several parents, too. You know how it is. I won't see them until after New Year's. Up till then, everything was normal."

Jade's voice was strained, and her words spilled out so fast that Letty had to listen carefully to catch everything.

"And then what happened?"

"I came home like usual. I rode my bike. You know I'm trying to get more exercise. Maggie told me if I get more exercise I'll feel better. Something about endorphins."

"And then what happened?"

"I came home and parked my bike in the backyard, and I went in and changed my clothes, and I got a beer and went up on the roof, and I guess I fell asleep."

An image of Jade's house in the historic Sam Hughes District of midtown Tucson came into Letty's mind. She had only been there a couple of times on those rare occasions when Jade had hosted Sunday morning coffee on her back patio. Usually the Sunday morning coffee was at Maggie's house, and once in a while at Seri's condo. Jade's house was a small, well-kept adobe with a backyard surrounded by a six-foot adobe wall. The house had been a gift from Jade's affluent parents when Jade and Carlos married. The newly-weds could never have afforded the neighborhood otherwise. The house was enhanced with native landscaping that included some very mature palo verde and mesquite trees.

The back patio with its ramada had plenty of shade during the heat of summer days. The patio was a comfortable place to sit with her friends and drink coffee on quiet mornings. Letty knew that both Jade and Maggie came to coffee from early Mass on Sunday. She didn't know what Seri typically did on Sunday mornings, but Mass was unlikely. Probably she was reading an obscure text on Australian aboriginal art or quantum physics or something equally esoteric. Not Letty. She didn't go to Mass. After all the things she had seen, she wasn't at all sure that there was a god, and if there were, he just might be a real bastard with a sick sense of humor.

"Okay, so you're on the roof and then you woke up?"

"Yes...and I heard something down below in the backyard on the patio, and I looked and there was this man coming out of my house!" Her voice got all squeaky and breathless.

"Who was he?"

"I don't know!"

"Did he take anything?"

"No, I don't think so. I don't know. He didn't seem to be carrying anything."

"Okay. So then what happened?"

"I ducked down so he couldn't see me, but I was watching as best I could. He just came out of the back door, looked around, and then went out the side gate."

"So now he's gone?"

"No! I mean yes, but there's the other man. Let me explain. I decided to go down the ladder and go into the house to see if he'd stolen anything. And I sort of slipped and fell off the ladder."

In her mind, Letty saw the heavy mesquite branch ladder that usually rested up against the back of Jade's adobe house. Letty thought it was just for looks. Many affluent folks kept things like that around as decoration, especially the snowbirds who came only in winter to escape their northern winters. But apparently this wasn't just for decoration if Jade was using it to climb up on the roof. Letty wondered if anyone knew this about Jade, that she was spending time on her roof. They were all worried about Jade. She didn't seem as sad as she had been, but she still wasn't the same since Carlos disappeared.

Jade's breathing got really shaky now.

"I slipped, and I was going to fall but he caught me."

"Who caught you?" Letty was alarmed now.

"This Chinese dude. Well, really I don't know if he's Chinese. He just looks Chinese. Or something Asian anyway. Japanese. I don't know."

"This was the man who was in your house?" Letty gritted her teeth. Get to the point, Jade.

"No! The second man! He held me for a just a second, and then he set me down on the patio."

"What's he doing now? And who is he?"

"He told me that he's a cop. His name is Joe."

"Joe? That doesn't sound very Chinese. Is he an American, a Chinese-American I mean? And where are you now?"

"I'm on the patio. He's standing here. I don't think he's American. He speaks with an accent. He said he's a good guy."

"A good guy?" Letty snorted. Jade was a real sweetheart but amazingly naive.

"I'm sorry, Letty. I didn't know who to call."

"It's fine for you to call me, Jade, but if your house was broken into, you should call Tucson police."

"Well....not exactly broken into."

Letty sighed again. How many times had she and Maggie and Seri warned Jade that she really should lock up her house and lock the side gate leading to the backyard when she left for school?

"Besides all that," Jade said in a low voice, "what good are the cops anyway. They don't do a damn thing."

Letty understood Jade's cynicism and felt a stab of guilt. Jade had no faith or trust in law enforcement. They hadn't been able to find Carlos, so they were useless in Jade's eyes. And Letty reminded herself that she hadn't found Carlos either, despite the fact that she was normally very good at finding people.

"Okay. Go in the house. Tell this Chinese good guy to stay outside in the back, and you lock the doors and wait for me," Letty told Jade. "Don't open the door again. Okay?"

"Okay," Jade agreed. "Okay. I'm in the house now. He's out there now on the patio. He just sat down on one of the patio chairs."

Oh, great, Letty thought. Making himself comfortable.

"I'll be there in fifteen minutes," Letty said.

"Oh, thank you, thank you, Letty."

The drive across the city went fast despite the Friday five o'clock traffic. Everyone was in a rush to go home or, more likely, to go out to dinner at one Tucson's eateries. It was still warm enough to sit out on the patio and have a drink with friends while waiting for dinner to be served. Letty caught every green light, which she considered a minor miracle. Night had fallen when she pulled up in front of Jade's house. Letty could see that Jade had turned on every light in her house and outside, too, on the front porch and along the side of the house where the unlocked gate stood open.

The residential street Jade lived on was quiet most of the time, and like many streets in Tucson, there were no street lights. The city, including the surrounding region, was an important center for astronomy, and astronomers had convinced Tucsonans that too many city lights or lights of the wrong kind caused a kind of light pollution. So many streets stayed dark. The payoff for this was the ability for anyone to just look up and see millions of stars in the clear, dry desert night. The downside was that nighttime thieves were harder to see. Of course, there were plenty of daytime thieves, too.

Letty walked along the side walkway and came around the back of Jade's house. She saw the Chinese man immediately. He had been sitting on a patio chair, but at the sound of Letty's footsteps, he rose to his feet and faced her. He nodded politely. Letty said nothing. She knocked on the back door without turning her back to the man. She called out to Jade.

She could hear Jade moving around in the kitchen….cooking, no doubt. Their friends Seri and Maggie had teased Jade about what a little homemaker she was, always cooking and decorating for holidays and loving on those little third-graders that she taught every day. That is, they teased her until Carlos disappeared. Jade didn't have anyone to keep a home for anymore. Letty thought maybe Jade cooked now to deal with her anxiety. It's a wonder she wasn't hugely fat, but somehow Jade had stayed slender, even thin. It occurred to Letty for the first time that Jade might be cooking, but she might not be eating.

Letty looked directly at the man standing about ten feet away.

"My name is Letty Valdez, and I am a private investigator. And you are?"

"I am Zhou Liang Wei. I am a Detective Inspector from the Ministry of Public Security, People's Republic of China."

Letty noticed immediately that the man spoke English quite well. His accent was Chinese, but also faintly British.

By this time, Jade had opened the back door. More light spilled onto the patio. Letty took a closer look at the uninvited foreigner. She guessed Zhou was about five feet nine inches tall in his bare feet, maybe even five feet ten inches. He was a couple of inches taller than Jade – but not slender like Jade. He was all muscle. He looked very fit in an athletic way, like someone who worked out regularly. He wasn't so much a pumped-up muscle builder but more someone who focused on the agility and strength needed to accomplish specific tasks, like taking out an opponent in hand-to-hand combat – the kind of skills a cop would need, Letty guessed. He probably outweighed Jade by thirty pounds but every pound was muscle. Although Zhou had to look up to Letty's six feet, Letty intuited that she would have a hard time bringing this man down despite her size and her training in martial arts. She was sure that he was a martial arts practitioner, and a good one, too. The man looked relaxed, but she knew he was sizing her up as well.

Letty gestured for Zhou to enter the house before her. Once in the kitchen, Letty and Zhou pulled out identification at the same time and traded documents with each other. Letty looked closely at Zhou's red leather passport with the seal of the People's Republic of China on the front. It looked real enough. His police identification – or at least that's what she guessed it was – also looked like a typical cop's badge and ID, but all the words were in Chinese characters. Like most passports and other official documents, his photo was bad. It barely looked like the man in front of her. He seemed indistinguishable from any other Chinese man in his age group, which Letty guessed was early 30s. His clothing was average – khaki pants, a navy blue t-shirt under a long-sleeved light blue cotton shirt rolled up at the sleeves. His clothing was chosen to not attract attention.

Jade said, "Your name is Joe?"

He nodded yes with a short, sudden downward movement of his head. "Not American name Joe, but Chinese name Z-H-O-U." He spelled the word, using the British "zed" instead of "Z". "I explain. My name sounds like your "Joe", but in pinyin, it is spelled Zed-H-O-U. Zhou is my family name, and LiangWei is my individual personal name. Reverse of western names."

"Zhou," Jade repeated. "Joe."

Letty and Zhou traded identification again, and both slipped badges back into pockets.

"Why are you here?" Letty asked sharply.

"Interpol informed the Ministry of Public Security in Beijing that possibly a Hong Kong triad criminal gang is moving into the Arizona region. I have experience working with Interpol. I was chosen to investigate."

"Interpol?" Letty sounded dubious even to herself. Interpol was short for International Criminal Police Organization. She had read about it on the web just because she was curious after seeing a film with Interpol agents. She remembered that Interpol was headquartered in France, and its purpose was to help the police of member countries to cooperate on problems such as organized crime and terrorism. Most countries in the world were members of Interpol.

The organization did not make arrests, but it kept extensive databases on criminal activity and provided that information to police to help them cooperate in bringing down criminals. She'd heard of triads but knew little about them. About the Ministry of Public Security in China, Letty knew absolutely nothing. In fact, this was the first she'd ever heard of it.

"So you are a detective?"

"Yes. I am one of the Detective Inspectors. Allow me to explain. I arrived at Tucson International Airport today. I arrived one day early. I expected to follow the triad gangster who is scheduled to arrive tomorrow. At the airport I saw the triad member. Not tomorrow. He came today. His name is Bao. I followed him. He did not lead me to see others in his gang. Instead he came to this woman's house." Zhou gestured to Jade. "Bao looks for something or maybe looks for someone."

Zhou turned to Jade. "Now I want to know why this man comes to your house," He looked at Jade directly. "Do you know this man? Do you have a business or a personal relationship with him?"

Letty noticed that Zhou's eyes had narrowed. His voice was quiet yet firm, and his body was an odd combination of relaxation and tension. Letty had a sudden memory of a rattlesnake she'd seen once across a dry wash in the shade of a scrawny mesquite tree. The rattler was relaxed into a coil, quiet, watchful, and yet ready to strike at the least provocation.

"Certainly not!" Jade said hotly. "I've never seen him before. I have no idea why he was here. I have *no* relationship of any kind with that man. He's a stranger!"

Zhou frowned and looked at Letty. "This is not good. Bao is a very dangerous man."

"This is hard to believe," Jade said. "This isn't California. We've had a small Chinese settlement here since the mid-nineteenth century, but these days, most of the Chinese in Tucson are students at the university. We don't even have a Chinatown."

"What exactly are you investigating?" asked Letty.

"The triads are involved in many illegal activities such as drug smuggling, people smuggling, counterfeit money, money laundering..." He shrugged his shoulders as if the list were too long to convey. "In recent times, an important triad gang called Wo Hop To is suspected of working in northern Mexico and southern Arizona. We do not know what they are doing. Possibly they are smuggling Chinese citizens into the U.S. across the Mexican border. Or perhaps smuggling illegal drugs. Or both. We do not know. We know only that triad members have been seen here. Interpol alerted the Chinese government to send an agent to investigate. I am the agent." He smiled.

Letty considered this. An immigration investigation was definitely plausible. Every year hundreds of illegal immigrants crossed the U.S. border into Arizona. Most of the immigrants were poverty-stricken Mexicans or Central Americans looking for a job, a minimum wage job, any job. They just wanted to feed their kids. Many of them got caught, but for every one caught and sent back, two made it across the border successfully. They eventually found the jobs that other Americans wouldn't do.

"I have heard that there were a few Chinese and some other nationalities, too, trying to cross the Arizona border," Letty admitted. "I read in the paper that a couple of our local Chinese American businessmen who still spoke some Mandarin were hired by the local police to talk to the Chinese illegals – to find out where they came from and who was trying to smuggle them in and, most of all, to find out where they were going."

"Yes, we have information about illegal smuggling. Also there are rumors of Chinese women forced to become..." Zhou hesitated, "sex slaves."

Letty nodded her head in agreement. Human trafficking and sex slavery were known problems.

Jade interrupted. "That may be," said Jade, "but right now I'm hungry."

Letty sighed. Jade didn't seem to be taking this seriously.

"Please, sit down," Jade gestured toward the table. "I made a little something to eat while we were waiting for Letty." The table was covered with dishes filled with food.

"I'm meeting Will later for supper, Jade. In fact, I need to go call him." Letty rose from the table and went into the backyard, closing the door behind her. She didn't want Zhou to hear her make her phone calls.

Zhou sat and watched Jade make a burrito. He followed her example, starting with folding one end of the tortilla up so that the stuffing couldn't escape and then wrapping it around the other ingredients. He ate with enthusiasm. Jade smiled.

"What is this?" he asked.

"What is what?"

Zhou gestured to the food, and Jade gave names for each food item…some in English and some in Spanish. "Tortilla, shredded chicken, lettuce, tomatoes, cheese, salsa. And you just made a burrito."

Zhou took a big bite and nodded. "Burrito. Very good."

"How long has it been since you ate?" Jade asked.

"Hmmm….two days...maybe three. I did not eat well before. Airport food is usually bad. I don't like it. I did not sleep well," His mouth was full. "I came from Beijing, before that, Zambia. Long trip."

"Zambia? That's in Africa," Jade said. "Do you travel a lot?"

Zhou nodded and filled his mouth again. Jade followed his example. They ate in silence.

On the back patio, Letty made a quick call to Will's cell phone and left a message that she might be delayed a little while. Then she called Marv Iverson. She could see Zhou and Jade in the bright light of the kitchen. The air around her had taken on a nighttime chill.

"Hey, Marv."

"What do you want? I'm watching football." He was always like that – gruff and short with her. Fact is that he was a teddy bear who had turned out to be someone that Letty could always count on.

"Big deal, Marv. You know you're always watching football. I need some help. Remember Jade Lopez, the woman whose husband, Carlos, disappeared about a year ago? She just called me. I'm at her house now. A Chinese cop is here...or so he claims. He says he's following a triad gangster. You know triads are those Chinese mafia-like criminal gangs. This Chinese cop says he followed a triad gang member to Jade's house. The triad member went into Jade's house. We don't know why for sure. Apparently he was looking for something."

"Well, well. That's different from the usual stuff we deal with. And it's not good if it's true. Triad gangsters are worse than the mafia from what I hear. They like to chop up people with hatchets. What was the intruder looking for?"

"We don't know. In fact, the whole story might be a bunch of bull. I'll call Tucson Police. Don't you know someone high up in the police department or in Homeland Security who could tell us if they are expecting a Chinese policeman?"

"Yeah, I'll call Sam Lambert. That dick head. He's not going to like this. Mere mortals like you and me are not supposed to know about Homeland Security business. I'll call you back in a few minutes."

That's what Letty loved about Marv. He would drop whatever to help her. And this time she could tell that he was interested in what she was telling him. It's not every day that Interpol and Chinese cops come into their conversation.

Next Letty dialed Adelita Garcia at Tucson police headquarters, but got voice mail instead.

"Hello, Adelita. This is Letty Valdez. Please give me a call when you can."

Letty went back into Jade's kitchen and sat down at the table.

"Jade, are you sure nothing is gone?" Letty asked.

"I didn't find anything obvious, but I can tell he got into my stuff."

"Like what?"

"Drawers opened. The bed covers are disturbed like he looked under the mattress. Books moved around on the shelf."

Why would some Chinese triad gang member be at Jade's house and what the hell was he looking for? Could it be something as simple as the wrong address? Letty could think of no possible connection Jade might have with Chinese gangsters.

"Here, Letty," Jade said. "Please have something to eat."

Letty half-heartedly put together a burrito, made it thin, and took a bite. She still had hopes of eating with Will.

Jade turned to Zhou. "Your English is good. Very good."

"Thank you. You are too kind," Zhou said. "My father was a businessman, and my family frequently lived abroad." Zhou paused. How easily the lie came. Actually his father had been heavily involved in espionage for the Chinese central government. His father's "business" was a cover while he collected as much information possible – all of which went directly back to Beijing. He was part of a network of spies from every nation that spent time in the world's major capitals. One of his assignments was to figure out which of the American and British embassy staff were actually spies for their own countries.

Because of his father's clandestine operations, Zhou had spent many of his growing-up years in the West although his father made sure he spent regular long periods in China as well. Later, working with Interpol led to long periods in France. As a result, Zhou knew he didn't completely fit into the West, but he didn't really fit into China either. Sometimes he felt homeless.

"My father moved our family around a lot," Zhou continued. "I went to an American high school for a brief time, and I earned my bachelor's degree from University College London. Also, I watched American television to learn slang. I watched *Friends*, *Sex and City*, *Desperate Housewife*. That's how I learned the traditional American lifestyle and language."

"Oh, Lord," Letty said. *Friends*, *Sex and the City* and *Desperate Housewives*. Traditional American lifestyles? Good grief.

Jade covered her mouth with her hand to hide her grin. Her eyebrows arched upward.

Zhou laughed at their reaction. His face, which had been all serious and professional cop demeanor earlier, was suddenly all dimples and flashing white teeth. Letty noticed for the first time that he was actually quite good looking. She also noticed that Jade was blushing. Hmmm…that's not good, Letty thought. But then again, her blush may mean nothing. Jade's red face was nothing new. Jade, the red-headed, freckled-faced Irish-American girl with the Mexican Spanish name, blushed at anything and everything.

"You, please. What is your name?" Zhou asked. He was looking at Jade.

"Jade. Jade Lopez."

"Jade?"

"Yes. You know, like the green stone."

Zhou repeated the word in Chinese. "Jade in my language is…"

"Yùe" interjected Jade.

"You speak Mandarin?"

"No. I wish. When I was a kid, we lived in Australia for one year. My dad had a consulting job. My parents hired a Chinese couple to cook and clean and organize everything and take care of me, too. They called me Jade… Yùe," she explained.

Zhou nodded.

Letty's phone buzzed. Marv. She left the table and went to the backyard again, closing the door behind her.

"Your boy may be legit," Marv said. "Lambert says that they were expecting a detective from the Chinese Ministry of Public Security to fly into Tucson tomorrow. He's supposed to report to their office. And Lambert was not happy to know that I knew about this cop, and that you made contact with him first. I had to listen to him rant about security leaks and interfering people – meaning interfering me and interfering you. He wants you to come in, too, to find out why you are involved. But I gotta tell ya, Letty, it gave me a hard-on to jerk Lambert's chain." He laughed.

Letty knew that Marv and Lambert went way back. There was bad blood between them that Marv had never explained. But they had both learned that helping each other out was in each man's own best interest. So they stayed in touch and shared info, always grudgingly.

"Well, if Lambert asks again, I'm not *involved*. I'm just trying to help Jade."

"You can tell him yourself. He wants you and the Chinese cop to show up in his office at eleven tomorrow morning.

"Okay. I'll go. Marv, do you have an experience with foreign agents, or detectives...or whatever? He calls himself a detective inspector, and he says this triad intruder is dangerous."

"Nope. I only have experience with local boys and the Mexican cartel scum. Anybody who lives near the border has to deal with those scumbags at some point. I've never been to China except a layover in Hong Kong once, but that was back when it was British. I know lots of Vietnamese but no Chinese. But I've heard about those triad gangsters. They have a rep for being really nasty, violent SOBs. Be careful, Letty. And let me know what happens."

"Thanks, Marv. I'll stay in touch. Go back to your football."

Back at the table, Zhou and Jade were finishing their burritos when Letty returned.

"Mr. Zhou, aren't you supposed to report in to authorities here? And Jade, maybe we should think about finding you another place to stay until we figure out what's going on here."

Zhou nodded yes, and Jade shook her head no.

"No way, Letty. I don't want to go anywhere. This is my home. Where would I go anyway? My parents are on a trek in South America, Maggie has a full house for the holidays, Seri won't be back from her trip until Sunday, and you don't have room for me. I'll be okay. And I promise, cross my heart, that I'll keep this place locked up, and I won't let anyone in. Promise."

Zhou and Letty exchanged glances.

Zhou turned to Jade and said, "The triad gangsters are very dangerous. We do not know why they came to your house. It is best to go to a safe place."

"There's no safe place," Jade said with a frown. "I'm staying here. That's it. Period."

Letty shook her head. She knew Jade was thinking of Carlos again.

"Zhou, what about you?" Letty said. "I want to go with you when you visit the authorities."

Zhou hesitated. "I must see your Homeland Security and Tucson police. I will call them tomorrow. Then I will call you. We can go together. You will see then that I am a good guy. Okay?"

"Okay, Mr. Good Guy," Letty said. "Let's make it tomorrow morning. How about eleven o'clock? I have a client I have to see tomorrow afternoon. But first we're going to take a walk around and make sure this place is secure."

Letty went room to room, Zhou at her shoulder, and together they made sure all the windows were closed and locked. Letty felt better seeing that all the windows had decorative wrought iron security bars that made a window break-in very difficult. The front door had a dead bolt on it. The back door also had a dead bolt and chain although the door itself looked old and easy to smash in.

"And you. Did you just walk in past the side gate, too?" Letty sighed when Zhou nodded yes. "And where are you going to be tonight?"

"I first came over back wall, I hid in trees, then I passed through the unlocked gate. My rental car is behind the wall. I will go to a hotel tonight."

Letty shook her head. For a place that looked really secure in a neighborhood that was supposed to be safe, Jade's house was surprisingly vulnerable.

"This place is way too easy to get into," she muttered to herself. Zhou nodded in agreement.

Finally Letty was as satisfied as she could be, and said goodbye to both. Jade started cleaning up from dinner. Zhou followed Letty into the backyard, closing the door behind him.

"Miss Leticia?"

"Call me Letty."

Zhou nodded. "Bao is a 49er. The 49ers are the foot soldiers of the triad organization. Bao is hot-headed and impulsive. I can confirm that he has killed several people. He plays with them before killing...like a cat plays with a mouse. Bao enjoys hurting people. He forces his prisoners to cry and beg for release from pain before he kills them," Zhou looked at Letty intently. "Also he likes women. He will....," Zhou seemed to struggle for a word, "He will abuse women first, then hurt them, then kill them."

Letty felt a chill go up her spine. A sensory memory exploded in her brain for about two seconds, leaving her shuddering. Then she was pulled back again to the present. "You mean he rapes them first, tortures them, then kills them in some really painful way."

"Yes," Zhou said firmly, "You understand my meaning. He is very bad guy."

"Yeah, a bad guy. Okay, then let's do what we can to keep Jade safe."

"I agree. We cooperate. Let us make Miss Jade safe."

CHAPTER 4

Letty's cell phone rang again just as she pulled into the gravel driveway of her modest home in midtown Tucson. She had chosen the neighborhood because it was centrally located, and it was easy to get to most parts of the city from here. There were rentals, small apartment complexes and duplexes as well as single-family homes on the streets nearby. Also the neighborhood had a higher-than-average share of immigrants and college students.

Letty was able to blend in easily in her neighborhood. A six-foot tall, dark-skinned Native American-Hispanic woman who kept odd hours could become the object of unwanted attention in more affluent parts of the city, and she didn't want that kind of energy. Nor did she want to deal with the petty criminals and gangbangers elsewhere in Tucson. Letty tried to remain as invisible as possible. These were the reasons that Letty told herself when she chose this house and neighborhood. But secretly she knew that the big mesquite tree in the front yard and two smaller mesquites and a palo verde tree covered in yellow blossoms in the backyard may have been the real reason for buying her little house. Most significant was that the house was affordable.

Detective Adelita Garcia was returning her call.

"Hi, Letty. Please tell me that you have single-handedly cleaned up the streets of Tucson, put all the criminals in jail, and you're calling me to tell me that I can retire now."

Letty laughed, "You are too young to retire, Adelita. So today I found a new bad guy just for you."

"Oh, yeah?" Adelita, who had made the rank of detective just one year ago, was assigned to the Violent Crimes Section of the Tucson Police Department's Central Investigations Division. Her response to Letty was all business now. "Anyone I know?"

"That's what I'd like to know. Are you acquainted with any Chinese triad gang members, or would you like to be?"

"No, can't say as I know any, and I think I'd rather not. I hear they are not very nice people."

Letty had made a point of cultivating contacts in all the law enforcement agencies, in the medical examiner's office, and in several agencies in state, county, and city government offices. She did what she could to give law enforcement helpful bits of information when she had them, unless confidentiality obligations prevented it. She also knew and kept friendly relations with a couple of attorneys who occasionally hired her to do investigative work for them.

Adelita Garcia was different. She and Letty had been friends since their student days at Pima Community College. Both came from poor backgrounds, both had aspirations to do better, both were smart and capable, and both knew that if they worked hard, they might have a chance at a decent life. Adelita had always wanted to be a police officer. She had a plan and a supportive family who chipped in when her part-time job wasn't enough to cover her tuition and school fees. Adelita earned an associate degree in criminal justice from the community college. Right after graduation, she entered the Arizona Law Enforcement Academy.

Letty's economic situation was just as dire as Adelita's, but she had little family support and no career calling like Adelita's. After some thought and talking it over with her best friend, surrogate mother and teacher Maggie, Letty decided to go into a medical field. She figured there would always be a job helping to take care of people. She managed to earn a certificate as an Emergency Medical Technician before things fell apart. Letty's mom took off – again – and left Letty's three younger siblings with their grandmother. The elderly woman could provide shelter and lots of love, but not much more. The old woman lived at a subsistence level out in the desert on the reservation. Letty's uncle Mando and her aunt helped out, but they didn't have much either, and they had their own kids to care for.

Letty Valdez was forced into being the matriarch of the family when she was only twenty years old. She had to step up to make sure her sister and two brothers had enough to eat, clothes on their backs, and shoes on their feet. She wanted to make sure they stayed in school.

Given the choice of a low-paying, dead-end job that wouldn't really cover the bills, Letty looked for another option – one that she hoped would provide a better future for herself and her siblings. The U.S. military was appealing because after her tour of duty, Letty would get help with tuition to return to college and finish her associate degree. Maybe she could even go on to the University of Arizona and get a bachelor's degree someday. If she joined the Army, she would get training and experience that would potentially be interest to a future employer. Best of all, she would earn a monthly salary while in the Army, and the Army would feed, house and clothe her. Letty considered a tour in the U.S. Army to be a good deal. Most of what she earned would go directly to her grandmother to support her brothers and sister. So Letty went to the recruiter's office and signed up.

Through these years, Letty and Adelita maintained their friendship. Adelita was one of the few old friends who bothered emailing Letty when she was in Iraq, and Letty would always be grateful for that. A couple of times Adelita sent Letty a box with luxuries so hard for a woman in a desert war zone to get – skin moisturizer, lip balm, and hair conditioner, and even some Mexican candies. In return, Letty sent Adelita some items from the Iraqi markets. Adelita's favorite was a square cotton head scarf called a keffiyeh in a black-and-white checkered pattern.

Letty filled Adelita in on the evening's events. She described her encounter with Zhou Liang Wei, who claimed to be from China's Ministry of Public Security, and his explanation that he was in Tucson to check up on the reported presence of triad gangsters.

"Marv got word for me from his buddy Lambert in Homeland Security that they were expecting a Chinese cop to arrive this week. Zhou Liang Wei is that cop. So I left him there with Jade because she refused to leave her house. I hope she'll be okay. He seemed like he was the real thing. But I'm not sure where to go from here. I can't help but wonder if this might have something to do with her husband's disappearance – just a gut feeling."

"No progress on that case at all?"

"No, colder than ice. Carlos Lopez just disappeared into thin air. It's been a year already. And that $100,000 grant money disappeared with him. I haven't been able to find Carlos, and there's been no sign of the money, either. I have a big file on this, and I've used all my tricks to find him. If he were a skip, I think the money would have shown up somewhere. It's difficult to have that much money in your pocket and not start spending it. I checked and rechecked all my sources."

Letty didn't mention it, but she had even looked into Jade's financial records to see if Carlos had deposited funds under her name instead of his own. Letty found a certificate of deposit made years ago by Jade's parents under Jade's name, Mary Catherine O'Reilly, before her marriage to Carlos. The CD for $3,000 had never been cashed. That was it. No sign of the $100,000.

"Well, everyone at the police department thinks he took off with the money. But you know what I think. I think he's dead, and whoever killed him took the money." Adelita's voice was flat.

"Yes," Letty breathed out. "I knew Carlos. There was no sign at all that he was unhappy with Jade or with his life here. He seemed very excited about being awarded that grant. He had all kinds of plans for the after-school center for kids on the south side. But he's the one who took the money out of the account just before he disappeared."

"Sure, but anyone willing to do violence could have forced him to withdraw the money," Adelita said.

"We looked at the surveillance video at the bank. He was alone. But I get your point. It would have been easy enough for someone to have threatened him...or more likely to have threatened Jade. Carlos loved her a lot." Letty paused, realizing that she had used the past tense "loved." "But people can fool you. Maybe he's lying around on some beach somewhere with a couple of babes on his arms, and a lot of money stuffed under his mattress."

"Hmmm....I'll look into this Chinese cop for you, and I'll find out if we've had any complaints or tips involving anyone that vaguely looks or sounds like triad gangs. I know one of the detectives working on Homeland Security intel in the department's Special Investigations Section. I'll talk to him."

"Thanks, Adelita. I have no idea at all why a member of a Chinese criminal gang would show up at Jade Lopez's house. I can't think of any connection to her husband's disappearance, but there's nothing else to go on. So anything you hear could help me a lot."

"Okay, will do."

Letty ended the call and walked into her house. All the lights were on, and the kitchen door to the backyard was open. She could hear the furnace running, trying to stay ahead of the chilly desert night. Not good for the utility bill, Letty thought.

"Will," she called. Her baby brother was named after Willie Nelson, the country and western star. Willie Nelson Antone Ramone. The twins had more normal names – Eduardo and Elena Antone Ramone. But when she was pregnant with Will, their mother had a big crush on Willie Nelson and, as a result, gave his name to her youngest son. Letty was just glad that her mom hadn't been infatuated with a Lady Gaga-type when she gave Letty her name.

Maybe Will was the youngest child, Letty thought with irritation. Their mom had run off with some Navajo cowboy from the rodeo several years ago. By now, she may have even more children, which would mean that Letty might have even more brothers and sisters. Letty and her siblings hadn't heard from their mother for ages.

"Yep, I'm out here with Millie."

Letty smiled. Their dog Milagro, a word which means "miracle" in Spanish, had somehow become Millie under Will's care. Millie was a beat-up, crippled runt of a pit bull with the sweetest nature in the world. The dog was content to stay in their backyard during the day, she barked a greeting at dogs that passed by, and she slept on her own padded doggie bed at the foot of the bed every night – sometimes at the foot of Will's bed, sometimes at the foot of Letty's. Millie had two doggie beds. Letty suspected that Millie ended up in Will's bed on cold nights.

Letty closed the back door to keep the heat in. She turned on the oven and slipped in the "healthy" pizza and "healthy" quiche she'd just purchased on her way home. The pizza and quiche were heavy on the veggies and short on the cheap greasy meat and cheese in typical pizzas. That must be what made it "healthy", Letty thought. She hoped that the food really was as healthy as claimed.

The O'odham people had been suffering from a serious problem with obesity and diabetes for many years now, since they started eating the white man's food. She had seen old photos of the People back before the change. They were tall and sturdy people, but almost never overweight, much less obese. They worked on their farms and in their fields growing tepary beans and corn and squash and other foods that kept them healthy. But that was before government food aid, television, food stamps, soda pop, white flour, and chicken nuggets led to rampant diabetes.

Since both his parents were O'odham, Will was as vulnerable as any tribal member to junk food. What he had in his favor was a big sister who made sure he ate right and his all-consuming passion for long-distance bicycling. Letty set out the ingredients for a salad and then went into the backyard. She sat down next to Will on the porch. It was full night now. She buttoned her jacket.

"Supper will be ready in about 20 minutes. Have you fed her yet?"

Will smiled and rubbed Millie's tattered ears. "Yes, and she ate like there was no tomorrow. She acts like every meal is her last meal. She has to eat every crumb and then she licks the bowl."

The dog, a red nose American pit bull terrier, moved over to sit where she could lean against Letty's legs. Millie looked up at Letty with adoring eyes as Letty stroked the dog's back. Millie had big patches of bare skin on her tan and white short-haired body. Her ears were chewed up, and there were scars all over her neck and chest. Her front left leg hung limp and almost useless from too much nerve, tendon, and ligament damage. The dog used the leg mainly for balance. Millie was small for a pit bull, maybe only 45 to 50 pounds. She had obviously been used as bait in dog fights. When the scumbags were done with her, they just dumped her out in the desert on the edge of town. They hadn't even bothered to kill her, but just left her to die a slow, miserable death in the hot summer sun.

No telling how long the dog had been out there before Letty found her. That was entirely accidental, too. Letty remembered suddenly that she had forgotten to return a call to one of the attorneys she occasionally worked for. She pulled over to the side of the road to look up the phone number when some movement in the hot sand about twenty feet off the road caught her attention. Letty got out of her car to take a look. She spotted the dog right away. It was emaciated and had several open wounds. The dog hadn't had any water for who knows how long. It was on its side, panting short, shallow breaths, eyes sunken and glazed. The dog shifted its amber-colored eyes to focus on Letty. Then the dog's tail began to wag feebly.

"Damn," Letty muttered to herself, but she didn't hesitate. Who could resist a dog on death's door that would wag its tail when it saw you coming? Letty checked and could see the dog was female.

"Okay, you pitiful mutt. Some asshole really did a number on you. I guess there must be some reason that I'm the one who found you. So don't you die on me. I had too much of that in Iraq already." Letty picked up the dog and placed her on the floor of her pickup truck in front of the passenger seat. Off they went to the vet. Fast-forward about six weeks, and after being cared for by a very generous and kind-hearted veterinarian who provided services at reduced rates for vets, Millie went home with Letty. The plan was to foster Millie and find her a permanent home, but Will and

Letty both fell in love with the good-natured little pit bull. And the feeling was mutual.

Letty and Will sat together in comfortable silence, taking turns rubbing Millie's ears and her chest.

After a few minutes Will said, "Letty, I have a chance to work longer hours over the Christmas break. My boss wants me to fill in for a couple of folks who will be on vacation. He said he would teach me some new bike-repair skills plus I'll make a few extra dollars. What do you think?"

"Sounds good to me, Will. You'll need to set aside some time for us to visit Grandma. Just remember when school starts in January, you'll have to drop down on the hours so you can keep your grades up."

"Yeah, yeah, I know.....I had all B's this last term except for chemistry. But I brought that D up to a C+."

"Much better than the term before. Now let's see some A's. You are capable of it."

Will laughed. "You're not gonna be satisfied until you see me win a Nobel Prize in physics, right?"

Letty grinned. "That's right. The People need a Nobel Prize winner. Might as well be you. But it doesn't have to be physics. Literature would be okay, or economics or…" Will laughed.

Letty felt real relief at Will's good cheer. Letty had been shocked when she'd first seen him after she returned from Iraq. Her little brother, whom she had carried around on her back as a child, had grown to nearly six feet three inches tall and had ballooned up in weight…not obese, but heading that way, like so many in the tribe. She didn't like the crowd he was hanging with either. She knew that there were gangs on the reservation, and she suspected that his friends were in a gang. Letty decided on the spot that her little brother was going to live with her. Grandma Antone accepted this with equanimity like most things in life. No one else was there to ask so Letty took Will with her back to Tucson.

When he first came to live with her, he was surly and rarely spoke to her. She ignored his bad attitude, and focused on what needed to be done. She enrolled him in the neighborhood high school, and she made sure he was eating right and doing his homework every night.

What really turned Will around was the day that Letty took him to see the start of El Tour de Tucson that first November that they lived together. Ten thousand bicyclists from around the world came to Tucson to bike the tour. Much to Letty's surprise, Will was captivated. He asked a lot of questions that she couldn't answer. They went home, and Will pulled her old bike out of the shed, then they went back to the tour. Will ended up riding a short leg in the last hour of the tour. That was all it took. Long-distance bicycling became his chief interest in life. He got a part-time job after school at the bike shop, and earnings from the job enabled the purchase of a good bike. Will brought his grades up, he hung out with biking geeks, he spent most of his free time training for races, and in the process, he dropped fifty pounds.

"So what's up with you? What have you been doing, Letty?" Will asked. This was new. In recent months, he'd become much more open with her and was now expressing interest in her life as well as sharing some things going on with him.

"Today I sent off the final report for that client in Phoenix. Remember? The one with the partner who skipped with all the money? I found the skip taking it easy on a Caribbean beach. Now I'm waiting for a big fat check in the mail." She smiled. "And tomorrow afternoon I am meeting a new client...or potential client. I don't know exactly what she wants me to do. She was pretty vague in the phone conversation. She lives up in the Foothills."

Actually Letty did know what the woman wanted, which was to prove that her sister's teenage son was innocent of murder, but she thought it best not to tell Will details of her work.

"Want to go biking with me tomorrow morning before your interview with the client?"

Letty hesitated. She was thrilled to get the invitation from him, and the idea of a relaxed bike ride sounded like fun. But she had to go with Jade and the Chinese cop to check in with the Tucson police. She didn't know how much she should tell Will about that.

"I wish I could, but I can't." She paused. "I have something else ...business-related...that I have to do in the morning"

Will grinned. "Big secret, huh? I wish you'd tell me more about what you do. I think it's so cool. My friends at the bike shop think you are just totally cool...a private investigator. Very hip. Like on TV. They love it when you come in the bike shop. They try to guess if you are packing heat."

Letty was genuinely surprised. She had no idea that he thought anything she did was cool. No one had ever had told her that she was cool. Well...no one other than Chava. She pushed down the stab of pain that inevitably came when remembering him.

"They'll be sorry to learn that I spend most of my time searching through public records or on the Internet. It's not all that exciting. And 'packing heat?' Your friends have been watching too many movies. Okay. I'll tell you more, but you can't talk to anyone about this. It's all confidential. I'm serious. We investigators have guidelines we have to follow to keep our licenses. We can't go around flapping our lips about the clients. Keep your mouth shut, okay?"

"Okay. I promise. I'll just tell my pals that everything is top secret. That makes you even cooler." He laughed.

"Remember Jade Lopez?"

"Of course. She's so smoking hot. All that red hair and those melons. Ai yi yi."

Letty laughed. "Don't get any ideas. She's too old for you. She's twenty-eight and you are only seventeen. And she's a married woman."

"Yeah, and her husband disappeared on her and took all that money. Right? She needs a younger man...one with no money. That could be me. I'm just saying." He grinned.

Letty sighed in mock exasperation. "So I guess that's how it is for seventeen-year old-dudes. You just think about one thing. Melons?" She raised one eyebrow.

"Pretty much," Will grinned. "Well, I think about my bike a lot, and I think about Millie, too." He stroked the dog's back.

Letty decided to give him a brief rundown about Jade's intruder and the Chinese cop named Zhou. "And tomorrow morning we're all three going down to the police station."

"Wow. That's totally weird. Mexican criminals I would expect, but Chinese?"

"Yes, I think it's weird, too. It's not every day that a Chinese cop shows up in your friend's backyard. And he seems to think Jade is in some serious danger. I'm going to keep an eye on her until I know what's up."

"I could keep an eye on Jade, too," Will said hopefully.

"No! You need to study."

Letty stood and opened the back screen door. "I think the food is ready now. Let's eat supper. Come on, Millie. It's getting too cold for you out here."

After supper and clean-up, Will went to his room and spent the rest of the evening as he often did, on his laptop reading websites about long-distance racing and doing a little homework. Millie followed him, her tail wagging.

Letty did the same on her laptop, but instead of reading about carb loading for a bike race or time trials for the Tour de France as Will did, Letty looked at the Chinese government's Ministry of Public Security (not much information there), then the Interpol website. Interpol was more forthcoming, but there was nothing about Chinese triad gangs in Arizona. Then she put the words "triad gangs" into Google, and started reading. After an hour of this, her sense of dread had grown considerably.

Triads were a group of secretive criminal gangs shrouded in myth and mystery. The story was that the society had formed originally during the Qing Dynasty as a patriotic effort to resist the rule of invading Manchus from the north and to reinstate the ethnic-Han Ming dynasty. There were different stories about where the term "triad" came from. The most cited was that the 17th-century group, the Three Harmonies Society, led to the name triad. No one could say for sure. Later when Mao and the Chinese Communist Party took over China, the triads had already become heavily involved in crime. Triads fled the mainland to set up business in Hong Kong, that beautiful city on the South China Sea. Hong Kong was still their primary center of operations, although triads had spread across the world to operate in places where there were large Chinese populations. That included North American cities like Vancouver, Toronto, San Francisco and New York.

Over the centuries, the secretive triads had transformed from revolutionaries to hardened criminals similar to the Italian mafia and Japanese yakuza. Triads were involved in everything from smuggling, money laundering and prostitution to the counterfeiting of a long list of goods and money. They were deep into just about every criminal activity known to man. And eventually the triad gangs had returned to mainland China, too. They flourished there, thanks to corrupt officials at every level who took bribes and looked the other way at triad operations.

Letty learned that there were numerous triad groups with names like Sun Yee On and 14K. Each had an elaborate organizational structure with officers carrying poetic names like "Mountain Master," "Incense Master," "White Paper Fan" and "Red Pole." Their initiation ceremonies involved animal sacrifice, and members were often easy to identify because of elaborate and extensive body tattoos.

But it was their brutality that really got Letty's attention. The triad gangsters had a favorite tool. It was a rectangular hatchet – a cleaver really – that was often found in the kitchens of Chinese restaurants. If the triad gangster met with any resistance, the cleaver was a quick and easy way to remove a finger from a hand as a warning, and if that wasn't enough, removing the hand usually did the trick. Swearing to adhere to the Thirty-Six Oaths was part of a triad initiation, and woe be to anyone who took those oaths and then violated them later. That person could count on being chopped into pieces, slowly, by the triad cleaver.

By the time she crawled into bed, Letty was taking the incident at Jade's home very seriously indeed.

CHAPTER 5

Before Letty left Jade's house to go home and eat with her brother, Zhou followed her around the interior to make sure all windows and doors were locked. The house looked moderately secure although they both knew that a determined intruder would have little trouble breaking in, most likely through the back door. Zhou was going to make sure that didn't happen. Zhou knew, too, that Letty Valdez was not entirely sure about him. That pleased him. If she were wary, then she would be alert and watch everything and everybody. And Jade would be safer because of the wariness of Letty Valdez.

Zhou complied with Letty at every point. He knew she was watching him as he went through the back gate, and he heard the lock click behind him. He knew she would be listening for him to start the engine of his rental car and drive away. And so he did exactly that.

He pulled away from Jade's house and headed to a convenience store on a nearby boulevard named "Speedway." He wondered briefly if motorists were allowed to drive faster there, but judging from the cars passing by, it did not seem that they were driving unusually fast, for Americans, that is. Drivers generally went faster here in the U.S. than in Chinese cities, maybe because there was just more room on the roads than in crowded China. Of course, neither country's drivers could compete with the Italians. He remembered the thrill of driving on the Italian Autostrada A-4 between Torino and Milano. Thanks to a grateful Interpol associate, Zhou had been lent a Lamborghini for a couple of days. He drove it on this section of the Autostrada with a speed limit of 93 mph. Yet, it seemed that no one was paying any attention at all to the speed limit, least of all Zhou. Fast and dangerous was the Autostrada. Yes, definitely a thrill.

Zhou waited a few minutes to make sure Letty wasn't following him. Then he left the convenience store and doubled back to a city park quite close to Jade's house. The park was deserted, and the library was closed for the day. Before traveling to the United States, Zhou had done some research about his destination, Tucson. He found that the city's public libraries had free wi-fi. He needed wi-fi now so he could contact his boss Yang using WeChat, the Chinese social media app.

Zhou chose the city park and library not only for the wi-fi. He had learned from his travels that Chinese people tended to speak louder to each other in normal conversation than the volume typically used by North Americans or Europeans. He had to find a place to speak at Chinese volume without attracting attention, and the alley behind Jade's house wouldn't do. A deserted park was a better choice. He checked his watch. It was almost 9 p.m. in Tucson. Beijing was fifteen hours ahead, which meant he would catch his supervisor in his office at the Ministry of Public Security in late morning unless Commissioner Yang was in a meeting. Zhou pulled his phone from his pocket and connected to Yang through WeChat.

Yang answered after a brief delay.

"Where the hell have you been?" Yang sounded even more irritated than usual.

Zhou explained briefly about following Bao from the airport to the American woman's house. He did not tell Yang that he was planning on returning to Jade's house to make sure she would be safe overnight. Yang would give him a direct order to abandon Jade and get on with his investigation. Zhou didn't want that.

Yang waited in silence, a subtle message that Zhou interpreted as Yang's disappointment with him. He let Zhou know by his silence that he thought by now his star investigator should have come up with something already.

"Tomorrow I'm going to report in to the local police and get some identification from them so that I don't have any problems with local law enforcement," Zhou added.

"All right, then," Yang said sharply. "Report back on a regular basis."

Yang hung up without saying goodbye.

Zhou frowned. Yang had a reputation for being rude and something of an ass, but in their recent interactions, he had been especially curt. Zhou remembered their last face-to-face meeting in Beijing two weeks earlier. It was a bone-chilling winter day in the capital, and thick smog from thousands of coal-burning heating units hung over everything. The streets were full of people, most with white paper masks over their faces in a futile attempt to protect their lungs. Yang's office was filled with cigarette smoke. A burning cigarette hung from his lips, and another waited in an ash tray. Their meeting was brief. Yang made it clear that Zhou had been chosen at the last minute for this assignment and against Yang's will.

Yang had been planning on sending another inspector, one that was a personal friend of his, whose name also was Zhou...in this case Zhou Li. Being sent to the U.S. was something of a treat for Chinese agents. After they finished their assigned tasks, most of them took a detour on the way home and enjoyed the casinos and prostitutes in Las Vegas for a few days. Yang wanted to reward his favorite inspector by assigning the case to Zhou Li. But the Deputy General Commissioner above Yang had intervened at the last minute. He handpicked the young, up-and-coming Zhou Liang Wei to go to America, find a missing girl, and stop the triad gang. Yang was annoyed as hell about being overruled by a superior, and also annoyed at being unable to give out a plum assignment that would increase his personal status among his staff. Yang made no effort to hide his irritation. Zhou was off on assignment when this decision was made, and on his return to Beijing, Yang informed him of his assignment in an American state known as Arizona.

After a brief and tense meeting in Yang's office, Zhou left to prepare for this trip. He hailed a taxi and directed the driver to take him down Chang'An Avenue past the Forbidden City, the Gate of Eternal Peace, and Tiananmen Square. Zhou often went that way before leaving China on assignment. He represented an ancient and advanced culture when he went abroad, and he wanted to remind himself to be the superior man that the Yi Jing described. He always tried to be the best man he could, but most especially when in another country. Despite all its many problems, Zhou believed that China, its people and its culture, would always endure. He wanted to always represent China well even if he often felt out of place in his own homeland.

Twenty minutes later, Zhou left the city park and cruised quietly past the front of Jade Lopez's house to make sure Letty was gone. There were no cars on the street at all. The neighborhood was quiet. He returned to the alley behind the house and tucked the rental car against the back wall.

Zhou retrieved a windbreaker from his backpack and quickly climbed the adobe wall into Jade's backyard. He had to avoid the nopal cactus that was almost as high as the six-foot wall, but the palo verde tree made it easy to go over the wall into the backyard for the second time that day.

Despite the pool of light around the back door, most of the backyard was in shadows. He silently moved the reclining patio chair into the darkest spot he could find against a side wall under overhanging branches of an olive tree. He put on the windbreaker, zipped it up, and settled onto the reclining chair for what he expected to be a long, cold night. He was surprised at how quickly the temperature dropped once the sun set. It was December after all. Although this region called Arizona had a reputation for wonderful sunny winters that attracted tourists, he knew he would be thoroughly chilled before morning. He thought about the western desert in China...Urumqi and Kashi. It was the same there. Wild landscape, gorgeous sunsets, dry air, cold nights, stars in the sky. He looked up. Yes, a sky just like the Taklimakan Desert. Beautiful. Silent. Peaceful. So wrong to see Bao in this place.

No way was Zhou going to a hotel. He figured that there was at least a 50-percent chance that Bao would show up again. And he might not come alone this time. He was the violent arm of a triad gang that carried out the will of the boss. Zhou believed that the triad boss in this case was Ting. Bao had a well-deserved reputation for being violent. Ting was worse. Ting was the handmaiden of violence. Violence was her middle name. She breathed violence. Zhou knew that many criminals acted out of a desire to improve their financial status. He thought that some of them could be rehabilitated. In Ting's case, she was ambitious and wanted to be wealthy beyond measure. But more than that, she enjoyed hurting people. Jiang Qing. That's who Ting made Zhou think of. Mao's last wife, Jiang Qing. Leader of the Gang of Four. Jiang Qing made recordings of the cries of people being tortured by her henchmen. Then she listened to the recordings again and again for her personal pleasure.

Zhou closed his eyes. He knew he was in a difficult situation. First, he wasn't supposed to be here like this. He was a Detective Inspector in the Ministry of Public Security, People's Republic of China, not a bodyguard. He had moved up quickly through the ranks to bypass Inspector Third Grade and become an Inspector Second Grade at the young age of thirty-two. Rumors floated around the Ministry that he might be in line to become Inspector First Grade after his recent superior performance in Zambia and at Interpol headquarters in France. So here he was in this desert city in the United States with the job of investigating what no-good Ting and her gang were up to. He had told Jade the truth, or at least part of the truth. Interpol had picked up rumors that Ting's gang was opening a new smuggling route into the United States and had passed this information on to the Ministry in Beijing.

Zhou had a second assignment, one that he had not mentioned to Letty or Jade. The teenage daughter of a Hong Kong government official had gone missing. Her dad finally went to the Hong Kong police and then to the Ministry in Beijing to ask for help in finding the girl. The triad gang had approached him, he revealed, and had offered him a huge bribe if he would make sure that the men under him would not obstruct triad illegal operations. The gang wanted assurance that their counterfeit goods and smuggled people could be moved from Shenzhen down the Pearl River to Hong Kong and then shipped off to ports around the world without interference from Hong Kong inspectors. The Hong Kong official had been educated in Britain. He had developed some idealistic views about China's need for "rule of law." He made a point of committing himself to ending corruption in the People's Republic. He turned the triad gangsters down. He refused their bribe. A few days later his daughter disappeared. She had been gone a month now. Her name was Victoria. Zhou wondered if she'd been named after the landmark peak on Hong Kong Island, and Queen Victoria before that.

There was no definitive connection between the girl's disappearance and Ting's gang, and there was no firm information at all about the girl's whereabouts. And yet whispers from informants on the streets of Hong Kong led the Ministry to believe that Ting might have taken her to America. Then they got a break. One informant came close to naming a place, claiming that Ting had the official's daughter and had taken her to an American city close to the Mexican border. San Diego came to mind first, but then a crucial bit of information was added only three days earlier. A triad member definitely identified as Bao had purchased a plane ticket from Hong Kong to Los Angeles, with connecting flights to Phoenix and Tucson. The final destination was Tucson, Arizona. Zhou had to look on the map to find this city because he had never heard of it. He followed in Bao's footsteps and arranged his own flight to Tucson.

Zhou guessed that Ting and her group were probably involved in sex trafficking. Young peasant girls and women from rural Fujian Province answered an ad for a job in Hong Kong, and then found themselves in a brothel somewhere in the world servicing fifteen or twenty men a day, seven days a week, with beatings in between if they complained. Death was the penalty for attempting to escape. It usually took just one dead girl in a brothel to convince the others to stay in line and behave. Zhou had already closed down one of Ting's girl trafficking rings in Australia a couple of years earlier. Ting knew who Zhou was, although the two had never met. Of course, Ting would like nothing better than to eliminate Zhou as an obstacle to her business plans. There was a chance that the Hong Kong official's daughter had been thrown in with the Fujian girls. It was an awful end for the daughter of an important Chinese official or for any young girl at all.....to disappear into the dark world of human sex trafficking...to be whored out to customers until she died from disease or exhaustion, probably before the age of thirty.

Why the triad gang had chosen Arizona and Tucson was a matter of speculation. Zhou knew that U.S. Homeland Security personnel had been much more careful in recent years about inspecting incoming cargo at the American ocean ports of Los Angeles and San Francisco. Homeland Security feared that terrorists would try to smuggle in a nuclear device. Because of this increased vigilance at the ports, smuggling people and goods by sea had become much more difficult.

Mexico's ports and beaches were easier. The beaches south of San Diego along the upper Baja Peninsula or the Sea of Cortez were not so well inspected or patrolled, and bribery was rampant. Once they had their goods in Mexico, Ting's gang would still have to make the trip across the international border from Mexico into the U.S. But that border was like a sieve, regularly breached by the drug cartels and those people-smugglers known as coyotes who charged a fee to take migrant workers north. They guided peasant workers from Mexico, and from Central American countries, too, across the Arizona desert to Phoenix where they were transported to other cities across the U.S. Often the migrant workers were forced by cartel operatives to carry drugs on their desert trek. The goal of the migrants was to find a job, and to send money home to feed the families left behind in Mexico. Too often the coyotes abandoned the migrants in the desert once the coyotes were paid. Over a twenty-year period, thousands of job-seekers had perished in the unforgiving Sonoran Desert.

Zhou figured that if he was right about what Ting's gang was doing in this region, then she had probably worked out some kind of deal with the Mexican drug cartels as well as Mexican officials. The Sinaloa Cartel controlled this region along the U.S.-Mexico border. He imagined bribes to the cartel were standard practice, or perhaps some cooperative business arrangement existed that involved sharing profits. He wondered how long that kind of business arrangement could last. The drug cartels were nearly as violent as the triad gangs and not very open to sharing anything. He wondered if Ting were brazen enough to openly defy the Sinaloa Cartel. True, the area just south of Arizona was somewhat disputed because the Sinaloa Cartel had lost some influence there in the last year or so. But if Ting went up against Sinaloa, it might be her undoing. Zhou sighed. Or maybe she was trying to create a partnership. There were too many unknowns at this point.

Up until the fight in Jade's backyard, Bao and Ting had not known Zhou was sent here. Bao also never saw Jade up above him on the roof. Good thing, that. She might be dead now if Bao had seen her. Zhou regretted that he'd been forced to fight Bao. He'd have much preferred that Bao not know he was on the scene. But it couldn't be helped. Zhou saw the woman on the roof before Bao did. Zhou had to distract him before he could hurt her – and knowing Bao, he would definitely have hurt her had he known she was there. So Zhou engaged him. Bao was good at his gong fu, but Zhou was better. Zhou's master at the police academy was the best in Beijing and one of the best in China. Zhou's master had learned from the Shaolin monks. Zhou learned from the best of the best, and he kept his skills honed with constant practice. Of course, if Bao carried a gun, it just made things a bit more challenging for Zhou. He welcomed the challenge.

Being in the uncomfortable position of acting as bodyguard and being unable to carry out his investigation wasn't Zhou's only problem. He was a self-aware person who had been trained to notice where his thoughts were going. Paying attention was important to survival. No, not "important." Paying attention was *crucial* to survival. If he wasn't paying attention, if he wasn't focused, if he allowed his mind to wander, the results could be lethal.

That brought him to his second problem. The young woman Jade definitely made his mind wander. She reminded him of that red-headed woman on a horse farm that he'd known when he was investigating for Interpol in Wales. Yet Jade was…herself…like no other woman he'd known. Or maybe it was just a case of deprivation. It had been a long time since he'd been with a woman, maybe nearly a year? He couldn't remember. Too much travel. Too much work. No personal life at all. Too many nights alone.

No, it wasn't just deprivation. It was her. This woman. Against his will, Zhou was attracted to her. When Jade slipped and fell off the ladder, and he reached out and caught her, holding her in his arms had an unexpected effect on him. She was soft and warm. She smelled good. She had this incredible wild halo of orange-red hair like nothing he had ever seen. The halo hung in ringlets around her face. Her skin was so fair with freckles across her nose and cheeks. Her face had the perfect shape of a watermelon seed so admired by the Chinese. Her mouth, her lips, her emerald green eyes….she was so beautiful. He wanted to know everything about her.

And therein lay the problem, Zhou thought. How could he protect someone for whom he had this instant attraction? A moment of inattention could be deadly to both of them. He would have to work diligently to keep his attraction in check so that he would not endanger her and himself by becoming distracted.

Zhou let his thoughts go over the events of the day. He had been completely surprised to see Bao at the airport. He ducked behind a pillar and managed to avoid being seen. He followed Bao out of the airport and across Tucson until Bao parked in front of Jade's house. Zhou drove past Bao, who never noticed Zhou in the rental car. Bao had always been an arrogant bastard who was so interested in himself that he often failed to notice what was going on around him. It wasn't that hard to understand how he had failed to notice

Zhou. Zhou found the alley behind Jade's house and went over the adobe wall without being detected.

Bao was tall and well-built with long dark hair that hung fashionably at his shoulders. He was considered very handsome. In fact, Bao had often been compared favorably to heart throbs like Huang Xiaoming. Bao wore expensive Italian suits and shoes and was often seen along the French Riviera and other upscale vacation spots in the company of beautiful women.

And Bao was a known triad 49er, which meant that he was at a lower level in the hierarchy. Even so, he was suspected of several assassinations. The word on the street was that he enjoyed killing.

Bao didn't stay in Jade's house long at all. Maybe ten minutes. Zhou speculated that Bao had something specific he was looking for, but he left empty-handed. That meant he would definitely be back. Again, Zhou wondered what Jade could have that was of interest to a Hong Kong triad gang. Zhou hoped he would have the opportunity to ask her some questions so he could find the connection.

Next he thought about Letty Valdez. He had never seen a woman like her either, but she was nothing like Jade. He guessed Letty to be almost two meters tall, close to 1.8 meters. Despite her height, she moved at times deliberately and with grace, like a cat, and at other times, with military precision. Her skin was dark with a reddish cast, her nose and cheekbones prominent, her eyes were black, as was her hair which hung long in a thick braid down her back. Letty was far from the Chinese ideal of fair-skinned, delicate beauty in a woman, and yet there was a presence about her that Zhou liked. She seemed very intelligent and capable. She seemed trustworthy.

It was quite clear to Zhou that Letty Valdez was far less open to him than was the gentle Jade, who took him into her kitchen and fed him like an honored guest. Letty had an unusual job as private investigator. Perhaps it made her somewhat suspicious of everyone. Or maybe she just didn't buy his particular story. Zhou was very curious about what kind of work she did as an investigator. This profession of private investigator was fairly new in China and typically associated with business investigations for corporations. It was obvious that Letty had phoned someone about him when she left Zhou alone with Jade in the kitchen. And Letty got an acceptable answer – for the meantime, anyway. He was going to have to prove himself to Letty eventually. He knew that. He also wondered why Jade had called her friend Letty before calling the police. He wondered if there were cultural differences he was missing, or if there were a deeper story here...something between friends. Overarching everything was the mystery of why a Hong Kong triad criminal had come to Jade's house.

He looked at his watch. Nearly twenty-two hundred hours now. It was getting colder.

Suddenly the back door opened, and Jade came out. She walked directly to him and laughed.

"I see you, Zhou," she teased. He found her so very charming.

Zhou stood and smiled. "I am watching. You are safe."

"You are so sweet to stay here and take care of me," she said, "but you're going to freeze to death. Come on inside. I'll make you some hot tea. I have some green tea. Would you like a cup?"

"Yes, please." He followed Jade into to her kitchen again. This would be a good opportunity to ask Miss Jade some questions.

She led him into her living room where a small fire burned in an adobe fireplace. The glow of the fire flickered in the darkened room.

"Sit here. I'll be back in a minute."

Zhou looked around. As best he could see in the dim light, her house was spare and simple, decorated in the Spanish style popular in this part of America. He read that the region was called The Southwest. Navajo Indian rugs covered parts of the Saltillo tile floor. He could see a short hallway and doors that led to what he guessed were two bedrooms and a bath. Moments later, Jade returned with two cups of steaming hot tea on a tray with sugar and lemon.

"You are not concerned that Miss Letty will be angry you invite me into your house?" Zhou said as he sipped his tea. Ah, so good to have real Chinese green tea again. No sugar. No lemon.

Jade shook her head from side to side.

"Oh, Letty and the others, Maggie and Seri, sometimes treat me like a child. I'm an adult. I can make decisions on my own. And I decided to invite you in, Zhou. I feel like I can trust you. Letty will just have to deal with that."

She paused and added as if she needed to explain.

"They've been very protective of me since Carlos disappeared. They just want me to be happy again."

"Who is Carlos?"

"My husband."

Zhou felt his emotions go flat. Ah, married.

"Carlos disappeared a little over a year ago."

Zhou sat up straight. Very interesting.

"Where is he now? Why did he leave?"

Jade sighed deeply.

"Okay. I guess I'll just start talking and tell you about me and my life. Maybe you can figure out what's going on. But if I tell you about me, then you have to tell me about you? Deal?" She smiled at him.

"Yes, but not many things to tell."

"Oh, I doubt that. You are a very interesting person, I think."

Zhou smiled again. Not good. He must stay focused.

Jade stood and went to a heavy wooden chest against the wall. She retrieved a thick photo album and brought it to him. She sat next to him on the couch and opened the album. Their knees touched.

For nearly an hour, Jade talked about her life. Born Mary Catherine O'Reilly, she came to be called Jade as a baby. Her parents had hired a Mexican nanny who treated Mary Catherine's colic by putting jade amulets on her stomach. The colic went away, and her grateful parents, who didn't believe for a minute that a jade amulet was responsible for the cure, started calling her "Jade." The nickname stuck. Then when she was only five years old, her dad was sent to Australia for a year to work as a business consultant. Her parents hired a Chinese couple to take care of their daughter and their home. The Chinese couple called her Jade, as she had already told Zhou. By the time the little red-headed Irish-American girl went off to elementary school, she had a new name, Jade O'Reilly.

Zhou surmised also from Jade's commentary that her parents were affluent and not very engaged with their daughter. They hired others to take care of her as a child. And now, though it was a significant holiday season in America – Christmas and New Year's – their daughter was alone. Yet they chose to go on a vacation without her.

Jade showed him her childhood pictures and then photos from high school. There was a boy, a Mexican-American boy who appeared for the first time in those high school photos. After that, he was in almost all the other photos in the album.

Jade and Carlos had been high school sweethearts from the age of sixteen. Two days after they graduated from high school, they had a big wedding at San Augustine Cathedral, and Jade acquired a new name, Jade Lopez. She pointed to the photos of her wedding.

"That's Maria, the mother of Carlos. And those are all his siblings and cousins. The Lopez family is big. They still treat me like one of their own even if ...," Jade frowned, then continued.

"My parents live back East now," Jade continued. "They moved after Carlos and I started college. They were both from Boston originally, and Daddy kept some business interests there. After I married, they decided to make Boston home base. They still keep a house here in Tucson and come out often especially when it's cold back East. By now they thought they'd have grandchildren, and Carlos and I planned to have a big family. But no kids came. I guess there's something wrong with me."

Zhou let her talk and when she got to the end of the photo album, he began asking questions.

"You work. What are you doing?"

"I am a teacher. I teach small children. They are third graders – eight and nine years old. Yesterday was the last day of school for fall semester. We have a two-week holiday now for Christmas and New Year's, then I'll go back to school in January. I have a ton of photos of my students, but I think I've shown you the most important photos already."

"Why were you on the roof?"

"I just like it up there. I go up after school often and drink a beer and watch the sun go down on the Santa Catalina Mountains. The view is very nice. I'll take you up there tomorrow."

"You said one year has passed since your husband disappeared. Please explain."

"I can't explain! He was here one day, and then he was gone. He went to work, and he didn't come home. By midnight, I was frantic. He had never done that before. He just didn't come back. Ever." Jade clasped her hands together in her lap. "There's something else you should know. Carlos had just won a big grant to start an after-school program for the kids on the southwest side of the city. Carlos is a social worker. He wanted to give the kids something fun and safe to do after school. Otherwise, a lot of them get involved in gangs or some other kind of trouble."

Zhou noticed that Jade began to rub her fingers nervously.

"When Carlos disappeared, the money disappeared, too. The cops think he skipped out with the money."

"Skipped out? I do not know the meaning of 'skipped out.' "

"The cops think he took the money and left to go live some rich person's life somewhere in a new place.......without me."

"Do you believe this?"

"No! Carlos loved me and I loved him. He would never steal that money."

"What does Miss Letty think?"

"Letty and my other two friends, Maggie and Seri, won't say so to my face, but I know what they think. They all think Carlos is dead. They think his body is out there somewhere in the desert. Even Carlos's mother, Maria, thinks he's dead. They all think that someone stole the money and killed Carlos. They think we'll never know what happened to him. They think I should get over Carlos and forget him. Recently Maria even suggested that I think about finding another man and getting married again. But I can't just forget."

She suddenly unclasped her hands.

"Don't get me wrong, Zhou. My friends and Carlos's family have all been very good to me. This would have been much harder without their support. But the bottom line here is that my husband disappeared without a trace and so did a huge amount money. I don't know what happened to him or the money."

Zhou decided to try another approach. "Do you know any Chinese people?"

"No, not really. Well, one year I had a little Chinese boy in my class. His name was Li. His parents were graduate students at the university. I went to the Chinese Culture Center last year for Chinese New Year's. I went with Letty and her brother Will. I didn't really know anyone there. Oh, and I met Seri's friend. He was a visiting professor this past year at the university. Professor Wen. I think he's returned to China already. That's all."

"Did Carlos know Chinese people?"

"No, he never mentioned anyone. And I knew most of the people he knew. I know what you're getting at. You're trying to find out why there was some strange Chinese man in my house. I have no idea!"

They sat together quietly.

Zhou said, "It's late. I return to sleep in your ...what do you say ...patio?"

"Yes, patio. It's a Spanish word. But it's cold out there. I think you should sleep on the couch."

"No, I think Miss Letty will not approve if I sleep here."

Jade laughed, too. "You are probably right about that. She'll have a fit if she comes over here in the morning and finds you asleep on my couch. Letty is a very serious person. I don't know if she's always been like that or not. I didn't know her before she went into the

Army. Maggie introduced us after Letty came home. I think she saw some terrible things there in Iraq. I wish I could make her smile more. But now I've just added to her problems. I called her because I didn't know who else to call. I don't trust the cops. They gave up on finding Carlos, and I think they suspected me for a long time when Carlos disappeared."

Hmmm, Zhou thought. So Miss Letty had been in the U.S. Army and had served in a war zone. Interesting.

Jade looked directly at him. "Okay. Your turn. Tell me about you."

Zhou felt a sudden pang of shyness. He opened his hands in front of him in a gesture of helplessness.

"I am a boring person. I work all the time. I don't have an interesting life. Not like you."

Jade laughed. "Most people wouldn't think an elementary school teacher's life is all that interesting. But an Interpol Chinese cop who travels around the world is most definitely exciting," She paused. "Okay, start from the beginning. Where are you from originally?"

"Before I was born, my parents lived in the countryside near a small farming town called Zhou Zhi, west of Xi'an. It is the mí hóu táo capital of the world."

"Mí hóu táo?"

"Yes, a fruit about this size," He made a fist. "Maybe a little smaller. Fuzzy…is that right? fuzzy?" Jade nodded yes. "Fuzzy on outside, green inside with small seeds."

"Kiwi fruit?"

"Yes, exactly! That's the word for it."

"Go on."

"My parents had been sent down during the Cultural Revolution. They worked on a farm there. Then Mao died, and Deng took the leader position. My parents were allowed to return to Nanjing, which is their home town. My father was rehabilitated soon after that. I was born in Nanjing. When I was at school, my coach identified me as a good prospect for a special school to study gong fu. At age 11, I entered the school to study."

"What is gong fu?"

"Martial arts. You Americans call it kung fu. Gong fu is Mandarin. Kung fu is the Cantonese language that is spoken in southern China and Hong Kong. You Americans watch Hong Kong movies so you call it kung fu. But really the more common term is gong fu. You know, like the Shaolin monks?"

"Yeah, I've heard of them. So you studied martial arts?"

Zhou nodded. "Yes, in school in China. Then, as I told you, my father was sent to live in the U.S., then in the U.K. and we lived briefly in New Zealand. My dad spoke English well, and that's why he worked in these English-speaking countries. This explains my English. Next I went to a British university. After university graduation, I returned to Beijing to attend the police academy. I have been in the Ministry of Public Security now for almost ten years. I travel often. My job is to find the criminals and stop them."

"Where do you live when you aren't working?"

"I have a small flat in Paris and an even smaller flat in Hong Kong – what we call a 'micro' flat. When in Beijing, I stay with a friend."

"Paris and Hong Kong! How romantic! And your family?"

"My father died when I was at University. I bought a nice apartment in Nanjing for my mother. She is happy there. Her sister and nieces and nephews live in Nanjing. My mother also has friends in Nanjing. She goes to the park every day to practice her tai ji. I visit her on my free time when in China. I have no brother or sister. One-child policy, you know."

"Do you have a wife?" Jade's voice was low. She avoided his eyes.

Zhou was pleased that she wanted to know this crucial bit of information about him.

"No. I was married briefly. I met her when I started my career at the Ministry. My wife is very ambitious. Later, she was not happy with me because she said I lack ambition. Two weeks after we divorced, she married another man, a rich entrepreneur. She lives in Shanghai now in what you call a 'penthouse.' She and her husband have a second home in Vancouver. She likes to shop."

"I think you dodged a bullet there."

"No, no, no. She did not use a gun. I freely agree to divorce."

Jade giggled. "I mean I think you are lucky to escape her, and she was really stupid for letting you go."

Zhou couldn't help himself. A surge of happiness washed over him. He realized then that he'd better get out of here fast and return to the dark, cold patio so he could calm himself. "Dodge a bullet" must be some kind of idiom or slang. Zhou would investigate that on his android phone before he slept.

"Okay. I go to patio now." Zhou stood.

"Wait a minute. If you insist on sleeping out there, then let me get you a sleeping bag. I put Carlos's bag in storage out in my studio so I'll let you use mine instead. It's in the closet. I'll get it." She rose and hesitated. "Oh, I forgot to tell you. My hobby is to work in clay. I make pots and cups and other things out of clay just for fun. Carlos made a studio for me in the garage. I'll show you tomorrow."

She left the room and returned shortly with a bright magenta and pink sleeping bag, an extra blanket and a pillow.

"Thank you, Miss Jade."

"See you in the morning, Zhou. Please call me Jade. No "Miss." And I believe you are definitely a good guy." She smiled and waved at Zhou as he closed the kitchen door behind him. He checked to make sure it was locked.

Settled in Jade's warm sleeping bag in the shadows again, he thought about what Jade had told him. There was no obvious connection between the triad gang and the missing husband. No connections to Chinese persons. It was a very intriguing fact that Carlos and $100,000 had disappeared at the same time. Interesting also that Letty believed Carlos to be dead. As for Jade, she seemed to Zhou to be a very warm-hearted person with a spirit as beautiful as her lovely face.

Zhou took a deep breath. Everything – the bag, the pillow and the blanket – filled his head with the fragrance of the lovely Miss Jade.

CHAPTER 6

Eduardo Ramone sat in his battered old black Nissan pickup on a side street in Barrio Santa Rosa south of downtown Tucson. He had parked the rust-and dent-decorated little truck facing north so he could observe the house at the end of the block. By parking carefully behind a large SUV and in the shade of a eucalyptus tree, he was pretty sure that he could not be seen by anyone in the house. The view of the Santa Catalina Mountains was great from this vantage point. It was late afternoon, the sun was setting, and long bands of copper-colored light were ascending upward along the ridges and canyons of the Catalinas. Eduardo's eyes moved back and forth between the house and the mountains beyond as he contemplated his problem.

The neighborhood around him was poor, and the people who lived here didn't have much. Even so, there was a character to it that wasn't found in the sterile suburbs to the north. Almost every house on this potholed little street was painted a different color, and each had a little garden in the back, and there were flowers in pots on porches and walkways. The barrio was so characteristic of Mexican-American neighborhoods. There were Indians in the neighborhood, too, mostly O'odham. In fact, some of Eduardo's relatives lived just a couple of blocks away.

Eduardo could hear a recording of Papago chicken-scratch music coming from one of the houses down the block. It was nice to hear some music because the radio in his truck wasn't working, and even if it had been, Eduardo wouldn't use it. He didn't trust the battery.

It was old and ran down fast. He didn't want to get stuck with a truck that wouldn't start because of a dead battery.

As he waited and watched, Eduardo went over again in his mind the events that led him to be sitting here in Tucson watching a stranger's house. It had been five days since he'd seen Esperanza. He was here now hoping to learn something that would help him find her.

Ban. Ban the Coyote. Eduardo had Ban with him on that day just before he found Esperanza. He'd just now remembered and wondered if seeing Ban meant something. Traveling between his grandma's house and his uncle's house, he had been riding along a rough ridge trail mounted on his mare Bonita. Mountains to the north were washed out in the late afternoon glare. Eduardo had been trying to hurry the horse without overheating her. He'd just crossed a low flat plain studded with cholla cactus when he went around a little curve in the rocky trail and started to descend into the wash. That's when he saw Ban.

The coyote stood silently at attention on a large boulder about 100 yards ahead. Eduardo reined in Bonita and watched Ban watching him. It was obvious that the coyote knew Eduardo was coming toward him, but the animal had not run. Why should he? Ban was the prince of the desert. Wind rippled fur on the coyote's shoulders. Ban stood his ground, and with his round golden eyes, he intently watched the man on horseback. After a minute or two, Ban turned and casually trotted away toward the Baboquivari Mountains. It was then that Eduardo has seen the fluttering of Esperanza's rebozo.

Although he had seen Ban in the wild more times that he could count, this encounter sent chills up Eduardo's spine. Ban the Coyote, he who was there with Elder Brother at the beginning of the world. He had shown himself to Eduardo.

It was only a few minutes after seeing Ban that Eduardo had discovered the young immigrant girl Esperanza dying of thirst under a palo verde tree. He revived her enough to get her on the horse with him, and they set out for Mando's house.

As Eduardo led the horse carefully through the mesquite bosque in the growing darkness that late December afternoon, he could see the light from his Uncle Armando's little flat-roof adobe house. The adobe bricks were so much the tan color of the surrounding desert that the house almost merged into the landscape. The soft glow from a kerosene lantern wasn't much light, but it carried a long way in the clear desert night.

Four dogs of various sizes and mixed breeds rushed up to Eduardo. They barked, then began wagging their tales furiously when they recognized Eduardo.

"Hola, you worthless mutts," Eduardo said with affection. "Come to greet us?"

Eduardo's mare picked up her pace. Even though Eduardo didn't live all the time with Mando and Valerina, he left his horse at their place most of the time. Bonita stayed in the little corral near the house with Mando's horses. The mare could sense the nearness of home, of food and water. One of Mando's horses whinnied, and Bonita answered.

Mando appeared, silhouetted in the light of the doorway. He peered out into the darkness.

"Hey, Uncle, it's me, Eduardo."

"I was wondering when you were gonna show up....What's that you're carrying?"

Mando came toward him just as Eduardo entered the dusty circle of light in front of the adobe house.

It had taken Eduardo almost an hour to get to Mando's. Only a few minutes after Eduardo started off with the girl, she leaned over precariously from her seat behind him on the mare and vomited. Eduardo dismounted, pulled her down and held her upright while she emptied the contents of her stomach.

This worried him. It was bad if she couldn't hold down water. Maybe it's just that she drank it too fast, he thought. When she finished, he wiped her face again with a wet cloth and got her back on the horse. A few minutes later, he felt her slump against him, and he knew that she'd lost consciousness again.

Eduardo didn't want her falling off the horse so he found a small piece of nylon rope in his side pack, pulled her arms around his midsection again, and tied her wrists loosely in front of him. That will keep her on this horse, he thought. She slumped against him, more closely this time. Hurrying as fast as he could without jarring her too much, they arrived at Mando's just after sunset. Already there were many stars visible in the sky. The night was cooling fast, but the girl's body still felt too warm against Eduardo's back.

Uncle Armando laughed softly when he walked toward Eduardo and saw that his nephew had a girl with him on the horse.

"Is this the only way you can get a woman? Knock her out and tie her to you?"

Eduardo grinned. "Figured it was about time to find a girl so I just went out there in the desert, and this is what I came up with."

Mando reached up and took the unconscious girl into his arms as Eduardo untied her hands.

"Hmmmm..." Mando looked her over. "Very pretty. But she's in bad shape. Days too hot, nights too cold. No telling how long she's been out there."

"Yeah, I found her about midway between here and Grandma's. I got her to drink a little water, but she threw it up. She keeps passing out."

"I heard there was a bunch of 'em out there the past couple of days. The Border Patrol found some of them, but I was afraid there'd be some stragglers. Looks like she's one that La Migra didn't find. I'll get Valerina."

Mando turned and went toward the house. He carried the unconscious girl in his arms.

"Valerina, Eduardo brought you un regalito, mujer." Their conversation alternated between Spanish and English in that unique language of the borderlands called Spanglish.

Eduardo slipped from his horse just as Valerina, all five feet four and two hundred pounds of her, appeared in the doorway. He could hear her laughter as she reached out for the girl.

"A little desert dove? Una paloma? Es un regalito that Eduardo brought me? A gift for me?" She led Mando, still carrying the girl, through the door.

"Let's get her in some water," Eduardo heard Valerina say as she and Mando disappeared into the house.

Valerina was one of the sweetest, gentlest creatures on the face of the earth. Eduardo figured if there really was an angel, Valerina was it. He'd spent half of his growing years here with Mando and Valerina on their little rancho miles from town. Uncle Armando Antone was the brother of Eduardo's mother Rhonda. Valerina was Mando's wife. Well...not really. Mando and Valerina never bothered to get legally married.

Valerina was from somewhere in central Mexico. She'd come north years ago looking for a job. She crossed the border in the night just like Esperanza. Valerina showed up at Mando's door one evening asking for directions to Miami. The coyote told her it would take her two days walking to make the trip. When Mando heard that, he slapped his forehead and told her that there was no way she could walk to Miami from Pima County, Arizona, in two days. He invited her in. She never left. Eventually they had a couple of kids who grew up and moved into Tucson. The kids came home for frequent visits. Mando and Valerina preferred life on the reservation.

Things got rough at home for Eduardo sometimes. That was mainly when his mom was drinking. Eduardo would take off then for a few days and go stay with Mando and Valerina. He spent most of his summers there, too. He would have moved in with Mando and Valerina except for his sister Elena. Eduardo couldn't leave his sister Elena. He and his sister were twins. Even though they were like day and night, they were very, very close. And there was their little brother Will they had to look out for, too. Their sister Letty was older and had been sent away by their mother because Letty had a different father. Eduardo never understood that.

Eduardo led the bay mare to the corral, slipped off the saddle and halter and spent a few minutes wiping down her reddish brown coat. He left Bonita munching happily on her dinner shoulder to shoulder with Mando's horses. As he walked toward the house, Eduardo could smell the sweet fragrance of tortillas, frijoles, and chiles coming from the adobe house. He stepped into the kitchen, his well-worn, sweat-stained cowboy hat still on his head in the O'odham way. His stomach growled.

Mando appeared, pushing away a heavy Oaxacan blanket hanging from the doorway between the bedroom and the kitchen.

"Valerina said her temperature was too high. It must have been even higher when you found her. Valerina got it down now to just 99 degrees. We don't know if she got too hot walking all that way in the sun, or if she got sick and has a fever from too much cold in the night. The girl's conscious, but she's pretty weak."

"Think she'll be okay? I could get my truck going and take her to the hospital. Or we could use that new phone of yours and call the ambulance out here." Eduardo said.

"She doesn't want us to do that."

"What? She's already giving orders?"

Mando smiled. "Begging is more like it. She's begging us to not call anyone. Says she'll be okay. She insists that the Angel will take care of her."

Eduardo grinned.

"And I suppose you would be the Angel?" Mando teased.

"I guess so. She's been calling me Angelito."

Mando shook his head, smiling broadly. "I think she's gonna be okay. She's young and healthy, and Valerina says she'll be fine. Valerina's giving her Gatorade and some of that manzanilla tea that she thinks is a cure for everything bad in the world. You wanna go talk to the girl?"

"Sure," Eduardo said. "Then I'd like to eat. I'm starving."

"She's probably ready now."

Mando lifted the blanket and Eduardo stepped into Valerina and Mando's bedroom. The first thing Eduardo saw was a big galvanized steel tub in the middle of the bedroom floor with Esperanza sitting in it. Valerina was pouring water over the girl's head. Her eyes were tightly shut against the streaming water. All Eduardo could see were the girl's face and two plump breasts, nipples erect, glowing bronze and wet in the lantern light.

Eduardo jumped back into the kitchen. His face was ruddy with embarrassment.

"Uncle Mando. She's naked!"

Mando chuckled. "She's still in the tub? Well...you didn't expect us to leave her clothes on when we put her in the water, did you?"

"You didn't tell me she was naked," Eduardo said accusingly.

"I didn't know ....but so what? What do you care? After all, you're an angel."

Eduardo looked down at his boots and blushed even more. Mando laughed again.

"Sit down and I'll get you something to eat."

Eduardo sat at the table. He didn't know whether to be annoyed with Uncle Mando for being the butt of his joking or grateful for having had the chance to see something so beautiful.

"The immigrants are getting to be a real problem for us," Mando said as he handed Eduardo a plate of beans and some tortillas. "Most of 'em are coming through the Chukut Kuk district because they can't get across the border anywhere else, and now they're breaking into people's houses and stealing food and water."

Eduardo nodded between mouthfuls. Chukut Kuk was a vast open desert area on the three million-acre O'odham reservation. It was impossible for the tribal police and the Border Patrol to adequately patrol such a huge area.

"So it's the 'very poor' stealing from the 'just poor,'" Eduardo said, reaching for another tortilla.

"Yeah, I feel sorry for 'em, but our people don't have enough themselves. You know old Garza that lives near Itak? Some of 'em broke into his place and took every bit of food he had. He's afraid to leave home now. He thinks they might steal everything he's got when he ain't watching."

Eduardo smiled, but he knew it wasn't funny. If you are at poverty level yourself, you can't afford to be robbed.

"But Esperanza isn't like that. She's no thief," Eduardo said. Mando nodded.

Valerina came into the room and sat down at the kitchen table.

"I got as much liquid down her as I could. Her temperature's almost back to normal so it looks like to me she'll be okay tomorrow. I don't think she's really sick. She just overdid it," Valerina said.

Mando handed her a cup of hot coffee.

Valerina smiled at him, then turned to Eduardo, "I dried her off and gave her one of my old gowns to wear. It just about swallowed her up 'cause she's such a little thing. I put her to bed in the other room and told her to go to sleep.

Eduardo nodded. The extra room was used for storage and as a place for visitors to sleep. This was where Eduardo usually slept.

"I put up another cot in there with her, Eduardo," Valerina added. "You want to sleep now?"

Eduardo turned away, blushing furiously, saying, "Nah, I think I'll sleep outside tonight under the ramada."

Valerina and Mando both grinned.

* * *

Eduardo and Mando rode away on horseback the next morning to round up some cattle and move them to a new pasture. When they returned to the little adobe rancho in the early evening, Valerina told them that Esperanza was well on her way to recovery.

"She got up after you two left this morning. I made her some *migas* for breakfast. She ate, slept some more, ate even more for lunch, then took an afternoon siesta. This evening she's been so energetic and so full of smiles that I could never guess how much trouble she was in yesterday. She's just about talked my ear off. I'm saying that girl hasn't stopped chattering since she got up."

"Yeah?" Eduardo asked. "What's she talking about?"

"She told me a little about her family and her village. It's like you thought. She's from southern Mexico, I think from the mountains of Chiapas. I'm not sure which indigenous group. Maybe she's a full-blood Maya."

"No kidding," said Eduardo. "She's pretty far from home then."

Valerina continued. "She asked a lot of questions about you......
Angelito." Valerina mimicked the name with a big grin." She wants
to know all about you."

"She does? Like what?" Eduardo asked. He was surprised and a
little embarrassed.

"Like does Angelito have a novia?" Valerina's laugh came from
deep in her chest and her belly shook. "Novia" was the Mexican
Spanish word for "girlfriend."

Eduardo laughed nervously. He shrugged his shoulders.

"Come on, Guapo. Supper's on the table." Valerina poked him
in the ribs, and Eduardo turned to follow. She had called him
guapo, handsome, since he was a little kid. He just hoped she didn't
call him that now in front of Esperanza.

Despite reports that she had chattered like a magpie all day, Esperanza said almost nothing at dinner. All through the meal, she
looked shyly at Eduardo, then down at her food, then at Eduardo
again. This amused Valerina and Mando to no end.

Later when they were in bed, Mando told Valerina that it was
about time that Eduardo found himself a woman.

"Good things come together," Mando said. "Elena got herself
that musician boyfriend and now it's time for Eduardo to balance
things out."

"Too bad we can't find a man for Letty," Valerina said seriously.
"I think she's lonely."

When the evening meal was finished, Eduardo announced that
he had to check on the horses. Esperanza offered to help clean up,
but Valerina and Mando both said no.

"You go help Eduardo," Valerina said.

The girl didn't have to be told twice. Off she went with a big
smile on her face.

Esperanza found Eduardo leaning against the corral rails slowly
rubbing Bonita's head and ears. The girl stood beside him silently.

"What will you do now?" Eduardo asked her softly in Spanish.

"The coyote gave me the name and address of a man in Tucson who has a job for me." She pronounced the city's name in the Spanish way - Took-Sohn.

Eduardo nodded. "Then I will take you there when you are ready."

They fell silent. Esperanza stepped closer and reached to stroke the mare.

"You know my people gave that town its name." Eduardo said. "We had a village there a long time before the *Milga:n* came. We called it 'Chuk-son.'" Eduardo didn't know if she was interested in a history lesson, but he also didn't know what else to say.

"Valerina told me your people are the Tohono O'odham, the desert people."

Eduardo nodded.

"Who are the *Milga:n,* Angelito?"

"Everybody else, I guess. Well...really the white people, the Anglos."

Eduardo looked down at Esperanza. Nearly six feet tall and broad-shouldered, Eduardo towered over her. Esperanza, five feet tall if she stood up straight, was fine-boned and slender.

He smiled at her.

"You know I'm not really an angel. My name is Eduardo Ramone."

"I know. Valerina told me." Esperanza hesitated and smiled shyly. "But you are my angel because you saved me from death."

Eduardo shrugged his shoulders nonchalantly, as if rescuing people were no big deal to him. His embarrassment was intense.

Esperanza smiled sweetly. "How can your people survive here for so long in this desert, Angelito?"

"The desert is full of food," Eduardo said. He was glad to change the subject.

She looked at him skeptically.

"Truly," he said. "There are many plants here that make delicious food. The mesquite bean makes a good flour for pancakes and muffins. Cholla buds are good to eat and so is nopal and the saguaro fruit makes wine for our sacred ceremony. Tomorrow I'll show you all the things to eat."

"And water?"

"When I found you, you were very near a spring that has water in it year round. You just didn't know it was there. If you are really desperate, you can get some water from young nopal pads or fishhook barrel cactus. This just for emergencies because too much cactus juice can make you go to the toilet a lot. You just have to learn the stories from the old ones and know the ways of this land if you want to survive here."

"Tell me the stories, Angelito, por favor. I want to know about you and your people."

"This is a good time. The winter is the right time for stories, not the summer. That's because in summer the snakes will hear us and maybe bite us. But if you go to town and take a job, I don't know when I can tell you the stories."

"I must find a job, Angelito. For my brothers and sisters."

"If you allow me to visit you….." Eduardo's voice drifted away. He looked intently at the horse, shy and uncertain and surprised himself at his own boldness. When he finally looked at her, Esperanza was smiling broadly.

"Yes, por favor, Angelito. I want you to come to visit me when I start my new job and my new life. I will be very happy to receive you."

Eduardo shook his head happily. "Good. You can call me when you are set up."

A frown flickered over her brows.

"Do you know how to use a phone?" he asked gently.

"No, Angelito. I am from the countryside."

"I will show you. In fact, I will give you a cell phone to carry with you."

Eduardo went into the house and returned with two cell phones and a charger.

"Here's how you turn it on. Be sure to turn it off after you talk, or you'll run down the battery. Here's how you dial my number.

Memorize the number." She practiced. Then Eduardo walked to the backyard and left her in the front. She called him using the new phone. She giggled uncontrollably when he answered. He also handed her a charger and explained how it worked.

He found old clothes belonging to his sister Elena for Esperanza to wear so she wouldn't look so much like an illegal immigrant peasant. Dressed in tight jeans and a red Arizona Wildcat t-shirt with her hair piled loosely on her head and a pair of cheap dangling earrings in her ears, Esperanza looked like an O'Odham teenager on her way to shop at the El Con Mall.

Two days later, Eduardo had driven away from the rancho in his dented pickup with Esperanza at his side.

He made sure that Esperanza put the cell phone in her bag.

"Call me right away when you are settled at your new job. Then when you are ready to receive visitors, you can use the cell phone to call me again. No matter where I am, I will come to you."

Eduardo delivered Esperanza to the address in South Tucson which Esperanza had carefully written on a small piece of paper. It was the same house he now sat watching in the growing darkness. After he'd left her there, Eduardo decided to give her a day or so and then try to call her to see if she was with her new employer. He hoped that she would call first. That would tell him that she was really interested in seeing him and not just contacting him out of gratitude for rescuing her.

Eduardo thought about her all the time. It was strange to him to realize how comfortable he felt with Esperanza. She didn't laugh or look at him like he was being foolish when he talked about the ways of his people. She showed every sign that she respected him and his effort to live the old ways. And why not? Esperanza was indigenous herself, so pretty, too, and so brave to have traveled from so far away. She was seventeen, old enough to know her own mind. She seemed to really like him, too. That was important. He wanted her to like him.

Eduardo dropped her off. The last thing he said to Esperanza was, "Don't forget to call me." She nodded her assent.

"I will not forget, Angelito."

After Eduardo left Esperanza at the coyote's house in South Tucson, he waited for twenty-four hours, but still Esperanza did not call. Finally, he couldn't stand it anymore and he dialed the cell phone's number, but there was no answer. He tried repeatedly but no one answered. Perhaps the phone was broken or lost? Had she forgotten how to use it?

Concern about Esperanza, and just plain missing her, pushed Eduardo to action. On Saturday, he drove into Tucson and went to the house where he'd dropped her off. An angry-looking man with an ugly scar on his face answered the door and told Eduardo that he didn't know any Esperanza and to get the hell out of there. Eduardo went back a second time and again was rebuffed. That time he was shoved off the porch, and the door was slammed in his face. On the third try, the man pulled a gun on Eduardo and told him to not come back.

Eduardo knew something was really wrong.

He began knocking on doors in the neighborhood and asked if someone had seen Esperanza. No one knew anything, or at least, they claimed they knew nothing. Eduardo knew that going to the police would be a mistake. Esperanza was an illegal, and if the man in the house got busted, then Eduardo knew he would never find her.

Why did things have to be so hard for some people? He would never understand. He just knew he wouldn't stop looking for Esperanza.

CHAPTER 7

Letty awoke later than her usual five a.m. on Saturday morning. The night had been too turbulent. There had been more of those Iraq dreams that didn't seem to ever go away. Maybe "nightmare" was a better word. The smell of human blood hung in the air. She groaned and pulled herself out of bed and went to the kitchen for a quick cup of coffee. There was a note on the kitchen table.

"Hey, Big Sister. I fed Millie and let her out and in again. She'll want to go out again. I got a call from one of the Tucson Bicycling Warriors. We're going to bike up to the top of Mt. Lemmon today. See ya, Will."

Letty sighed. Even the thought of cycling from the desert floor all the way up a nine-thousand-foot-plus mountain exhausted her. Warriors indeed. Of course, they had it easy on this trek up the mountain. No one was shooting at them, and there were no IEDs on the Mount Lemmon Highway. Letty gulped down a banana and a cup of black coffee and tried to empty her mind of the nightmares. She put on jogging clothes and laced up her running shoes.

"Out you go, Miss Millie, you big baby," she said. Millie wagged her tail, so Letty rubbed the dog's ears and gave her a dog biscuit. Millie went out, and Letty closed the kitchen door and locked it behind her.

After a five-mile run in a big circle around her neighborhood, Letty felt better. She took a shower and brewed a second cup of coffee. She called Jade.

"Everything okay over there?"

"Yes! I'm learning tai ji."

"What? Is that Chinese cop already at your house?"

"Yes, he is. He's teaching me tai ji, and everything is just fine, Letty."

Letty frowned. Jade was talking to her in that reassuring voice that elementary school teachers use when talking to eight-year-olds. Letty decided not to make an issue of it.

"Well, okay. Can you two meet me at the police headquarters at eleven a.m.?"

"Sure. See you then." Jade hung up.

Letty looked at her phone. Jade was so trusting. He might act like a nice guy, but as far as Letty was concerned, the jury was still out on Zhou Liang Wei.

* * *

Earlier that morning just as the rising sun began to lighten the sky, Zhou rose from his resting place on the reclining patio chair. He rolled up the sleeping bag and stripped down to his t-shirt and long pants. In bare feet on the flagstone patio, he began doing the morning tai ji exercises, just as he had been doing since the age of nine. Many Westerners were familiar with this ancient practice although they typically used the Cantonese term, "tai chi," rather than the Mandarin words used most often in China, "tai ji." In recent years, Westerners had begun to practice tai ji for health reasons, yet most did not realize that the practice was actually a martial art in slow speed. For a man like Zhou, who was already a skilled martial artist, tai ji was a way to practice his defensive skills and to build inner strength.

Zhou closed his eyes. He emptied his mind and focused on his breath. Slowly breathing in and out, he raised his hands in front of himself several times. After a final downward motion, Zhou moved his arms and hands slowly to the right, and at the same time he stepped to the right. His arms moved gracefully to form a circle. The movements progressed slowly, elegantly, with a sense of purpose that went beyond the problems of the current moment. He quickly felt himself settling, feeling calmer and stronger as he moved through the twenty-minute short form. All the while he kept the qi balance in the center of his torso. His hands and arms thrust sharply forward to deflect an opponent's intrusion. As he turned, he bent deeply at the knees from the center of his body. Yin and yang. Male and female. Heaven and Earth. Finding balance in all things. In the final movements of the form, he returned to slow, deep breathing as hands rose and fell in front of his body. His qi was strong today.

Zhou opened his eyes.

Jade was there watching. He didn't know how long she'd been watching. She smiled that radiant smile, and he felt himself growing warm.

"You are very graceful. Will you teach me?" she said.

"My pleasure," and for ten minutes Zhou did just that, starting with the initial centering pose and focus on breath.

"Remember. Start with qi. Do not resist force with force. Follow the motion of force and redirect it. Maintain balance. Willow bends in the wind. Willow does not break. Redirect force away from you."

The phone interrupted. It was Letty. The conversation was brief.

Jade put the phone down and said,

"Come on, Zhou. I'll fix you some breakfast."

"May I use your water closet?"

Jade giggled.

"Yes, you may use my water closet. That's British English. You may use my bathroom, or my restroom. "

Zhou took his knapsack with him, and she gave him a towel as she closed the bathroom door. He stripped to the waist and quickly washed, brushed his teeth and ran an electric razor over his face. He had a clean t-shirt in the knapsack. He put it on and added his long-sleeved shirt.

He made a quick call to his contact in the Tucson Police Department and asked for Sam Lambert. When Lambert came on the line, Zhou introduced himself and apologized for his tardiness at contacting his American counterpart. Zhou wasn't surprised when Lambert suggested an eleven a.m. meeting. He guessed accurately that Letty had a role in that particular hour.

At breakfast, Zhou learned some new words: "huevos (eggs) con papas (with potatoes) y frijoles refritos (refried beans)." He was learning that, although Tucson was an American city, Mexico had a very deep influence here. As they were eating, Zhou said, "Please tell me about this money that disappeared."

Asking Jade a question was like turning on the radio. She talked, and Zhou listened. He suspected that she was lonely, and since she spent all day with eight-year-olds, she missed talking to adults.

"Carlos won a big grant...well....it seems like a lot but really it's not so much. You'd be surprised at how fast one hundred thousand dollars can go. The plan was to put a down payment on an old warehouse and refurbish it into a community center. There would be an indoor gym, a dance studio, and an arts and crafts room. There was a small kitchen to provide an afternoon snack and drinks, too. A lot of these kids just don't get enough to eat. Upstairs there was a tiny room that was an office for Carlos. He had just moved into the office. He created a budget using the grant money to guide remodeling the facilities. His next step was to find funding to pay for staff. He needed money to buy sports and arts equipment, supplies, and other things like a photocopier for the office. He also planned to recruit volunteers to work with the kids. The grant was just the first step. He was writing more grant proposals, and he'd gone to the city council to see if he could get funding there. Carlos had been in the building only a month when he disappeared. "

Jade looked at Zhou directly. "I've gone over this a million times in my mind. I can't understand it really. This project was all Carlos talked about. It's impossible for me to believe that he would steal that money and take off."

"Did you find any helpful information in his office?"

"No, Letty went through everything very carefully. She interviewed everyone he worked with, the people in the warehouse district, the people who gave him the grant. She treated his disappearance as if I were her client. She told me once that she was treating him both as a 'skip' and as a 'missing person.' She has big files on Carlos, just as if I had hired her. She did her best, and she found nothing. I think that's why she thinks he's dead. She has no idea who killed him. The police searched the office and took the computer, but I think they decided early on that he had taken the money and then run off. I don't think they tried very hard. Letty did most of the work."

"What will Bao find in your house?"

"You mean that Chinese man who was here? I don't know! I don't know what he was looking for."

They both fell silent.

"Hey, I think you should search and see what you find. Want to do that?" Jade said.

Zhou was glad that she asked. He had been trying to think of a way to ask her if he could search her home.

"Yes, I will do this."

"Okay, let's start in the living room."

For nearly an hour, Zhou went from room to room in the house. Next he planned to search the garage and Jade's pottery studio. In every room of the house, he looked in drawers and on shelves, he turned over furniture to see if anything had been hidden underneath, he looked behind art on the wall, and even went so far as to remove the grates on vents to check inside. He looked up inside the chimney flue. He checked panels in the ceiling and tiles on the floor to see if any were loose. Jade followed him and handed him tools when he needed them.

In the second bedroom that served as a small office, Zhou noticed a traditional Chinese ink drawing on the wall. It was done in the flowing style known as grass calligraphy. The two characters were "long" and "feng," dragon and phoenix, male principle and female principle.

Jade said, "I bought that on a cruise on the Yangzi River."

"You visited China?" Zhou was surprised.

"Yes, last summer. I went with Seri. See, Zhou, for the first month after Carlos disappeared, I was frantic. Then I sort of became numb. After a couple of months, I went back to teaching again. Then when summer came, I had nothing to do. I was depressed. Maggie was worried about me. You'll meet Maggie. She's like everyone's mom or big sister. She's also a senior teacher and assistant principal at my school so she's my teaching mentor, too. She and Seri got together and decided that I should go with Seri on one of her trips. Seri travels a lot."

"Who is Seri?"

"She's a research librarian at the University. She's kind of like Mycroft to Letty's Sherlock Holmes."

Zhou frowned and shook his head. He knew Sherlock Holmes, but not Mycroft.

"Mycroft was Sherlock's brother. He occasionally helped solve mysteries, but he never left his room. Seri sometimes consults with Letty, but she never gets involved directly. They are both really smart. So I went to China with Seri."

"Where did you go?"

"Beijing, Xi'an, a river cruise, Shanghai. The typical tour. Then we took a little side trip to Hong Kong"

"You like China?"

"I loved it! The people were very friendly. The farther we got from the big cities, the more curious they were about us. They liked Seri especially – she's a blondie, and they found my red hair fascinating. Seri and I felt like movie stars! People took our pictures!"

Zhou smiled. He remembered his first time to touch a Western woman's hair. So soft. "Later I ask about trip, but now we search."

There was a large floor-to-ceiling bookcase in the office. He systematically took out each book, opened it and shook it for loose papers. Nothing fell out but for a few odd scraps of paper acting as book marks.

In the bathroom Zhou looked through a large cabinet holding towels. He looked under the sink, and in a medicine cabinet over the sink. There were feminine products there, make-up, sunscreen, bottles of female things for skin and hair, a hairbrush full of tangled red hair, and one prescription bottle. He took the prescription bottle out and looked at it. Jade's name was on the bottle. It was empty.

"Oh, I should have thrown that away. I had to take antibiotics last winter for a respiratory infection that I got from the kids. I was in such a stressed state that I seemed to catch everything that came along. I'm doing better now."

Zhou nodded, smiled, and returned the bottle to the shelf.

Jade's bedroom was next. He tried his best not to be embarrassed in this intimate space. Like the sleeping bag, the entire room was filled with her fragrance. He checked under the mattress and the bed, in the drawers where he carefully moved aside lacy lingerie, and then turned to the large walk-in closet filled with her clothing and shoes. There was no sign of a man at all in the room.

As if she could read his thoughts, Jade said, "Maggie thought that it would be better for me if I packed up Carlos's things. His mother, Maria, thought so, too. So I put his clothes and other things in boxes in the garage."

Zhou nodded. The kitchen was next, but like the rest of the house, he found nothing. No hidden cameras watching Jade, no secret hiding places, nothing at all unusual except that she had visited China.

"Jade, in China, did you form a friendship with Chinese people?"

"Not really. We were on the tour the whole time. We did visit some friends of Seri's in Hong Kong. They used to live in Tucson, and now they live in Hong Kong and teach English." Jade paused. "I sort of became friendly with the tour guide when we were on the mainland. His name was David. That's not his real name. I don't remember his real Chinese name. I brought some pearls home for his girlfriend."

"Please explain."

"David has an American girlfriend in Phoenix. They met when she was on a tour about a year ago. They fell in love and decided to marry. He asked me to take a gift to her when I passed through

Phoenix. When I stopped at the airport in Phoenix, she was there to receive the gift, which was a red-velvet box with a pearl necklace. Actually, I sort of broke the rules. I didn't declare this at customs. But it was all for love so I thought it would be okay."

Zhou considered this. It could be as she said, a simple gift from a Chinese man for his American girlfriend. But he knew that Chinese men were usually not interested in marrying foreign women, especially Americans. Women were considered carriers of the culture. They were the ones who taught children how to be truly Chinese. American women could not do that. Also, American women were thought to be too wild. As one of his friends put it, "American women are too hard to control." Usually relationships worked the other way. That is, Chinese women married American men. This, of course, created a great deal of resentment among Chinese men. So the story seemed possible but unlikely.

Could Jade have inadvertently carried some contraband or counterfeit jewels or something illicit without knowing it? He wondered if the triads had found a way to disguise heroin as pearls, or injected inside pearls. Or perhaps the case carrying the pearls had something illicit hidden in it. Jade's trip had occurred months after the disappearance of her husband. Perhaps Bao being here at her house had nothing at all to do with the missing husband. Maybe he was looking for that pearl necklace. Jade's voice interrupted his thoughts.

"We'll search the garage later. It's time to go meet Letty."

* * *

The meeting with Homeland Security agent Sam Lambert was tense from the outset. Zhou was immediately separated from Letty and Jade and escorted alone into a separate office. Through the office's glass windows, Zhou could see the two women sitting on a couch in the hallway. There was also a Tucson policeman present with Lambert in the office. The policeman represented Tucson Police Department's Homeland Security Intel section of the Special Investigations Section. However, Lambert didn't bother to introduce the TPD cop to Zhou.

Letty saw him, though, and made a note to find out what his name was. The Tucson cop might be a way to bypass Lambert later.

"So, Mr. Zhou, I received a fax from the Ministry of Public Security in Beijing. Almost all of this is in Chinese and might as well be hen scratches on a paper as far as I'm concerned. I can't read a word of it." He shook the papers as if they were covered in ants. "But finally on the last page I see here that your Ministry is sending an agent, I guess that would be you, right? You're here because you have information from Interpol that a Chinese criminal gang may be operating in our city."

Lambert tossed the papers on his desk, and then glared at Zhou as if challenging him to contradict anything he'd said.

Zhou politely introduced himself for a second time. He handed over his Inspector Second Grade identification card and his passport. He outranked Lambert by several levels in official hierarchy, but the Homeland Security agent would never realize that. Lambert gave only a cursory glance to the ID and passport. More Chinese hen scratching.

"I am very sorry not to have a translation of the documents. Perhaps the triads are in Tucson. Perhaps in Arizona or perhaps elsewhere. We do not know why they are here or where they are headquartered."

Zhou observed Lambert as he spoke. The Tucson cop was tall, about the same size as Letty, but outweighed her by forty or fifty pounds. He had blue eyes and short blond hair. He wore a rather rumpled light-colored suit. Beneath the jacket, his shirt was unbuttoned at the collar. Lambert's skin was patchy and florid, as if perhaps he got too much sun or drank too much alcohol, or a combination of the two.

"Explain how you got involved with those two?" Lambert tossed his thumb toward Letty and Jade.

Zhou briefly explained how Bao had showed up a day early, and luckily, Zhou had spotted him. He told Lambert about following Bao to Jade's house and watching Bao enter, then leave the house. Zhou did not expand on this. He did not tell Lambert about the brief physical altercation with Bao, or about catching the beautiful young teacher as she fell from the ladder, or about eating dinner with her, or about spending the night in her sleeping bag in the back yard, or about meeting Letty and talking to her as well. Zhou had the sense that there was some tension here, but he didn't know what was causing it. Did Lambert have some kind of history with Letty or Jade? Or was it simply that Lambert liked to be in control and he didn't like having some foreign cop show up on his doorstep with an unconfirmed story about Chinese criminal gangs in his territory?

"They claim they know nothing about this?" Lambert demanded.

"That is correct."

"What do you plan to do?"

"I will find these criminals. Stop them."

"You're pretty sure of yourself, aren't you? I want you to report in regularly. Got that? No independent action. You have no authority here."

Zhou nodded. "I understand."

Lambert motioned to one of his officers to bring Letty and Jade into his office.

"So what do you have to say for yourselves?" Lambert demanded.

"I am very grateful to Mr. Zhou for his concern about me," Jade said. She tossed her head back. "I do not know why that intruder was in my house."

Letty said nothing.

"You didn't see him?" Lambert asked.

"Yes, I saw him but from above. I was on the roof."

"On the roof?"

"Yes." She tossed her head again. Those red curls went flying.

"Okay," Lambert decided to let that pass. "Call us if this guy shows up again."

Jade said nothing.

"And you," Lambert turned to Letty. He was frowning and sounded very irritated. "What have you got to do with this?"

"Jade is my friend. She called me."

"That's right," Jade said. "I called her and asked her to come over."

"Did you see this intruder?"

"No." Letty wasn't about to add anything. She didn't like this guy. Not just because Marv didn't like him, but because she could see he had a very inflated opinion of himself.

"All right, then you stay out of this. You understand? And tell Marv Iverson to stay out of this, too. This is Homeland Security business. Got that?"

"Got it," Letty said. "Any chance of getting protection for Jade Lopez?"

Zhou wondered who Marv Iverson might be.

Lambert continued. "Not much to go on here. You told me yourself that it wasn't really a break-in, and no one has threatened Mrs. Lopez. I'm too understaffed to assign an officer to protect her. I think she can call us if she has a problem. And keep in mind that Zhou is off limits to you, Valdez. He's here on official business so don't waste his time. Not that you would understand him anyway. His English isn't all that great."

Jade's face turned red. "His English is excellent! And way better than your Chinese," she blurted out.

Lambert glared at Jade and said, "All of you. Get out of here."

Out in the parking lot, Jade fumed. "Can you believe how incredibly rude he was! What a jerk!"

"Yes, Marv and Lambert don't get along and I think it's easy to see why. Look. I have to go to work now," Letty said. "I haven't actually seen this guy Bao. I can think of no reason why he should be at your house, Jade. Maybe it's all some kind of mistake. But it pays to be careful. I think you should seriously consider leaving town for a while or staying with a friend or maybe just going someplace safe until we figure out what's going on here."

"My parents are off on a trek in South America so I can't visit them now. If there is some kind of danger, I don't want to get my friends involved by staying with them. If there's any sign of this Chinese man again, then I'll seriously consider staying somewhere else for a while. Maybe I could go up on Mt. Lemmon and rent a cabin or something like that. But for now, Zhou is here. I feel safe with him, and I'd like to try to help him. And maybe we will discover that this is all some kind of gigantic mistake. It wouldn't be the first time that criminals got the wrong house."

Zhou said nothing, but he knew it was no mistake. Ting sent Bao, and Ting didn't make mistakes. He was pleased that Jade felt safe with him, though. Yet being her bodyguard was only going to slow him down.

"I want to go to airport car rental and find information about Bao and the rental car," Zhou said.

Letty nodded. "That's a good place to start. We need to find out where this Bao is and what he's doing, before he comes looking for Jade again. As for me, I have to see a new client this afternoon. I still have to make a living. I'll call you after that, and we can meet later."

Letty got into her little sand-colored Toyota pickup truck and left the parking lot first. She headed north. Jade and Zhou followed in Zhou's rental car, turning south.

Behind the midtown police department complex and parking lot was the municipal golf course. Beyond that, stretching out to the west was a large urban park, Reid Park. Neither Letty, Zhou, nor Jade saw the slender, well-dressed Chinese man under the trees watching them through his high-powered binoculars.

CHAPTER 8

JADE directed Zhou south toward the airport.

"What are we going to do?" she asked.

"We ask about Bao's rental car."

"They may not want to tell you anything. A lot of businesses won't give out information about customers."

"We could give a gift of money."

Jade laughed. "You mean a bribe? No, I don't think so. We should make up a story so they'll give us the info." She fell silent for a while as he maneuvered through traffic.

"You are my sister," Zhou said, and grinned. "We look for lost baggage in a car."

"Hmmm..." Jade returned the grin. "Brother through adoption? Somehow I don't think you will pass as Irish-American."

"Seriously. I have a plan." He explained and Jade listened intently.

"Remember, Jade," Zhou said. "If clerk is a woman, you talk to her like sister. Ask for help. If clerk is man, you ask for help in flirt way."

Jade laughed. "Flirt way? You mean flirtatious. I don't know. I'm not sure I know how to do that."

Zhou smiled. "You will do very well, I think."

They arrived at the airport and went into the terminal. Zhou led Jade to the area outside the terminal where car rental companies were located. He had been there when he first arrived in Tucson. The clerk at the car-rental agency was a young Mexican-American man dressed in dark pants and a neat white shirt. He was staring intently at a computer screen.

Zhou faded into the shadows. Jade entered the car rental office.

He couldn't hear them talking, but it was clear from the smile on the young man's face that he found Jade attractive. Who wouldn't? Zhou could tell that the clerk was resisting the idea of leaving the desk unattended. The clerk frowned, looked around and said something to Jade with a slight shake of his head. She persisted, leaning over the desk toward him. Zhou couldn't see her face, but could easily imagine a seductive smile coupled with a persistent request.

Finally, the two left the office together and walked quickly into a large parking garage. The young man did not look back. He didn't see Zhou slip quietly into the office, nor did he see Zhou go behind the desk and insert a USB drive into the company's computer. Zhou stared intently at the computer screen for a few seconds. Then he began clicking commands with the mouse. Two minutes was all it took, and he was out of there.

Five minutes later, Jade and the clerk reappeared.

"Well...I don't know what happened to my purse. I'll look at home again. I'm very sorry to have bothered you." She walked away, turning briefly to wave goodbye to the clerk. Once out of sight, Zhou rejoined her and they returned to his rental car.

"We will go to your house now and use your computer. I will look at the record of rentals for yesterday," Zhou said.

They went through the booth at the airport exit where parking tickets were paid. The line of cars was longer than usual, and they had to wait. Out of habit, Zhou periodically checked the rearview mirror. He noticed the small gray car in the line about five cars back, but because of the angle in the road and cars passing in front of his view, he couldn't tell much about it. It appeared to be a Honda but he couldn't be sure.

After paying the parking fee, he pulled over to the right lane and slowed to about twenty-five miles an hour, ten miles under the speed limit. Most of the cars zipped past him, but the little gray sedan fell back at least ten car lengths and maintained the same speed as Zhou. Not a good sign, Zhou thought to himself.

"Why are you driving so slowly?" Jade asked. "Do you see something back there?"

"Not certain." He turned suddenly without signaling into a hotel parking lot and quickly pulled into a spot facing the road. The gray car suddenly picked up speed and zipped past. Zhou pulled and followed. The little gray car, definitely a Honda that looked suspiciously like the one Zhou had followed the day before, was now at a major intersection, still in the right-turn lane. Before the light changed to green, the Honda took advantage of a lull in the traffic and turned right. Zhou had to wait for a car to pass. Then he turned right. The Honda was well ahead of him and changing lanes as needed to keep moving fast.

At the next major intersection, the Honda was first in line in the left-hand lane waiting for the turn arrow. Zhou was several cars back in the same lane. When the arrow turned green, the Honda didn't turn. The driver waited a good five seconds, which caused all the cars behind him to sit on their horns. Then he turned just as the arrow changed from green to yellow, then red. That left at least five cars, including the one driven by Zhou, waiting for another cycle of the traffic lights to change. The traffic was too heavy for Zhou to do a run-around the lights and pursue. It was too dangerous. So he waited, knowing that it was very likely that he'd lost the car. He was right.

Zhou was left with a very unsettled feeling. He had not seen the license plate on the car, and so he could not confirm that it was the same car he'd seen yesterday driven by Bao. And he wasn't able to a good look at the driver. Even so, his gut told him that it was Bao.

How could he have known Zhou would be at the airport again? Had Bao been following him earlier and Zhou just hadn't seen him? Did Bao know that he'd met with Homeland Security and the police this morning? Or was it all some gigantic piece of luck for Bao to spot Zhou and follow him? Zhou had this kind of luck himself the day before. But his intuition told him that it wasn't luck. Bao was there following him and Jade, which meant that Bao was either incredibly lucky or he'd been tipped off. By whom? Were there more triad gang members here than Zhou knew about? Had they been watching him? Again, he felt regret that he'd been forced to reveal himself in Jade's backyard. It couldn't be helped. If he hadn't been there, Jade would have been Bao's first victim after his arrival in Tucson.

Zhou shifted focus to the Tucson Police Department meeting that morning. Had someone in the police department or Homeland Security known that a triad gang member had arrived the day before? Was there someone passing on information to Bao? If there was someone taking a bribe from the triad gang and failing to report Bao's presence, how was Zhou going to figure out who it was? And the fundamental question remained. What were Hong Kong triads doing in this unlikely part of the world? It made no sense.

He realized with a start that Letty was one who knew that Zhou was here. Zhou didn't think that she would do anything to jeopardize her friend's safety, but she may have made a casual remark to someone. Would she do that? She seemed very careful about her speech. In fact, she had hardly spoken at all during the meeting. Yet she knew everything. She knew that he was in Tucson, that he was meeting with the cops, and that he was on his way to the airport with Jade. She knew about the triads. Maybe she knew more than she was letting on.

And now Bao knew not only that Zhou was in Tucson, he also probably knew that Zhou was tracking him down at the car rental agency. And worst of all, Bao knew that Zhou was with Jade.

Zhou realized that Jade had become very quiet.

"It's okay," he said. He wanted to reassure her.

"Was that Bao in that little gray car?"

"I do not know, Jade. Maybe."

They didn't speak again until they arrived at Jade's home. She turned on her desktop computer and logged in.

"It's all yours. I'm going to make some tea."

Zhou inserted the memory drive and looked at all the transactions at the car rental place from the day before. He didn't have anything to go on but the approximate time that Bao rented the car, plus his own memory of what the car looked like. He found it fairly quickly. As he thought, it was a gray Honda sedan, the kind of car that would easily disappear in traffic unless you were looking for it. He entered the license number into his smart phone and memorized it.

The person to whom the car was rented was not Bao or Ting. The name on the form was Kevin Kwok.

When Jade came into the room with tea, Zhou pointed to the form on the screen. He said, "Bao is using this name. He's using an alias."

"If it's an alias, he's using the name of a well-known Tucson family."

"What?" Zhou was surprised. Using the name of a local family might explain why Bao had escaped notice by the local authorities.

"Yes, the Kwok family has been here in Tucson for a long time, maybe 100 years or more. I don't know if you know about this, but Tucson had a large Chinese community from …oh, I don't know exactly…maybe the 1880s and after. A lot of them came here to work on the railroads and in the mines. Back then, the Chinese immigrants were mostly men. They would work for a while and then go back to China. Most of them were from southern China around Hong Kong and Canton."

"Today we say Guangdong, not Canton. How do you know this?"

"I have lived here for most of my life, and you know how it is. You pick up information at school and from reading the newspaper and talking with people. Also I learned from Seri. She likes history and especially she knows a lot about the history of Tucson. She told me a lot about the Chinese in Tucson when we were traveling around in China."

"Tell me more, please."

"Some of the Chinese decided to stay in Tucson. So they sent for their wives, and they started families. They became part of the community. A bunch of them lived in Barrio Viejo, down where the convention center is now. Some of them established little farms over there under A Mountain on the other side of the Santa Cruz River. They produced a lot of Tucson's vegetables and fruits. Later the Chinese opened grocery stores and restaurants. They lived in the Mexican barrios. 'Barrio' is the Spanish word for neighborhood."

Jade paused, "Am I talking too fast?"

"I understand. Thank you for the Spanish translations. I speak French, but no Spanish. You use many Spanish words."

Jade continued, "There was a lot of discrimination against the Chinese back then. Seri said that in 1901, a law was passed that made it illegal for a white person to marry a Chinese person. There were restrictions on certain land ownership and other restrictions, too. Letty bought an old house built in the 1940s. In the original deed, it says that the owner can't sell the house to anyone who is a Mexican, an Indian, a Negroid or a Mongoloid." Jade shook her head. " 'Mongoloid' means an Asian person. It's ironic that the house is now owned by a woman who is half Mexican and half Native American."

"Letty is two races?" Zhou asked.

"Sort of. I guess you could say that. It's complicated. Depends on how you define the word 'race.' She's half Mexican and half Tohono O'odham. Her little brothers and little sister are full O'odham. They have different fathers."

"They are American citizens?"

"Yes, of course. I'm just talking about race, not nationality or citizenship. We're all American citizens. Except for you!" she grinned.

"The Kwok family is one of the first Chinese families in Tucson?" Zhou asked

"I think so. I'm pretty sure that the Kwok family was one of those early immigrant families. More Chinese came from Mexico after the 1910 Revolution. Then more came after World War II and later, even more came, but they were from all over China, not just that small area in the south. Some of the families did quite well and became wealthy."

"And the Kwok family?"

"Yes, they are among the wealthy or at least quite affluent. There are a bunch of Kwoks. Every generation had at least four or five kids. I don't know Kevin Kwok personally. I just know the family name. There are doctors and lawyers and owners of different kinds of businesses. They are an important family in Tucson."

"Very interesting. Perhaps Bao has a relationship with the Kwok family."

"But why would Bao use the Kwok name? Wouldn't he try to hide their relationship?" Jade asked.

"Maybe. Maybe not. Maybe Bao does not care. He is very arrogant. Maybe he assumes that no one will know. Maybe he feels safe. Perhaps he thinks he moves around without being observed. I am not certain now what Bao thinks and knows. There could be a simple explanation. Maybe he stole the Kwok name."

"Identity theft. But wouldn't Kwok know that his identity was stolen?"

"If Bao does not attempt to use a credit card with the Kwok name, or if Bao does nothing illegal using the Kwok name, then there is no warning to Kevin Kwok. You see here on this record, Kevin Kwok paid cash for the car rental. No credit card record. No advance reservation."

"Usually you have to show identification to rent the car."

"No problem. It is easy to get counterfeit identification."

"How do you know so much about this guy Bao?"

"Two years past, I worked to stop human sex trafficking from Hong Kong to Australia. A triad gang took young teen girls from the countryside, often Fujian Province, promised them a good job, and then forced them to work as prostitutes. Sometimes they serviced twenty men each day. The gang takes all the money. The girls never see home again. They often die of AIDS or another disease. Many kill themselves from despair."

"Oh, that's horrible."

"Yes. Very bad life for girls. This triad gang is part of the old Wo Hop To group. This gang's leader is a woman named Ting. Chong Ma is her Red Pole. Bao is a younger member. They are known as 49ers."

"Red Pole?"

"What you call 'enforcer.' Red Poles are often former military men. They typically lead a group of fifty 49ers who are the foot soldiers. Ting gives orders to kill. Chong tells Bao or another 49er to kill. Or sometimes, Chong does the killing himself."

Zhou returned to the computer. "Where I should look to find information about the Kwok family? A simple Google search?"

Jade sat beside him. "Yes. Do that and also let's look at the local newspaper archives. But we should ask Letty when we see her again. She's really good at finding out details about people. She does background checks all the time as part of her investigative work."

After a half hour of searching the archives of Arizona newspapers, they managed to put together a folder of articles and other documents on the various branches of the Kwok family. Many lived in Tucson, others in Phoenix, and a few had migrated to cities across the U.S., including San Francisco, San Diego, and New York City. There was scant mention of Kevin Kwok. According to his Catalina Foothills High School graduation announcement, he had won a scholarship and was headed for the University of Colorado. After that, there was a gap of four years, then Kwok returned home and opened a real estate office in Tucson.

Jade counted on her fingers. "That was twelve years ago so he will be thirty years old now. He's two years older than me. I went to Tucson High so I didn't know him. Look. Here's the website for his real estate business."

The website had little information about Kwok. There was a photo of a smiling young man dressed casually in a white knit polo shirt and khaki pants. Most of the information on the site was about homes for sale in and around the city. Everything on the website was out of date.

"Please look on Facebook," Zhou said.

Sure enough there was a Kevin Kwok, several Kevin Kwoks, in fact.

Zhou shook his head. "So many. This will take some time. Some of these people give out their private information so easily."

Jade laughed. "Right. That's one of the problems. I'm a teacher, and I was warned to be careful about what I put on my Facebook page. I've been thinking about going to Google Plus because my students are not there. They aren't supposed to be on Facebook either, but they are there anyway. They are too young. That's why teachers should be careful about what they post. It's too public."

"You are on Facebook? I want to see." Zhou grinned.

Jade smiled and logged into her account. They spent some minutes looking at the photos and her recent postings which were few and mostly about meetings with friends. There were photos of her with a group of women eating together at what looked like some kind of outdoor festival. The photo album was titled "Tucson Meet Yourself," and it dated back three months to October. Jade was smiling. As he went back in time, postings became fewer and stopped altogether, then there was a flurry of messages about a year earlier. All were pleas for help in finding Carlos.

Zhou looked at Jade. "I am sorry. I make you remember."

"It's okay. I just wish I knew what happened. If Carlos is dead, I wish I could have his remains so we could have a memorial service for him. Then I could let go and move on."

"Carlos knew Kevin Kwok?"

"I don't know Kwok, and I know a lot of the same people that Carlos knew. But I guess anything's possible. Carlos was very outgoing and friendly. He knew tons of people. But Carlos never mentioned Kevin Kwok. I really don't know, Zhou. I don't remember anyone by that name."

Zhou turned to the computer again. "You would I think find now maybe?"

"Say what?" Jade giggled.

"Sorry, Jade. I'm speaking Chinglish. Please help me to improve my English."

"Your English is great. You have a degree from a British university!"

"Yes, but that is all academic English, and British English as well. Your American English is different. American English is very dynamic. It changes constantly. You Americans create new words, and you borrow words from other languages. You have slang and idioms. And those dreadful things called phrasal verbs. You know? You combine a verb and a preposition to make an entirely new meaning." Check in, check on, check out, check up, check for; throw on, throw at, throw up. 'Throw up' means to vomit! Listen to this with the verb 'turn' and the preposition 'on.' 'She turned on him' and 'she turned him on.' Same words, the order changes, the meaning changes significantly. Impossible language! I need your help."

"Of course I will help you," Jade responded immediately. "But, you know, pillow talk is the best way to learn another language."

Zhou looked at her, a blank look on his face. Pillow talk?

Jade stood up abruptly.

"Oh, my god. I can't believe I said that. Never mind. Forget I said that. I'm so embarrassed. I'm such an idiot." Her face was very red.

Zhou had no idea why she was behaving this way.

"I'm going to fix some lunch." Jade hurried out of the room.

As soon as she was out of sight, Zhou turned back to the computer and searched for the definition of "pillow talk" in an online slang dictionary. A big grin appeared on his face when he read the definition.

When Jade returned to the room later with sandwiches, Zhou did not look at her directly. He didn't want to embarrass her.

"I think we are finished here now. Let's go to your garage after we eat. Okay?"

"Okay!" Jade replied, thankful that Zhou said nothing more about pillow talk.

CHAPTER 9

LETTY stopped off for a quick sandwich and a bottle of water at the grocery store in her neighborhood. Then she headed north along Swan Road. The potential client, Mrs. Baird, had given directions to her house that took Letty across the Rillito River and upward into the foothills of the Santa Catalina Mountains. Here is where the primarily affluent white people lived, many of whom kept lovely winter homes in Tucson and then returned to their homes up north during Tucson's hot summers. Snowbirds, they were called. Letty was no longer within the city limits of Tucson but had entered unincorporated Pima County to an area known as Catalina Foothills.

Swan Road narrowed as Letty climbed. She began looking at the street signs for those streets that led off Swan on curving lanes to million-dollar homes. Letty had always thought it amusing that the streets in the Foothills so often had elegant-sounding Spanish names like Avenida Cerro del Falcon and Camino del Cazador. Yet in the poorer, Mexican-American part of town far to the south, the streets were named after U.S. states – Iowa Street, Louisiana Street, Montana Street, Nebraska Street.

Here in the Foothills, most houses had expansive grounds with desert landscaping. That included various mesquite, palo verde and desert willow trees, plus the iconic saguaro and ocotillo. In the south, houses were on smaller lots with fewer large trees. After all, who could afford the water to maintain elaborate landscaping? Many of these yards in the southside homes were graced with old, broken-down cars instead of swimming pools. Yet kitchen gardens that produced real food plus flowers in colorful pots were much more common on the south side. The two Tucsons, Letty thought to herself. One with plenty of money; the other not so much.

She finally found the street she was looking for, which turned out to be a graveled lane leading to a huge Spanish-style home at least a quarter mile off the Swan Road pavement. The house was done in the adobe Santa Fe style with vigas visible all around. She parked her truck, turned off her cell phone and went up to a heavy, carved oaken door. The door opened before she could ring the bell.

A short and somewhat plump middle-aged Hispanic woman with elegantly-coifed hair, dressed in an expensive lavender-colored suit, opened the door.

"Are you the private detective?" she asked curtly.

"Yes, my name is Letty Valdez."

"I'm Consuela Baird. Come in."

She turned and led the way. As she followed, Letty got a glimpse of a huge living room with a polished Saltillo tile floor and a floor-to-ceiling window that provided a glimpse of the entire city and the Santa Rita Mountains forty miles to the south. A maid was dusting sculpture that adorned the room.

Mrs. Baird led Letty into a smaller, book-lined room with a large desk. She gestured to a chair. Letty sat down.

"You probably know that there was murder in the Sam Hughes neighborhood a few days ago," the older woman began.

Letty nodded. In fact, Letty habitually scanned the online version of the local newspaper first thing when she arrived at her office. She had seen a report about a Mrs. Barbara Lyle who had been murdered in her backyard in the historic Sam Hughes neighborhood of Tucson.

The murdered woman had been shot in the head from a distance, most probably from the side yard near the street. The very brief news report said that a group of teenagers, mostly Mexican Americans from Tucson High School and led by José Maria Gomez, had been in an altercation with a group of University High School Anglo teen boys earlier in the evening at a fast food restaurant on Speedway Boulevard. The police had to break up what had escalated into a fistfight, but no arrests were made. The teens from University High School included Travis Lyle, son of the dead woman. The report went on to say that police thought that Gomez followed Lyle to his home, attempted to shoot Lyle, and shot Mrs. Lyle by accident. A gun had been found at the site. Gomez was arrested and booked into the Pima County Jail. The investigation was ongoing, the report concluded.

"My sister's son, José, has been accused of this crime. He is innocent. I want you to find the real killer and clear José's name. Will you do this?"

"Mrs. Baird, I can investigate, but I cannot guarantee that your nephew will be found innocent of the crime. Are you willing to accept that?"

"Yes, and I will pay you no matter what you discover. I believe in my heart that José is innocent."

For a moment, Letty considered turning the job down. After all, she had this problem with Jade to deal with. But that was for a friend and involved no money. Letty had to pay the bills, and make enough to give some to her grandmother, and to her brothers and sister if they needed it, and to save a little from every paying job for emergencies and for Will's college tuition. It was obvious that Mrs. Baird had money and could afford to pay top dollar for Letty's services.

"Okay. I'll get started on Monday."

"Here is my attorney's card. He will be defending José. You will be working with him and reporting to him. Is that clear?"

"Yes." Letty looked at the card. The name on the card was Frederick Clark, a well-respected Tucson attorney.

Letty was about to rise from her chair when a teenage girl came into the room. She had long, dark braids, and she was dressed in a Catholic school uniform – dark plaid skirt and long-sleeved white blouse.

"Grandmother?" the young girl asked.

"Miss Valdez, this is my granddaughter Elizabeth, and this is my husband, Colonel Baird. He's retired U.S. Marine Corps."

A tall, fit man with an erect bearing entered the room directly behind Elizabeth.

Letty rose to her feet. "Sir." Old habits die hard, Letty thought to herself. Commanding officer. Stand up. Say "sir."

"You come well recommended, Miss Valdez. You were on the ground in Iraq. Correct?"

"Yes, sir. I served as an Army medic, sir."

The Colonel nodded gravely.

Letty noticed that Elizabeth had a look on her face best described as bored.

"Miss Valdez, here's something to get you started," Mrs. Baird handed her a check. "If you need more, let me know. Make contact with my attorney, and keep me informed."

"Thank you, Mrs. Baird. I'll do that."

Letty made her escape. The room had become very claustrophobic.

Back in her truck, Letty looked at the check and gasped. It was for five thousand dollars, and it was made out to Leticia Valdez. Once over the initial shock of having so much money available to her all at once, Letty began thinking about what she'd just experienced. She wondered who had recommended her to the Bairds, and she also wondered how an Anglo Marine colonel had met and married a Mexican-American woman who was presumably a native of Tucson. There's a story in that, Letty thought.

She drove directly to her office where she checked her phone messages.

"Miss Valdez, this is Jessica Cameron from Mr. Clark's office. I'm calling about the Gomez case. I understand you've met with Mrs. Baird already. I emailed you a link to a folder with the paperwork on our client. I've arranged for you to interview José Gomez this afternoon. After you've spoken to him, call me for a Monday appointment. We'll meet at my office to discuss this."

The voice was polite but at the same time, very assertive. Letty got the feeling that Jessica Cameron didn't like to take no for an answer, and it was already obvious that Cameron was very organized. Letty wondered who Cameron was. She did a quick search on her computer. Clark was the head of a large law firm. Cameron was listed as a shareholder in the firm. Her photo suggested that she was fairly young, mid-thirties, very blonde, and rather pretty. Maybe that explains the assertiveness, Letty thought. She's getting her bluff in before someone tries to push around a pretty girl.

Letty retrieved Cameron's email and saw that there was a file attached. She glanced at her watch. She had just enough time to make it into the jailhouse before Saturday afternoon visitation ended. She'd have to look at the documents later.

* * *

Letty never liked going to the jail. It reminded her of her childhood when she had to visit her mother in jail on more than one occasion. Drunk and disorderly. That was always the reason. And there was something about it that reminded her of Iraq, too – a pervasive sense of despair and the ever-present threat of sudden violence.

She went immediately to the front desk and announced her purpose. After a brief wait, she was ushered through the security process fairly quickly. Jessica Cameron had handled all the paperwork and made the right connections so Letty's path was open. It was clear to all that Letty Valdez was there on business on behalf of the influential Clark law firm.

Letty was led to a room with rows of booths. Each had a television screen and two telephones. She eased herself into an uncomfortable plastic chair. Only a minute later, Gomez appeared on the television screen, a telephone receiver at his ear. Letty picked up her telephone receiver, too. She knew that any interaction she had with José Gomez was being monitored and recorded.

The teenager was slumped down in his chair, waiting.

"Who are you?" he demanded sullenly.

Letty took in his appearance. He had a wiry build, not especially tall, with a dark complexion and long dark hair in cornrow braids. Tattoos were visible on his right arm and both hands. She didn't recognize the tattoos as belonging to any gang she knew. He glared at Letty with angry eyes.

"My name is Letty Valdez. I'm a private investigator. I've been hired by Mrs. Consuelo Baird and your lawyer to help you. You have been charged with murder."

José Gomez looked away toward the wall.

Letty waited.

Nothing.

"The police report says that you and some of your friends got into it with another group of teens, one of whom was the dead woman's son. Is that true?"

He shrugged.

"The police report says you were arrested outside the Lyle house. A gun was found discarded nearby. Is this true?"

José hesitated. "If the police say so, it must be true. Right?" He snorted derisively.

"Is the gun yours?"

"No."

"Did you kill Mrs. Lyle?"

"No!" José spit the word out.

"Then who did?"

He fell silent. He looked away at the wall.

Letty waited.

Finally José said in a low voice, "I don't have anything else to say."

Letty waited.

"Look. Your family is spending a lot of money on you. They want to help you. I want to help you. My guess is that you didn't kill this woman. I have a feeling that there's something else going on here. But you have to help me. Give me something to go on. Some information that no one has. Someone to see. Some question to ask. Help me help you."

More silence.

Finally José Gomez turned to Letty. His eyes were bright, and he looked very sad.

"I can't talk."

Letty waited, and then finally she said, "Okay. I'll be back." She stood, turned around and walked out of the room without a backward glance.

* * *

Back in her truck again, Letty clenched the steering wheel. It was very obvious that Gomez was hiding something. She had a strong sense that he wasn't talking because he was trying to protect someone. Who? One of the other boys in his group of friends? It had to be one of them. But why? Simply because Gomez didn't want to be seen as a snitch? Was he willing to go to jail for life to avoid being labeled that way? Or was there more to it than that?

The sun was getting lower in the sky when Letty made it back to her office again. She opened the email from the attorney Cameron again and saved the attached file folder to her hard drive. She opened the folder. The first document contained rather sketchy information that repeated what Mrs. Baird had told her. José Gomez was eighteen years old – old enough to be tried for murder as an adult. A gun had been retrieved at the scene. It appeared to have been thrown by the shooter into a hedge next door to the Lyles' home. Ballistics tests were underway to see if the bullets in the gun matched the bullet that killed Barbara Lyle. Her body had been transported to the morgue and made ready for an autopsy in the coming week.

There was a second document, a police report that included the names of individuals who had been at the dust-up on Speedway. She saw Travis Lyle's name as well as four other boys from University High. The other group, the one including Gomez, was larger and included four boys and two girls. On Monday, Letty would contact the dead woman's husband and try to get an interview with him and with the son, Travis Lyle. Then she'd start on the others in both groups of teens and attempt to interview them as well.

One more possibility for today was to talk to José's mother, Mrs. Baird's sister, and see if she knew anything. Letty found her number listed on the arrest papers as Mercedes Gomez. She dialed the number and got a quick response and an invitation. Fifteen minutes later, she was in Mercedes Gomez's living room south of downtown Tucson.

With Mercedes were two daughters, both younger than José, and a third teenage girl that Mercedes introduced as Emily Castro.

"You can call me Em," the girl said to Letty. She was a Mexican-American girl, very pretty, about Jose's age.

"Em is José's girlfriend. She's been trying to comfort me," said Mrs. Gomez, "but I'm just too upset." She started crying.

Letty attempted to ask a few questions, but Mrs. Gomez had little to add. It was clear that her son, at the age of eighteen, was not at home much. His mother knew very little about what he was up to most of the time.

"He has a job at the tire place. He patches tires and takes them off cars and puts them back on. His dad is dead but if he were here, he would be so proud of José," Mrs. Gomez said. "José is a good boy. He's a good boy." She started to sob.

Letty waited patiently but felt that she wasn't going to get much more out of Mrs. Gomez.

"Em, would you mind coming out to my truck with me?" Letty asked José's girlfriend.

"Sure."

Letty had to be careful. This girlfriend might be the one who did the shooting. Maybe she's the one José is trying to protect from the police.

"Em, I'm trying to help José, but he's not helping me. He's just not telling me anything. Do you know anything that could help get him out of jail?"

Letty watched her reaction.

Em looked directly into Letty's eyes. She appeared to be hiding nothing.

"No. I don't believe José would kill someone. I just don't believe it."

"Then why did he follow Travis Lyle back to his house?"

She shook her head and said, "I don't know."

"What were they fighting about?"

Em sighed. "Oh, everything and nothing. They just don't get along. Those boys from University High were calling us names … racist names. I know most of the kids that go to that high school are okay. I'm even good friends with a girl there. But Travis is a real ass. He likes to start trouble. He's thinks he's such hot stuff."

"Can you remember some of the things they said to each other?"

"Well, like I said, they were calling us stupid names like greasers." Em hesitated.

"This could be about me, I guess."

"What do you mean?"

"Travis has been bothering me. He knows I'm José's girlfriend. But Travis keeps asking me out, and once he grabbed me and tried to kiss me. I pushed him away. But then I told José, and it made him really mad."

"So what did José and Travis say to each other?

"Travis stopped talking to José. He started flirting with me instead. He said in front of everybody that he had something I needed…something José couldn't give me because José's wasn't big enough."

Em sighed heavily.

"Then José yelled at Travis and called him a pinche cabron and he said…" she paused.

"José said, 'It's not enough that you got those Chinese girls. You want my girl, too." That's when they started throwing punches."

Letty breathed in. She felt herself grow tense.

"Are you sure José said something about Chinese girls?"

"Yes, but I have no idea what he was talking about. José has never mentioned anything to me about Chinese anything."

"Then what happened?"

"A police car just happened to be cruising by. The two cops saw what was going on and stepped in. They stopped the fight, took everyone's name and phone number, and told us to grow up and stop acting like little kids. Then they told us all to go home. I left because I have a part-time job, and I was due for my shift. I work at a local restaurant, and we were starting to serve a new ice cream flavor that day. I had to be there because it was going to be really busy."

"Do you remember anything else?"

"No." Em hesitated. "Is José okay?" There were tears in her eyes.

"For now," said Letty, "but he really needs to start talking and help me find the real killer. Does José have a gun?"

"No, not that I know of. I've never seen him with a gun. He's never talked about a gun."

Em reached out and touched Letty's hand. "Thank you," she said sincerely.

"Thank you, Em. You've been very helpful."

As Letty drove away, she felt a sudden thrill that was somewhere between excitement and dread. This might be the break she and Zhou had been looking for. She might have found a local connection to the triads who had appeared so recently in Tucson. She had to call Zhou. She headed for her office.

* * *

Not far away, Zhou and Jade had just finished searching Jade's garage. The garage was so full of stuff and junk that Jade's car was left outside in the driveway. Zhou systematically went through everything. He looked through the tool box and a wooden cabinet with tools and supplies that Carlos had used. He looked under the base of Jade's pottery wheel. He opened the door to the wooden cabinet where she kept pottery supplies, and he moved bottles and sacks around to see what was under and behind everything. He went through a big box filled with clothing and personal items that had belonged to Carlos. He climbed up a ladder and looked above the rafters to make sure there were no boxes hidden away. He peered behind every container and knocked on the walls, looking for empty spaces that might hold something.

"I find nothing," Zhou finally said to Jade.

"That's what I expected," Jade said. "Come inside and I'll make us some coffee…or more of that green tea you like."

Seated again on her living room sofa, Zhou decided to show Jade some photos of known Hong Kong triad members. He pulled a notebook from his backpack and set it on the coffee table.

Jade returned with two cups of hot tea.

Zhou looked up at her. "Jade, will you please look at my photo album?"

"Oh, how nice! Do you have pictures of you when you were a child?"

Zhou laughed. "No, not that kind of album. This is a policeman's photo album. What you call 'mugshots.'"

She sat beside him, and Zhou opened the album. Each page had twelve mugshots. The faces looking back at Jade were all known members of various Hong Kong triad groups.

"Look carefully and see if you recognize anyone."

Jade did as instructed. She turned the pages slowly after observing each photo carefully. She came to the end of the photo album, then turned suddenly back to the third page. She tentatively pointed to one photo. It was of a middle-aged man with graying, short-cut hair.

"This man looks a lot like a termite inspector who came here. I'm not sure."

"Termite inspector? When did he arrive here?"

"Maybe a three or four weeks after Carlos disappeared. This was about a year ago."

"Describe everything you can remember."

Jade closed her eyes, and then she opened them and looked directly at Zhou. "He came to the front door. His panel truck was out front. It was white and had some kind of business logo on the side. He was dressed in khaki uniform with a logo on the pocket.

He said Carlos had ordered a termite inspection for our house. He talked kind of like you. Sort of Chinese with a British accent. Oh, my god. I never thought about him again until you showed me this photo. I didn't tell the police or Letty about him. I just didn't think of it. I was very upset then."

"Not to worry," Zhou patted her hand. "Tell me more."

"He had a clipboard and an order form. He showed me the order form. Carlos had signed it….or it looked like Carlos's signature. I let him in, and he did the inspection. He inspected everything… inside and outside the house and the garage…everything. It took him over an hour. When he was done, he came and told me that he found no evidence of termites. He asked me to sign the form. I did. Then he left. Come to think of it, I never received a bill for the inspection."

"Did you have a conversation with him?"

"No. After just a few minutes, I went back in the house. I didn't even watch him. You know, at that time I was so distressed because Carlos had been gone for a while, and no one could find him. That was all I could think about. It never occurred to me that Carlos might not have ordered this inspection."

Zhou nodded his head. "I understand."

"Who is this man?" Jade pointed to the photo.

"Do you remember I told you about the Red Pole?'

Jade nodded.

Zhou said, "This is Chong Ma, the Red Pole."

Tears filled Jade's eyes. She leaned against Zhou and put her head against his shoulder.

"Zhou," Jade said softly.

Zhou knew what she wanted. He pushed her away gently. "We must not allow ourselves to be distracted with this…..this attraction between us. This is dangerous. We must be very watchful."

* * *

Letty sat back in her chair at her office to think about what she'd learned from the interviews she'd done that day. Mrs. Baird, Jessica Cameron, José Gomez, Em Castro.

The phone rang. It was Eduardo.

"Big Sister, I need some help. I rescued this migrant in the desert this week, and I brought her to town. Now she's disappeared. She promised to call me, but she didn't. I need to find her. Uncle Mando said maybe you could help me."

"Whoa. Slow down." Letty wondered why Eduardo had so much interest in this particular person. He'd found migrants before in the desert. After helping them when he could, he had let them go on their way. What was different about this one?

"I'm heading home now," Letty continued. "Come to my house and we'll talk about it. Will has been talking about connecting with you anyway. He'll be glad to see you. We can eat supper together."

After getting Eduardo's agreement, she hung up. The phone rang again immediately. This time it was Zhou.

"Miss Letty, Jade has identified one of the triad members from my police photos. I want you to see the photo so you will be able to recognize Chong Ma."

"Fine. We'll meet tomorrow morning. I have some important news for you, too. I think I found a local connection to the Chinese criminals. I'm not sure. I want to discuss this with you."

They made plans for the next day. Again, the phone rang.

"Hello, Miss Valdez. My name is Clarice. You don't know me, but I'm friends with your brother Will. We're in the cycling club together. Will was attacked earlier this evening."

"What!?" Letty was immediately very alarmed.

"He's okay. He's at the hospital, and the docs say he can go home now. I can bring him to your house. Is that okay? I can be at your house in ten minutes."

"Yeah, that's good. That's faster than I can get there, so please don't leave him alone until I arrive. Okay?

"Of course. I wouldn't leave him. Never. He's sort of stoned anyway. They gave him midazolam before they put his shoulder back into the socket, and the drug made him silly. He giggles about everything."

"His shoulder! What happened?"

"He was on his bike and stopped at Himmel Park. He said he tried to help this girl, and some Chinese dudes jumped out of a van, grabbed the girl, and one of them came up to Will and dislocated Will's shoulder. That's the extent of his injuries. He'll be okay except he has to keep his arm in a sling for a while. It's going to hurt, too, when the drug wears off."

"Okay, I'll see you in a few minutes. Thank you."

Yet another Chinese connection, but this time the connection was way too close to home.

Letty locked her office and headed home as fast as she could safely drive.

CHAPTER 10

Letty made it back home in record time. She arrived just as Will's friend Clarice was opening the passenger door of her silver-colored Volkswagen hatchback. To Letty, the car looked like a newer model that had seen some country backroads in its brief life, probably transporting bicycles and riders. Dried mud and dust decorated the car, and a long scratch could be seen in the paint of a rear passenger door. Clarice held Will's arm as he lifted himself to his feet. He staggered against the open car door. Clarice was medium-height, about five feet eight inches, and slender, not really big enough to keep Will upright if he fell. Letty moved to his other side and slipped her arm around him under his non-injured arm.

"Oh, there's my big sister! Hi Letty!" Will was grinning. "See! There's Clarice. She was at the hospital, too. I don't know why."

"I was at the bike shop when you called for help, so I volunteered to come and pick you up and take you to the hospital."

"You did?" Will look confused. "I went to the hospital?'

Clarice laughed. "Yes, you did. Your shoulder was dislocated, and you had to see the doctor. Remember?

"Oh, I just remember playing basketball in the bed. That was fun."

Clarice looked at Letty and grinned.

Letty asked, "What's this drug you mentioned on the phone?"

"Midazolam, also called Versed. They give it to patients just before surgery, or in this case, before putting his shoulder back in the socket. It reduces anxiety and pain. Also it's sort of an amnesiac drug. He's already forgotten a lot of his hospital experience. The drug will wear off soon."

"Yeah, I can see he's out of it. Why do you know so much about this drug?"

"My dad's a doctor. Let's get him inside and see if he can tell you what happened to him. He told me he was trying to help a girl get away from some bad guys."

They entered the house just as Millie came rushing forward to greet them, tail wagging enthusiastically.

"Hold on, Millie," Letty said. "I'll feed you in just a minute."

"Oh, my god. What happened to this dog?" Clarice asked.

"She had a rough time before we adopted her. I'll tell you about her later."

They helped move Will toward the couch and managed to get him seated. Clarice sat down next to him, and Letty sat in a chair opposite.

"Will, do you need any water or anything?" Letty asked.

"No. Where's my bike?"

"It's in the back of my car. I locked it up. Don't worry. The bike is fine." Clarice answered,

"Will, what happened?" Letty leaned forward.

"I'm so tired, Letty." Will leaned back and his eyes closed.

Clarice took over. "Will told me he was in Himmel Park when he saw a girl trying to get away from three men. They were all Chinese, he said. Two of them grabbed the girl and forced her back to their van. They pushed her in while a third man came up to Will. He grabbed Will's hand and pulled. Will said it was a quick, violent move that dislocated his shoulder. Will said the other guy just laughed when he saw the look of pain and shock on Will's face. Then this man turned and walked away. He got into the van, and they all drove away. That's when Will called the bike shop."

"He didn't call me?" Letty asked. She was dismayed at the thought that he considered his bicycling pals his go-to people, not his big sister.

"Will said he tried calling you first, but your phone was on voice mail."

Oh, damn, Letty said to herself. She had turned the phone off when she was doing those interviews, and she'd forgotten to turn it back on until only a half hour earlier at her office.

"Will called the bike shop. I happened to be there so I said I'd go get him and take him to the emergency room. He was hurting pretty badly by that time. Later, I tried to call you, and you answered."

"That's all he said?"

"Yes, as soon as we got there and Will was examined, they gave him the drug. He was pretty goofy after that. They took him in and put his shoulder back in the socket. It didn't take long at all. He couldn't tell me anything else. He just kept saying that he had to tell his sister Letty something important."

Letty took a good look at Clarice. She was about Will's age, young, athletic, and self-possessed. She was very fair with dark hair and green eyes. She was pretty in a quiet kind of way, not the type you'd notice up against a glamorous blonde. She radiated self-confidence and intelligence.

"Thank you, Clarice. You've been a really good friend to Will."

"Oh, he'd do the same for me. All of us in the bike club know we have to be ready to help in case anyone gets hurt. I always thought that would be a bike wreck, but I was there for Will when he called. I took a first aid course, and I know how to do CPR. My dad made sure I know the basics."

"Okay. Let's leave him alone for a while so he can sleep. I have to feed this dog now." Millie had been at their feet the whole time, listening and wagging her tail.

As Letty prepared Millie's food, Clarice asked, "What happened to this dog? She's really beat-up looking."

Letty conveyed the story of how she'd found Millie in the desert, and her guess that Millie had been used as bait in a dog-fighting ring.

"Assholes," was Clarice's response. "So how did she get the name Millie?"

"Really her name is Milagro, but Will shortened it to Mille."

"Milagro? That's a Spanish word, right?"

"Yes. It means 'miracle.'"

"I need to learn Spanish. It's on my list."

Letty smiled. So Clarice was a no-nonsense, make-a-list-and-get-it-done kind of person. Letty liked her already. She took the dog bowl out to the back porch with Millie at her heels.

Letty offered Clarice something hot to drink. Clarice chose hot chocolate. A few minutes later, Millie returned through the doggie door with a full stomach and a grin on her pit bull face.

"Come here, baby," Clarice said to Millie in a soft voice, and Millie happily complied. Clarice began stroking the dog's head and ears and back. Millie leaned against Clarice's knees.

"Clarice, did Will have enough sense to show the hospital his insurance card?"

"Yep. I helped him with that. Your family is covered by the ACA, right?"

"Yes, and let's hope Obamacare survives. No way can I afford regular insurance costs."

Clarice sipped her hot chocolate and continued to caress Millie.

"So, are you a student at Will's high school?"

"No. I'm a student at the University of Arizona. I'm actually only six months older than Will. The difference is where our birthdays fall on the calendar."

"Where are you from? You have some kind of accent. I don't know what it is."

Clarice smiled. "I'm from Boston, and I spent a lot of time in Connecticut. Boston is what you are hearing."

"You came all the way to Arizona to go to college?"

"Yes, I needed to get away from home. I have a big family. Every single one of them has a strong opinion about me and what I should be doing. I want to decide for myself how to live my life. I spent my junior year abroad in France, and I got a taste of freedom there. When it came time to go to college, I wanted to go far away from Boston. I chose Arizona because I like to do outdoor things, and I wanted to escape the snow. My parents are still pissed off at me. Everyone in our family goes to…," she hesitated, "to some Ivy League school. I decided on Arizona. I've been here since August. I met Will at the bike shop soon after my arrival in Tucson."

Letty appreciated Clarice's openness, although she wondered how two such different individuals could become friends. Was it long-distance bicycling that brought them together or something more?

Suddenly, Letty and Clarice both heard a thump. They ran into the living room.

Will was removing his shoes, and he had tossed one of them across the room.

"I can make a three pointer," Will said.

"Will, try to focus. What happened to you?" Letty asked.

Will still looked a little confused.

"Okay, I'll try." He rubbed his eyes.

"You were at Himmel Park," Clarice prompted.

"Yes. On the way home from the bike shop, I got something caught in the gears. I stopped off at Himmel Park to get it out. It was dark already. I have this little flashlight. So I was over on the south side of the park. You know where all those trees and oleander bushes are? It's pretty dark there."

"Yeah. Then what happened?"

"I bent down with my little flashlight to adjust the gear, and all of a sudden this white van pulled up in the parking lot across the park. The side door slides open, and this girl jumps out. She started running away from the van and toward the south side of the park but not directly toward me. I don't think she ever saw me. She tripped and fell, then got up and ran again. In the meantime, these three dudes jumped out of the van and chased her down. One of them slapped her a couple times, and then they picked her up and put her back into the van. She was struggling the whole time."

"Did the men see you?" Letty asked.

"Not at first. My flashlight was off then. They weren't looking my way anyway. They were focused on the girl. Those dudes were really serious about getting her back in the van. Then I came out of the shadows and yelled at them."

"What happened?"

"Two of them ignored me and carried the girl to the van. The third guy came toward me smiling. Yeah, he was smiling," Will frowned. "Before I could say or do anything, he grabbed my hand and arm, and he jerked really hard. The next thing I knew, I had a dislocated shoulder. Then the scumbag laughed. He turned, and he just walked away. Very casual-like."

Letty shook her head. She didn't like this.

"That's not all. The girl was dressed in one of those tight Oriental-style dresses with the slit up the side and a high collar. The light was low, but I could see that the dress was made of red silk. She looked Chinese, and the men did, too. And really they looked a lot like those Chinese people in that movie that you and I watched."

Letty knew he was referring to Wong Kar Wai's art film classic *In the Mood for Love.*

She felt a sense of dread fall over her. Too many coincidences in one day. Too many Chinese people in one day.

Will looked at Letty and said pointedly, "Remember what you told me yesterday about those Chinese dudes?"

Letty nodded, avoiding Clarice's questioning gaze. "Anything else you can tell me? We're going to have to make a police report. What more do you remember?"

"The man who jerked my arm had on a white suit. Good looking. His hair was a little longer, enough to make a short ponytail. Not as long as yours or mine, but not like you usually see on Asian men." Will slumped back against the couch. "I'm tired."

Letty turned to Clarice. "I'm working on a case that could involve some Chinese gangsters. It's best you forget what you've heard here from Will. And both of you. No talking to your co-workers at the bike shop. We don't want to get them involved. After this is all over, you can tell them all the gory details. And Will, if you run into these guys again, *do not* approach them. Don't try to rescue anybody. Got that? You, too, Clarice."

Both Will and Clarice nodded their heads in assent.

"Actually, I'm the only one who knew about the Chinese," Clarice said. "Will told Ron at the bike shop that he'd fallen off his bike and was hurt. It was after Will was injected with the Versed that that he told me about the Chinese men and the girl. Then the drug took over. He was out of it after that."

Letty was relieved. "That's good. The fewer people that know about this, the better. I'm sorry you got involved, Clarice."

"No problem. I know when to keep my mouth shut."

Will sat up and dug into his back pocket. "Oh, yeah. I forgot. Letty, I found this on the ground where they picked up the girl." He opened his hand to show her a necklace. It was a jade amulet on a red silk string. The red silk string was broken.

Letty took it and turned it over in her hand. "Good. I'll try to find out what this is." She pocketed the necklace. Zhou would see this tomorrow.

"I'm going to call the police now and report what's happened. They will likely want to come by here in the morning for your statement." Letty went into another room, made a quick call to the police, and set up an appointment.

When she returned to the living room, Millie was sitting between Will and Clarice on the couch.

"Good grief," Letty said. "That dog knows she's not supposed to be on the couch. Will, I think you need to rest now."

Clarice stood and reached into her backpack. "Your sister is right. You need to go to bed. Here are the meds your doctor gave me. Read the instructions and follow them. The meds are for pain."

"This is going to hurt?" Will made a face.

"Yes, tomorrow especially, but you'll get well fast," Clarice said reassuringly. "Okay. I'm outta here. I'll bring your bike back to-morrow when I come to check on you."

"Don't forget me," Will looked worried.

Clarice laughed. "No, silly. I won't forget you. I'm not the one taking drugs."

She leaned down and gave Millie a goodbye pat. "Bye, bye, miracle baby."

Just at that moment, Eduardo knocked and walked in the door.

"Clarice, this is my brother Eduardo Ramone. He has a twin sister named Elena. Eduardo, this is Clarice, a friend of Will's."

Clarice shook Eduardo's hand. "Eduardo Ramone," She looked at the ceiling and repeated his name as if it were the first word of an epic poem. "What a great name." She looked at all three siblings. "You three are all so good-looking!"

Will laughed. Eduardo laughed. Letty felt herself grimace. One of those unexpected and unwanted memories came back suddenly to haunt her. Those memories felt like a knife in her gut. She'd never thought of herself as good looking until Chava came along. He told her that and more. He called her "chulita." Sexy girl. She could feel his arms around her. So much pain came with the memory. The grief of knowing that he was gone forever, lost in the sands of Iraq, was almost too much to bear.

Clarice said her goodbyes again and closed the door behind her.

Letty turned to Eduardo. "Help me get Will to bed, and then we can catch up." Letty and Eduardo pulled him up and steered Will to his bedroom. They maneuvered him into bed and covered him with a blanket. Safe in his bed with Millie in her bed nearby, Will fell asleep almost immediately.

"Want something to eat? I haven't eaten and I'm starved," Letty asked her brother.

"Sure," Eduardo responded.

Letty threw together a quick meal. They ate in silence for a few minutes. Then Letty gave Eduardo a review of what had happened to Will. She left out the part about Chinese criminals, and only described the assault as involving a possible abduction that Will had the misfortune of encountering.

Then she said, "Okay, what's up with you? You said you need my help."

Eduardo, normally a calm, very quiet young man, suddenly looked very anxious. "I rescued this migrant in the desert about a week ago. She had run out of water, and she was in bad shape. She's a bit younger than me, only 17. She's from Chiapas in southern Mexico, and her name is Esperanza. She stayed with Uncle Mando and Valerina for a few days to get stronger. Then she asked me to take her into Tucson to her coyote. When they were still in Mexico before crossing the border, he told her that he had a job for her in Tucson. I was really reluctant, but she said her family was desperate for money. Her little brothers and sisters aren't getting enough to eat. So she was determined to find a job. I gave her a cell phone and taught her how to use it. She promised to call me. But she never called."

Letty shrugged her shoulders. "Are you sure this is a problem? Maybe she just found a job and decided to move on."

"No," Eduardo hesitated. "I don't know how to explain. This is different. She's different. We have something between us. I'm sure she would have called if she could." He looked down and pressed his palms together.

Letty couldn't remember a time that she'd seen her normally serene brother so distressed.

"Earlier today I went to the place where I dropped her off. This rough-looking guy answered the door. He said he didn't know anything about any girl named Esperanza and that I should get lost. When I pressed him, he pulled a gun on me and slammed the door in my face."

"I sat in my truck for a while, then I started knocking on doors. No one would tell me anything. They were mostly women at home with kids, and mostly they looked scared. They would glance at his house and then tell me that they hadn't seen anything. So I went off and had something to eat. Then I remembered Denise, my cousin."

"I went back to the neighborhood to find Denise. Remember her? She doesn't come out to the reservation very often. She pulled me inside really quickly. She told me that the coyote did a lot more than just find jobs for the migrants. She said she was pretty sure he was involved in trafficking humans. For months, she'd seen groups of young girls come out of his house and be put into vans. She said there were these Asian-looking guys that always came with the van, and they seemed to be in charge. But she said that about a year ago, she stopped seeing the girls."

This was about the time Carlos disappeared, Letty noted to herself.

"So, no more girls?"

"Denise said she couldn't be sure because she didn't always see what was going on, but either there weren't any girls or far fewer than before. The vans still came, but now boxes were taken into the house. Later a moving truck would come and the boxes would be carried out of the house and put into a moving truck. The Asian men are still there, Denise said. She said once she saw an Anglo man, too."

"Did she have any idea what's in the boxes?"

"No. She said she doesn't want to know. She stays away. She told me that I should forget the migrant girl and go back to the rez. The coyote and his pals are too dangerous, and I should stay out of what they are doing."

Letty sat back in her chair. She was dismayed. How both her siblings could have gotten mixed up in this was a truly awful development. She wished she could send them away until this was all over. But there was nowhere to send them, and they probably would resist going anyway. They weren't little kids any more, and she couldn't just tell them what to do.

"And they aren't telling the cops because they are all too scared?"

"Right. Denise said that a year ago some of them had even been sending their teenage girls to live with relatives so the Asian dudes wouldn't see them. There are a bunch of undocumented workers in the neighborhood who are afraid to call the cops. That includes Denise. She's O'odham born on the reservation, but on the other side of the border. Her husband, Alonzo, is undocumented, too. He's been here twenty-three years. He's made a good living working for a plumbing company. He and Denise raised four kids. They see this stuff going on, but they are afraid to report it these days, especially since there's all this hysteria now about illegals. They are afraid they might be arrested and deported if they contact the police. So nobody's talking."

Eduardo looked very unhappy. "I have to find Esperanza, Letty." He paused.

"After I talked to Denise, I called Mando and Valerina and asked their advice. Valerina suggested going south across the border to look for the coyote smuggler who had originally brought Esperanza across the border. But Mando didn't like that idea. He suggested I talk to Hu'ul. She will help."

Mando had used the O'odham word for Eduardo's maternal grandmother.

"Mando also said to call you, Letty. He said you'd know what to do."

Letty sighed. She wished she knew what to do, but it just wasn't that simple.

"Eduardo, this is bad. I didn't tell you the whole story. But first, you have to agree not to talk about this with anyone until we figure out what's going on. There is a gang of Chinese criminals called triads operating here. I'm trying to help Jade Lopez, remember her? They broke into her house. And the man who assaulted Will was one of them — a triad gangster. Now we're learning that there's a connection to human smuggling. I assume that they are selling these young girls as sex slaves. Probably they are being transported to Las Vegas or maybe the West Coast. Maybe there's something else, too, in those boxes, something illegal."

Letty paused.

"There's more. I'm working with a guy from the Chinese police and Interpol who is trying to stop them. His name is Zhou. It sounds like "Joe" but spelled Z-H-O-U. I'll meet with him tomorrow, and we'll do our best to figure out what happened to Esperanza. Okay?"

"Thanks, Letty. You are the best big sister in the world. This is really important to me. Esperanza is really important to me."

"We can't do anything more tonight. I'll get you some blankets and a pillow and you can sleep on the couch. Okay?"

After she got Eduardo settled down for the night, Letty went to her bedroom. She turned on her computer and started searching about the sex trade and about the triad gangs' role in it and other crimes. The list was long: counterfeiting, money laundering, extortion, kidnapping for ransom, illegal gambling, credit-card fraud, and software piracy were big, along with various types of smuggling – people, endangered animals and plants, drugs, weapons, you name it. Triad love of violence was notorious. Torture, mutilation, murder, arson, and bombings were common.

Over an hour later, Letty turned off her computer. She pulled a box down from the top of her shelf of her closet and retrieved her handgun, a semi-automatic Glock. She took the gun apart, cleaned it, reassembled it, and loaded it.

Letty hated guns. She hated handguns and she hated rifles and she hated artillery and rockets and she hated bombs, and she especially hated IEDs. She hated violence. She hated war. Waves of Iraq memories washed over her as she worked, leaving her with a tremendous sense of grief.

Starting tomorrow morning, Letty Valdez would be packing heat.

CHAPTER 11

Letty woke Will and managed to get him out of bed and into the living room with a cup of coffee in his hand by eight a.m. She handed him some pain medication to take with the coffee.

"Does it hurt a lot?" she asked sympathetically. Letty had a sudden memory of carrying Will in her arms when he was just a toddler. Her feelings toward him were as much motherly as sisterly. Motherly usually won out, considering that neither she nor her siblings had been mothered very well at all by their real mother, and god knows, little Will had needed a mom.

"Yeah, a little. Not too bad. It's okay unless I move my arm." He snorted. "Guess the solution is not to move my arm for a while. I'm not sure I can ride a bike. My shoulder won't support my weight on the handle bars…unless I get one of those recumbent bikes. Hmmm…that might be fun."

Oh, my cheerful baby brother, Letty thought. Always looking on the bright side.

"Better wait on bicycling right now. We'll need to take you to the doc and see how you are doing before you try anything too physical."

"Letty, I like Clarice," Will blurted out.

"Yes, she really helped a lot."

"I mean, I really like her. Do you think she likes me?"

"Yes. I do."

"I mean….really *like*?"

"I don't know if she would make so much effort for someone she didn't really like. And remember? She said she thinks you're good-looking."

"Oh, she said that about all of us," he said dismissively. Will hesitated. "I think I might …you know…see if she wants to spend some time with me."

"Good idea. Now when the cops come, just tell them what you did and saw. Don't speculate on anything."

They heard a knock on the door a few minutes later. Letty knew one of the officers slightly, and to her relief, the other was her friend Adelita García.

"Sorry to make you come out on a Sunday," Letty said.

"I asked for this assignment. I'm here to help." Adelita was every inch the professional detective, dressed in a trim navy blue suit and a white blouse. Her dark hair was cut short, and she wore pearl earrings A bulge at her waist suggested that she was wearing a holstered gun. Adelita sat down opposite Will and took out her notebook. Will gave his statement, and Adelita took notes. Will described seeing the girl trying to run from the three men and how she was pushed back into their van. He described them all as "Asian." He went into some detail about how his shoulder was dislocated by one of the men and about his trip to the hospital.

When he was finished, Letty asked, "Do you have any reports of missing persons? We're wondering if anyone is looking for the girl."

"No," Adelita responded. "But we're spreading our net wider to see if she was reported missing elsewhere. We're starting with southern Arizona and extending into metro Phoenix."

Just as they were leaving, Clarice drove up and parked.

"Adelita," Letty said in a low voice.

Adelita turned toward her and stepped closer.

"I have more. I'll fill you in later."

Adelita nodded. "Later," she said. Then she turned and walked to the squad car where her patrolman was waiting to drive her back to police headquarters.

Millie greeted Clarice like a long-lost friend.

"Hi, Millie!" Clarice patted Millie's head. Then she leaned over Will, who was still on the couch, and pecked him on the cheek.

"How are you doing?" she asked him.

Was Will blushing? Letty laughed to herself. So their friendship is not just bicycling.

"Oh, my shoulder really hurts," Will, who had just a few minutes before told his big sister that the pain wasn't so bad, was now doing his best to get Clarice's full sympathy.

"Poor baby," Clarice said.

Well, that worked, Letty thought to herself.

"Clarice, I just gave Will his pain meds."

"Okay, I'll sit with you for a while, Will." Clarice plopped herself down on the couch next to Will. Millie joined her.

"That dog is not supposed to be on the couch," Letty said. She was ignored. "Okay, I'm off to Maggie's house. Call me on my cell phone if you need something."

* * *

Zhou looked at his watch. Early morning in Tucson meant late evening in Beijing. He called his boss Yang and got him relatively quickly.

"What have you to report?" Yang was his usual abrupt self.

"I met with the local authorities. A man named Lambert. He was not happy to see me. I'm not sure he even believes the Interpol reports about a triad gang here. Actually he was almost hostile. He expects me to report to him."

"Stupid laowai. What do they know about these Hong Kong criminals?" Yang snorted.

"Right now I'm trying to track down how many of the triad gangsters are here and where they are headquartered."

"You're not making much progress."

"I don't have much to go on. The woman here, Jade, identified Chong Ma from a photo. And you know I had a brief encounter with Bao."

Yang fell silent. Finally he said, "Chong Ma?"

"Maybe. The photo was bad, and it's been a year or more since she saw him. I can't be sure that it was Chong Ma."

"Okay. Keep me informed." Yang abruptly hung up.

Zhou hesitated. Something wasn't right. He couldn't say what. Just a vague, uncomfortable feeling. After some thought, Zhou picked up his cell phone again and connected to a number in Paris. He spoke briefly with his friend and Interpol colleague Jean-Pierre Laurent.

* * *

For at least two years, maybe nearly three, Letty had joined her friends Maggie, Seri, and Jade at Maggie's house on Sunday mornings for coffee. Maggie's husband, Brian, always disappeared with their kids during what he called "The Girls' Coffee." The four women – or three if Seri was off on one of her trips – would gather around Maggie's dining table in a wonderful room that Letty loved. The dining room was small and intimate, and it seemed that the fragrance of delicious foods lingered. There was a big sliding glass window at one end of the dining room that led outside to a deck and a view of the garden beyond. Sometimes on cool winter mornings, they sat out on the deck in the sun.

Letty had known Maggie for nearly fifteen years. Letty had been only fourteen years old and Maggie's student in English class at Tucson High when it became apparent that Letty was on the verge of becoming homeless. Since she was nine years old, Letty had been living with her dad, Neto Valdez, and his second wife and kids. But her dad got tired of being a father and husband and took off for Los Angeles in the middle of the night. Later, after Letty had been in Iraq for a while, she came to understand her dad's abrupt departure. He was a Vietnam War vet. He had always been distant. He drank too much during the years Letty lived with him. She remembered very clearly that he went camping alone in the desert every New Year's Eve and Fourth of July. He said he couldn't handle the sounds of exploding fireworks. Now after Iraq, Letty totally understood. After Iraq, she had come to forgive her dad for abandoning his family – twice. He left Letty's mother, and then he left his second wife and their kids. He suffered from untreated PTSD, and he just couldn't handle family life.

When her dad left, his wife, Letty's stepmother, had small kids of her own to take care of. She told Letty that Letty better find another living arrangement. The stepmother insisted she couldn't support her kids and Letty, too. Letty's only choice was to go back to the reservation and live with her grandmother, who was struggling to care for Elena, Eduardo, and little Will. Somehow Maggie found out about this and asked if Letty would agree to be fostered by Maggie and Brian. So Letty moved in, and Maggie became a best friend, a big sister, and the caring mother that Letty had never had. Over time, more children appeared at Brian and Maggie's house – two were Maggie and Brian's biological kids – and two more were fosters. Maggie made sure Letty saw her siblings on a regular basis, a practice Letty continued into adulthood. Letty lived with Maggie's family until she entered the U.S. Army.

Those years with Maggie were Letty's easiest years. Earlier in her life, before going to live with her father, Letty had lived on the reservation with her mother. But then, her mother married a man named Rudolfo Antone. He would become the father of Eduardo, Elena, and Will.

"You're going to live with your dad," her mother abruptly told Letty when she married Rudolfo. "My new man shouldn't have to live with another man's child." So off Letty went to her father, Neto Valdez, whom she barely knew. She coped by becoming a very quiet child who tried to disappear from view. That was hard to do when a girl is six feet tall in the eighth grade. Years later, she would learn from her brothers and sister that their father had actually wanted Letty to stay with the family. It was her mother's rejection that led to Letty being turned away. Occasionally Rudolfo would pick her up and take her to the reservation on weekends to visit. Letty quickly fell in love with her new siblings and missed them terribly when she had to return to Tucson.

Sadly for them all, her siblings' father was killed in a car accident. During a summer monsoon rain storm, another driver hydroplaned his car on the narrow road through the reservation. He hit Rudolfo head on. Rudolfo was dead before the emergency medical team arrived. The children's mother tried to cope. But she couldn't seem to live without a man. Elena, Eduardo and Will went to live with their grandmother, and their mother took off with that Navajo cowboy. None of her children had heard from her since.

That meant that Letty had lived her early life on the reservation as an O'odham, the years nine to fourteen in an extended Mexican-American family, and after fourteen, with an Anglo-white family. Chava teased her about being multicultural. "You fit in everywhere, Chulita," Chava told her, when she said she didn't really belong anywhere in particular. He hugged her and told her, "Most of all, you belong with me, mi vida. Don't forget that."

Maggie put her arm around Letty's shoulder and kissed her on her forehead. "Hello, my sweet Letty. How are you?"

Letty smiled. "I seem to be doing better than my friend here." She gestured to Jade. "She's got Chinese gangsters after her. Have you met Zhou yet?" Maggie nodded.

Seri nodded. "Jade told me he's a Chinese cop here because of Interpol information. Impressive. It looks like he's become Jade's bodyguard. And he looks like someone you don't want to mess with. He's handsome, too." She waved her hand at Zhou, who was out on the deck.

"That's exactly what he's doing, Seri," said Letty. "He's trying to keep Jade alive and well and so am I. We're in a difficult situation right now."

"Yeah? Tell me more," Seri's natural curiosity was awakened.

Letty gave Seri a summary of recent events, including Will's being attacked.

"Maybe we could talk about something more pleasant," Jade interrupted. "Tell us, Seri, what did you do in New York City?"

Letty only half-listened to Seri who recounted trips to art galleries and jazz clubs and various libraries and museums. Letty was watching Zhou who was alert as usual. He seemed to be looking everywhere and nowhere at once. Letty realized to her surprise that she was very glad he was there. She didn't know if she could manage the triad gangsters on her own.

"It's time for me to catch up with our Beijing-by-way-of-Paris detective inspector," Letty left her friends and joined Zhou on the deck.

"You start. What have you learned?" Letty asked.

"Jade and I discovered that Bao is using the alias of a Chinese-American from Tucson named Kevin Kwok. I googled him. Very interesting. There were occasional small news particles about him until one year ago and then nothing."

Particles? Letty thought about that. She decided "news particles" made as much sense as "news articles."

"Hmmm…that *is* interesting," she said. "That was around the time Carlos disappeared. I'll look into this tonight and see if I can find more information."

"Also," Zhou continued. "I showed Jade some photographs – mugshots – of triad gang members. She identified one as Chong Ma. He is a Red Pole, what is called an 'enforcer.' He came to Jade's house a few weeks after Carlos disappeared. He was dressed as a termite inspector. He told Jade that her husband had ordered a termite inspection. Jade allowed him entrance. She said he stayed longer than one hour and looked everywhere."

"Those guys are definitely looking for something, and they think Jade has it."

"Correct," Zhou frowned. "They will not stop looking until they find it."

Letty crossed her arms over her chest. "We have to watch her 24-7. What they do next may lead us to where they are headquartered and what they are up to."

"Yes, but they have a history of killing a person if they cannot find what they want."

Zhou hesitated. "Letty, do you believe that Jade's husband, Carlos, is alive?"

"No. I did a very thorough search for him, and in the months since, I've checked in again and again. He took the money from the bank. We know because he showed up on surveillance video. Then nothing. He could have created a separate identify or stolen someone's identity, but if that happens, there's usually some evidence that surfaces eventually. In his case, he disappeared off the face of the earth. I'm almost certain Carlos is dead, and his body was dumped in the desert somewhere."

Zhou frowned. "It would be good to find the bones. This would help Jade have…what do you call it?"

"Closure."

"Yes. Maybe a final memorial service also."

"Yes. Any other news?"

"No. And you? What have you found?"

"First, I was hired to investigate a murder. The client's nephew, his name is José, is accused of killing a woman who lives here in Tucson not too far from Jade's house. His lawyer arranged for me to interview him. I spoke to him, but he told me nothing. I think he's trying to protect someone. Then I talked to his girlfriend. She told me that José got into a fight with the son of the murdered woman over her, the girlfriend. She told me that José said to the boy Travis, 'You've got all those Chinese girls. Why do you want my girlfriend, too?'"

"Ah. Very interesting," Zhou mused. "Now we see maybe connection to this local family and triad gang."

"Yes, an Anglo and very affluent family."

"By Anglo, you mean white people?

"Yes."

"You have more?"

"Yes. I have two younger brothers and a younger sister. One of my brothers, Eduardo, lives on the reservation. He rescued a migrant lost in the desert last week. She is from southern Mexico, and her name is Esperanza. She insisted that Eduardo bring her to

Tucson to meet her coyote who promised her a job. She told him that her brothers and sisters don't have enough to eat so she's eager to work."

"Coyote?"

"This is a wild animal that lives here. The coyote is very much like a wild dog. The native peoples call them 'song dogs' because they howl to each other at dusk. You'll see one sooner or later. They are quite common. The men who smuggle migrant workers across the border also are often called 'coyotes.' They smuggle drugs, too, or they force the migrants to smuggle drugs."

Zhou shook his head. This was an America that he knew little about. In fact, he guessed most Americans who lived away from the U.S.-Mexico border knew little about this as well.

"Eduardo and Esperanza developed an attachment to each other. He became very worried when she did not contact him, so he went to the house where the coyote lives. He was turned away rather roughly. The coyote claimed that he didn't know any Esperanza. So Eduardo started asking the neighbors, but got no answers because everyone was too scared to talk. Then he got to the home of Denise, who is our cousin."

"Why afraid?"

"Many are undocumented workers with families who have been here for years. They are afraid that if they report crimes to the police, they will be found out and deported."

Another aspect of the America most people do not know, Zhou thought to himself.

"Denise provides information?"

"Yes, she said the neighbors had seen vans full of girls brought there. Asian men, Denise said, brought them to the coyote's house. Then about a year ago, that stopped. Now she sees the Asian men and the coyote, who is Mexican, and once, she saw a white man. Now they are moving boxes in and out of the house."

"This also is the time when Carlos disappeared," Zhou said.

"Yes, and it looks like they have cut back on the girl smuggling and now they've moved into smuggling something else."

"Letty, I must tell you that I have a second assignment that I did not mention earlier."

Letty frowned. "Don't hold back on me, Zhou."

"I will not. I also am sent to find a kidnapped young woman named Victoria. She is the daughter of a high official in the Hong Kong government. The official refused to pay bribes to gangsters so they took his daughter to sell into sex slavery."

"Wow, these guys are real scumbags. I have another story to tell you — something that just happened last night." She went on to relate how her brother Will had encountered a group of Asian men — Will was sure they were Chinese — who were in the process of taking a young Asian woman dressed in that traditional Chinese dress."

"'Cheongsam' in Cantonese, 'qipao' in Mandarin. You think this may be the young woman Victoria?"

"Could be. My brother called out to stop them, and one of them came forward and dislocated Will's shoulder. Then they got into the van with the girl and drove off."

"Your brother is okay?"

"Yes. His friend Clarice took him to the hospital last night. She's with him now."

"Your brother described the man who harmed him?"

"Chinese, fairly young, longish hair, white suit."

"Bao. His name is Bao. We can conclude then that perhaps they continue to smuggle girls but on a smaller scale. Now they are smuggling something different. What could it be? Triads have a history of smuggling counterfeit money, weapons, and drugs, of course. In recent days, we find they smuggle fentanyl and other opioids into the U.S. Also they smuggle chemicals from China to the U.S. to produce meth and to Europe to make the drug known as ecstasy. I worked on a case for Interpol that involved smuggling the chemicals into several European countries."

"We need to find out where they are headquartered…in Tucson or across the border or somewhere out in the desert," Letty was feeling the urgency. "And we need to figure out what they are smuggling and where's it going. And we need to find those two girls – Victoria and Esperanza. And soon."

"I agree."

Letty reached into her pocket. "Will found this on the ground after the girl was picked up in the park and shoved into the van." She showed Zhou the necklace. It was a green stone with a red string tied into a circle.

"This is a Buddhist jade amulet, Guan Yin. Goddess of compassion. She is said to protect women and children." Zhou knotted the broken red string together again.

Again another memory thrust itself into Letty's consciousness without warning. Chava with a St. Christopher medal on a chain around his neck.

Zhou tried to return it to Letty.

"You keep it. You can give it to her when we find her," she said.

"What will you do now?" Zhou asked.

"This afternoon I'm going to go see my uncle who lives on the other side of the border in Nogales, Sonora. His name is Miguel Valdez. He's been mixed up in things," Letty hesitated. She didn't want to go into Miguel's occasional illegal activities. "He knows a lot. I hope he's heard something about the triad gang."

"You have good guanxi, Letty."

The word sounded like "gwan-she" to Letty's ears.

Her puzzled look led Zhou to continue. "'Guanxi' is what you call connections or networking. You know many people, and you are in a large family."

Letty smiled. "I hadn't thought of it that way. That's good. What are you doing this afternoon?"

"Jade and I go to visit the family of Carlos. I want to see if any of his family members maybe remember something helpful. I will ask about the Chinese connection. This is something no one here knew about until Bao and I met in Jade's back yard."

"Good idea. Let's talk tonight."

"Letty, I don't hold back now. I have a problem."

"What's that, Zhou?"

"I am like your brother Eduardo who has attachment with the migrant girl. I feel this attachment for Miss Jade. I do not know if she feels this also, but I think maybe yes."

Letty laughed. "Oh, she does. Definitely. She looks at you like a big bowl of ice cream that she wants to gobble up and then lick the spoon."

This made Zhou smile.

"And that's how you feel about her? Like a big bowl of ice cream?"

"No," Zhou said seriously. "Jade is a fine French wine best to savor slowly."

Letty's eyebrows went up. Who knew this ass-kicking Chinese cop was such a romantic? Sweet.

Zhou frowned. "This is an unfortunate development. I make a strong effort to not be distracted. I must be very careful. I must be awake and watching at all moments. I cannot let this fine wine distract me."

"You'll do great, Zhou. You are a good cop." Even as the words came out of her mouth, Letty was taken aback. She didn't know why, but she had a good feeling about Zhou.

Letty smiled broadly. "And when this is all over, you can give your ice cream to Jade, and you can drink her wine."

Zhou couldn't help himself. He laughed, delighted at the thought.

CHAPTER 12

Letty headed south on I-19, the major four-lane highway that leads straight to the border between Arizona and the Mexican state of Sonora. Normally she enjoyed making this drive. Right now, she was tense, and she hoped the drive would help her calm down and focus. At a distance of nearly seventy miles, it was far enough to allow her to center into her thoughts. She wanted to get away and have an opportunity to think about recent events.

The day was one of those clear, warm, sunny winter days in the Sonoran Desert. A deep ultramarine blue sky stretched to the horizon. Behind Letty were the Santa Catalina Mountains on the northern edge of Tucson and ahead were the Santa Rita Mountains to the south, just two of the Sonoran Desert mountain ranges known as "sky islands." She deftly passed through the traffic congestion at the southern edge of the Tucson metro area. Finally traffic began to give way to open desert with sand, mesquite trees and saguaro cacti.

Soon after leaving Tucson, Letty could see on her right to the west the White Dove of the Desert, that beautiful eighteenth-century church of Mission San Xavier del Bac. The Mission church was considered the best example of baroque architecture in the United States – thus the White Dove designation – and Letty couldn't help but be proud that the Mission was built by the native people, Tohono O'odham, the maternal side of her family.

She liked to imagine what it was like for the people living in the O'odham farming village of Wa:k to see a stranger on horseback appear without warning in the late 1600s. He was Father Kino, an Italian Jesuit priest sent to New Spain, the Spanish colony in the New World. His task was to establish a string of Catholic missions that stretched up into what would become known as California. San Xavier del Bac was one of twenty-four outposts that he established for crown and church in his lifetime. Father Kino was an explorer, cartographer, astronomer and agronomist. What did Letty's people think of this strange man from a faraway world with his wide-brimmed hat and dark robes? How could they have known that he was just the first of so many Europeans who would follow and who would change everything forever?

Letty was not a practicing Catholic, but she loved going into the sanctuary of the Mission church. She liked sitting in the quiet silence where generations of O'odham had prayed. Seeing the Mission to her right as she drove toward the border helped to settle Letty into a quieter state of mind. Her thoughts turned to the problem she was facing now – the presence of a group of Chinese gangsters who were quite willing to use violence against her brother and her friend, for what purpose she did not know.

She considered the possibility that the Chinese triad gang members had developed a relationship with Mexican gangsters, probably from the Sinaloa Cartel. After all, the cartel controlled this part of northern Mexico, and not much escaped them. Were the Chinese gangsters paying off the cartel? Or were they working together? Sinaloa had competitors, of course. The Tijuana Cartel, the Juarez Cartel, and Los Zetas Cartel were in play, and any one of them could be trying to get an edge against the Sinaloa Cartel.

The possibility of some kind of connection between any of the cartels and the triad gang terrified Letty. She had made a point of avoiding any investigation that might push her into the sphere of the Sinaloa Cartel. Like the triads, they were known for a long list of crimes, chief among them drug smuggling, and like the triads, they were no strangers to violence and murder. Or it might be possible that cartel members hadn't noticed the triad gang yet, in which case there would be hell to pay when they did. A turf war would surely follow, one that would lead to multiple deaths.

While working with Marv Iverson before he retired, Letty found that she was really good at finding missing persons. Most often, those cases involved individuals who had engaged in some illegal financial dealings, especially fraud or embezzlement. These were the skips. She had become more and more efficient at finding them, typically because they couldn't stand waiting another minute to spend those misbegotten funds. She followed the money, and because of that, it was often easy to track them down. She was not typically responsible for bringing these criminal skips to justice. That was left to others. There was a distance between her and these white-collar criminals, and she liked it that way. It wasn't just her own revulsion to violence. She had her siblings to consider now. She did not want them dragged into her work.

Occasionally Letty would take another missing-person case that had nothing to do with financial misbehavior. Tracking down a missing child who most often had been abducted by a noncustodial parent was on her list of completed assignments. She had once found a demented missing father who had wondered away from home and had been taken in by a neighbor. The neighbor viewed her new house guest, who was not allowed to leave her house, as an opportunity to raid the helpless father's financial resources. Letty's client in that case was the elder son of the man suffering from dementia. Once found, the father was sent to a more secure nursing home and the neighbor to jail.

Infrequently, and only because she needed money to pay bills, Letty would engage in a stakeout. Usually this involved being hired by a person who believed his or her spouse was being unfaithful. Proof was needed in the form of photos that would help her client in divorce court. Those stakeouts often meant long hours in her pickup truck watching outside a motel or apartment where she could get photographic proof of marital misbehavior.

Letty's biggest failure as an investigator was her inability to find Jade's husband, Carlos Lopez. There was a point at which she had to accept what seemed obvious. He was dead. She had no proof at all that he was alive. She had no proof that he was dead, either. But based on her experience finding missing persons, everything about his disappearance pointed to his death and possibly his murder.

So now there was this thread connecting Jade and Carlos and a missing girl from the highlands of southern Mexico and her brothers Eduardo and Will that led to some Chinese gangsters and possibly some Mexican gangsters, too. Letty sighed in frustration.

Hearing from the girlfriend of José Maria Gomez that there might be a tie between the triad gangsters and a local white family living in an affluent neighborhood of Tucson was disturbing as well. If she closed her eyes and hoped for the best, this might mean very little. It could be something very simple. Perhaps "those Chinese girls" that José had spit out in the argument with Travis Lyle simply referred to some girls at school who happened to be of Chinese ethnicity.

But Letty had this feeling in her gut that it had to be more than just a jealous fight between two teenage boys. If it were more than just a reference to some local girls at school, wasn't it just logical to connect "those Chinese girls" to the triad gangsters' crime of sex trafficking? And if that was the case, then what the hell was the teenage son of an affluent white family doing? How could he possibly know about this? He couldn't, unless, of course, the triads were running a house of prostitution patronized by local boys. That was possible but unlikely, because the Chinese girls were probably not being kept in Tucson. Zhou seemed to think that these girls, typically from peasant families in rural counties, were taken to Las Vegas or some other location where it was more difficult to distinguish the unwilling prostitute from the willing.

Letty had to find out more about Travis Lyle and about his mother. Why had Barbara Lyle been murdered, and by whom? Was she involved in some criminal activity herself, or did she just know about it and someone was trying to shut her up? How had her son become involved in this? Most parents wouldn't want their kids involved in such dangerous illegal activity. And what about the father, Fred Lyle? Did he know what was going on? Did he play a role in any illegal activity?

On Monday, Letty would go to the Lyles' home and try to speak to both father and son, This would be after she spoke to the lawyer Jessica Cameron, who needed to be informed immediately about the complexity of this case. It was not a simple matter of Cameron's client being accused of murder. Letty's gut feeling was that José had not shot and killed Barbara Lyle. But he wasn't helping Letty at all. If José was trying to protect someone by not talking, who? And why? And who did kill Barbara Lyle and why?

And then there was Zhou. He was from another world. He seemed entirely legitimate, and there was no doubt that he was deeply concerned about Jade's welfare. But Letty had no way of verifying anything he said or recognizing any mistakes he might be making or anticipating any shortcomings he might have that would affect what was becoming a joint investigation. She was entirely dependent upon his knowledge of the triads. Yes, she had a good feeling about him, but feelings can be very misleading. What did she really know about Zhou?

The biggest mystery of all — and the one fact that made Letty most uncomfortable — was that she had never yet encountered a single one of these Chinese gangsters. She just had no idea how she would react when meeting one of them or especially more than one at once. Letty had her military training, and she had taken advanced martial arts classes while in the Army and after her honorable discharge, too. She had done quite well at defending herself when attacked. But she didn't have confidence that she could compete in a one-on-one with a Chinese gong fu expert bent on killing her, Jade, or her brothers. Letty was not eager to find out.

* * *

Miles went by, and the town of Ambos Nogales appeared before her. Nogales, Arizona, USA, and Nogales, Sonora, Mexico — one town divided by an invisible border made real by the profanity of a high metal wall. "Ambos" translates as "both" and that's what she was looking at, both of them. The elevation was higher here, and she could tell the temperature had dropped, even though the day was still sunny.

Letty found a place to park her pickup truck, and she walked across the border at the pedestrians-only crossing. She had every bit of identification she owned: a U.S. passport, a tribal identification card, her old Army ID, her Arizona driver's license, plus a small plastic card with photo identifying her as a licensed private investigator in the State of Arizona. She also had a card indicating that she would be a tourist during her time in Mexico. Going into Mexico was not a problem. As a U.S. citizen, she didn't need a visa to enter Mexico this way. Coming home would be a different story. She was dark-skinned with Native American features. She didn't look "American." Customs and Border Protection agents would stop her and question her. The irony never escaped her. She was from a tribe that had lived in America long before the whites came. Some anthropologists say that the People had lived in the Sonoran Desert for four thousand years. And yet the Customs agents definitely would want proof that she was a U.S. citizen. She had to prove that she was a "real American."

She walked across the border and tried her best to ignore "The Wall." Down into the town she went, past the big market that attracted tourists, deeper into the little city of Nogales, Sonora, with its hilltops surrounding the downtown area. Occasionally she would pass by some older Americans seeking less expensive dental care or cheaper prescriptions at a Mexican pharmacy. Prices were better on this side of the line. She wandered around a bit, looking into shop windows, and stopped to talk to street merchants. The entire time, she watched. She wanted to make sure no one was following her.

Eventually Letty walked casually down a side street and slipped into a small restaurant with the sign Café Heroica above the door. The café was the only tenant in a two-story building. She moved casually to pick up a menu at the counter and glanced upward to the balcony above. A narrow staircase led upward. The balcony was wide enough that small tables and chairs could be placed against the wall, making it impossible to see if anyone was seated there. Letty ordered a coffee and when it came, she started up the stairs.

Sure enough, there was her Uncle Miguel sitting at a table against the wall.

"Hola, Tío," Letty said with a big smile. Hello, Uncle. She put her coffee down on his table.

Miguel stood and gave her a bear hug. Letty couldn't help but notice that he was watching the door the whole time. They sat down at a table that had two empty beer bottles and a third that was half full. He took a sip.

"How have you been, Tío?"

He shifted his substantial girth in the little chair. "Not much to tell. My woman left me, but I found a new one." He laughed and shrugged his shoulders again. His eyes twinkled with mischief.

"You are a bad boy, Tío. Treat those women better and maybe one of them will stick around."

"Nah, eventually they all want too much money, and when I can't come up with it, they go. This new one will, too." He laughed again. "How is your family? Still enjoying your private eye work?"

"I like the work just fine. The best part is that I'm actually making a living, and so far no one has shot at me."

"Heard from your dad?" Letty's father, Neto Valdez, was Miguel's little brother. Miguel showed a big brother's concern.

"I call him once a month or so. He doesn't answer. But then in a day or two, he calls back. I guess he's okay. I don't know. He never has much to say."

"He won't talk to anyone else in la familia. Why do you think he calls you?"

"Because I was in Iraq. He and I had a conversation once about it. I'm using the term "conversation" loosely. Not many words came out. He wanted to know what it was like in Iraq. I tried to tell him, but after a few minutes, I just stopped talking. I couldn't say anything. It's like my tongue and throat got frozen. He said, 'I know. I know. Like 'Nam. It sucked, didn't it?' I just said, 'Yes. It sucked.' We never talked about it again. He's got PTSD, Tío, and he's had it for years. He told me once he thinks I have it, too, and that's another reason why he talks only to me. I'm the only one who can understand what happened to him in Vietnam."

"Do you have PTSD?" Neto asked her softly.

Letty hesitated. She wasn't ready to talk about Iraq. She wasn't ready to talk about Chava.

"I'm not here now about Iraq or about myself. You asked about my family. We're in a world of trouble right now, and it looks like it might get worse before it gets better. There are these Chinese dudes who are after a friend of mine. Will got in their way, and one of them dislocated his shoulder. They may have kidnapped the novia of my other brother Eduardo."

Miguel frowned. "Chinese?"

"Yes, Tío. They are real bad guys, a criminal gang from Hong Kong. They are called triads. A Chinese cop showed up here, too. He says he's here to find out what the triad gang is doing and to stop them. Do you know about the disappearance of Carlos Lopez about a year ago?"

"Not much. I read about it in the newspapers. Some money disappeared, too. Right?"

"Yeah, one hundred thousand dollars. We think there may be a connection between that and triad gangsters showing up at his wife's house looking for something. We don't know what they are looking for. The money is not there. That's for sure."

Miguel sipped his beer.

"Then my little brother Will had an encounter with them…well …we don't know if it was a triad member or not but it seems very likely. My other brother Eduardo came into town looking for a migrant he'd rescued in the desert. He thinks the Chinese may have her as well, but we don't know. There's a lot we don't know. But it seems to have something to do with smuggling – smuggling people or smuggling something else."

"So this isn't just a social visit," said Miguel quietly.

"No. You know a lot, Tío. You always know what's happening on both sides of the border." Letty didn't want to get specific about how much she knew about Miguel Valdez and his illegal activities. She was fairly certain that he'd done a fair amount of smuggling himself, primarily marijuana, and an occasional migrant as well.

Miguel said nothing.

"So I'm asking, Tío. Do you know anything about these Chinese dudes and what they are doing? I need your help."

Miguel fell silent. He stared at the wall opposite the balcony for a long time. So long, in fact, that Letty began to wonder if she'd offended him somehow. She waited.

Finally after long minutes had passed, he turned toward her and said, "Yeah, I know about them. They are very dangerous, mija." He used the abbreviated term "my daughter" indicating affection and care.

Letty sat up straight. "Truth is, Tío, I'm scared for my brothers. And my friend Jade, too. She's the wife of Carlos Lopez. I don't want anything to happen to them. I usually can keep my brothers and sister out of my work but not this time."

Miguel continued to drink his beer and stare at the wall.

"The more I know, Tío, the better I'll be able to deal with whatever they bring."

"Okay, but there are limits on how much I know. I figured out pretty quickly that I needed to stay away from them. That's what you should do, too," he sighed deeply.

"I'm trying. I just want my brothers to be safe."

Another long pause followed.

"They showed up here in Nogales a couple of years ago," Miguel began. "They opened a Chinese restaurant, but we think that was only cover. It became clear pretty quickly that they were moving Chinese migrants in and using them as workers in the restaurant. Then those migrants disappeared and more migrants would be brought in to take their place. Almost always the workers were female and fairly young. Teenagers. We believe they brought them into Mexico at the port of Guaymas. I had some reports from someone I know at the port that they were seen there coming and going. We think they transported these girls north to Nogales. We don't know how, but probably in a big truck. It's easier to get people and cargo into Mexico at one of the Pacific ports than trying to get them into California ports, so the Chinese are taking the longer but easier way."

"At first we didn't know what the Chinese were doing exactly, but then reports came through that they were moving these girls across the border into Arizona at a crossing west of Nogales in the desert. One of the O'odham men out there told us that the Chinese had been seen moving cargo across the border on more than one occasion. There are so few people out there, and the Border Patrol can't see everything that goes on. But the O'odham often see even if they don't say anything. They try to stay away from the smugglers. We don't know what happened to the girls after that. Took them north, I guess."

Letty shook her head in agreement.

"A couple of smugglers from Altar got in their way. Challenged the Chinese. Big mistake. The Chinese dudes took them out pretty quickly. Shot them both in the head, assassination style."

"Then a year or so ago, things changed. The Chinese stopped bringing girls north. Now they're moving some kind of cargo, but we don't know what. None of us has the huevos to look inside their trucks to see what it is. But it's not like the girls going north. Now they are moving the cargo south from inside the U.S. into Mexico, to Guaymas where it is shipped to god knows where."

"And I'm guessing that everyone along the way is getting a piece of the action."

"Right. These Chinese dudes don't mind paying a bribe. Just the cost of doing business. If anyone refuses the bribe or crosses them in any way, it doesn't end well. One Mexican cop who refused a bribe got his arm chopped off. That put an end to anyone going against the Chinese. They pay their bribes, and they go on their way."

"Are the cartels involved?"

"Don't know for sure, but I'm guessing by now Sinaloa knows about this and is getting its share. Otherwise, there would be a lot more shooting and chopping going on."

Letty fell quiet.

After long minutes, she said, "So we need to figure out what they are smuggling into Mexico and where the shipments are going."

"There is this rough dirt road, barely better than a horse trail. You need a 4-wheel drive. This dirt road is a little north of the border road where you see normally see la migra, the Border Patrol. The rough dirt road is higher up on the ridge, and it leads into a wash that goes south across the border. The wash is dry most of the year and has a pretty hard bottom, not real sandy so it's easier to walk. The road is south of Topawa and west of San Miguel in the Chukut Kuk district. I haven't been there myself, but as I said, O'odham out there chasing their cattle have seen them coming and going. Not often. Maybe once every three months or so. The one I talked to speculated that they unload the truck and carry the contraband down into the wash, then south across the border. He's seen truck lights on the other side. No doubt someone is waiting for them. We don't know where they take the shipments after that or what they are carrying."

"I have family in Chukut Kuk district."

"Ask someone you trust. The Chinese bribes are hard to resist, and you don't want them to know you are onto them."

Letty nodded gravely. She trusted her Uncle Mando, and he was the person she would ask.

Miguel sighed. "I think you should turn this over to the Border Patrol. Or better yet, the Shadow Wolves."

The Shadow Wolves were a special patrol unit in the U.S. Immigration and Customs Enforcement, known commonly as "ICE." The Shadow Wolves were experts in tracking smugglers. The Shadow Wolves unit was made up of Native Americans from several tribes, including the O'odham, Yaqui, Navajo, all from Arizona, and non-Arizona tribes Blackfeet, Lakota, and Kiowa. Their name came from their tracking ability – like wild wolves.

"I'm in over my head," Letty sighed.

"Yes, you are. Give this to the feds, mija," Miguel urged.

Silence prevailed for a few more minutes.

"One more thing I know."

"Yeah, what's that?"

"The Chinese have a house on the U.S. side on Ironwood Street. I don't know if they bought it or if they are renting it. It's only a few doors down and across the street from where I used to live. You know my old house, right? The one the Chinese have is a white house with red trim, a red door, and a pitched roof. We're not sure why they have that house on the U.S. side."

"Okay. I can check that out, too."

"Do you need a gun?"

"No, I have one," Letty said. She couldn't keep the sadness out of her voice.

Miguel reached out and squeezed her hand.

After a while, Letty said her goodbyes to her uncle and headed back to Tucson. As she expected, the ten-minute walk across the border from the U.S. into Mexico earlier that day took two hours going back north.

On the drive home, Letty thought about what the Chinese might be smuggling. If they were moving cargo south across the border into Mexico, it wouldn't be drugs or girls. Zhou mentioned counterfeit money. That's a possibility, she thought. But far more likely was the possibility that they were running guns. The U.S. was drowning in guns. There were roughly one hundred twelve guns per one hundred residents in the U.S., compared to thirty per one hundred residents in Canada and fifteen per one hundred residents in Mexico. Weapons smuggling had long been a preoccupation of the cartels.

Letty decided to talk to Zhou about this. Could it be that the weapons were not for Mexico but for a much more distant destination? A destination where there were only five guns per one hundred residents? Where gun ownership among private citizens was illegal? Could the triads be smuggling guns into China?

CHAPTER 13

THE morning coffee at Maggie's home wound down rather quickly after Letty left.

Jade joined Zhou on the deck. "Okay, Zhou. Let's go visit Carlos's mom, Maria. There are usually several family members there on Sundays. We can show them your book of mugshots. Maybe one of them remembers Chong Ma or some other Chinese person."

"Will you allow me to drive your car?"

Jade was surprised. "You must have a driver's license!"

"I do. I have an International Driver's Permit and also a Chinese driver's license. I show you."

Zhou pulled two cards from his pocket.

"This is a first for me. I've never seen this international permit. Sure, take the wheel. Where did you learn to drive?"

"I learned first in China. Then in Europe, I received more training for my police work."

"I see." Jade was smiling broadly again. "You're such a tough guy."

Zhou wasn't sure what it fully meant to be a "tough guy," but Jade seemed to like it. And if Jade liked it, then it was fine with Zhou.

Thirty minutes later they were in the very large backyard of a rambling older home in the Barrio Viejo neighborhood of Tucson. There were nearly thirty people of all ages at the family get-together. Some were eating at a long table filled with food. Others sat in lawn chairs with plates on their laps. People were laughing and talking in both Spanish and English and that unique combination of the two called "Spanglish." One young man, in his early twenties Zhou guessed, was sitting nearby very softly strumming the strings of an acoustic guitar. Children were playing an informal game of soccer in the far back of the spacious yard.

The entire family affair was presided over by a plump, dark-eyed older woman with long, dark, gray-streaked hair wrapped in a bun on her head. She was seated in a chair under a big olive tree holding a baby in her arms. She smiled constantly.

"Mija!" Maria Lopez called out when she saw Jade enter the backyard with Zhou.

Jade leaned over her and the two women kissed.

"Quisiera presentar mi amigo Zhou. I would like to present my friend Zhou." Jade said softly to Maria. She gestured to Zhou who came forward and shook Maria's hand. They exchanged smiles but no words because neither knew the other's language. Maria spoke little English.

Jade took Zhou around and introduced him to the others, most of whom spoke English. She explained to family members that there was a new lead in the case of Carlos. She told everyone that there was a possible connection to some Chinese criminals. She explained that Zhou was an investigator from Beijing. She asked them all to look at the Zhou's photo book and tell her if they recognized any of the mug shots.

Family members passed the book of photos around. Zhou watched carefully to see their reactions, both to when Jade mentioned the possible Chinese connection and to the mugshots in the book.

Finally Jade took the book of photos to Maria. At the same time, a couple of boys about twelve years old came to stand in front of Zhou. One said with some juvenile bravado, "Hey, are you Chinese? Do you know any kung fu?"

"Yes," Zhou smiled at the boy who was called Memo.

"Will you show us some?"

Zhou looked at Jade. She smiled and nodded her encouragement as she turned again to Maria and the book of photos. Zhou went away from the group of seated family members to a group of children. They quickly gathered around him. He began to show them some of the most basic defensive moves. Soon enough he was throwing the small children, boys and girls alike, in an arc and landing them gently in the grass. They squealed in delight, lining up quickly to be thrown again and again.

Jade watched Zhou as Maria looked at the book. He had so much grace and power. Jade found him fascinating. His moves were very elegant. She knew there was lethal power in those hands, and yet, he was so gentle with her nephews and nieces.

Maria handed the book back to Jade and said quietly in her native tongue, "I know none of these people." She sighed, "Jade, mija, Carlos is with God. I feel it in my bones."

Jade sighed sadly.

"Time for you to live your life now," Maria said comfortingly to Jade. "How about that one?" Maria gestured with her eyes toward Zhou. "El Chino is very handsome and good with the children. You like him?" Maria's eyes twinkled. Jade blushed furiously and looked down at her hands. Maria laughed delightedly and said, "Remember, chica, you will always, always be a part of the Lopez family and El Chino will be, too, if you choose him to be yours."

As they drove away from Maria's home an hour later, Jade said, "Hey, Zhou, you are really good with kids. You would be a good teacher of martial arts."

"I think of this," Zhou agreed. "I am older now. It is maybe the time in my life to stop this work and teach others." He didn't have all the words to tell her how tired he was, how he longed for another life. He had been traveling for years. He frequently had been in dangerous situations, and his life had been threatened more than he cared to remember. He had no permanent home, not since he and Siu Lin were finished. The work was taking more out of him physically. He was thinking now of a home, a wife, children, and passing on his skills.

"And just how old are you?"

"I am thirty-five on my next birthday."

"Oh, you are such an old man," Jade teased him.

Zhou smiled. He had been told that Americans had a reputation for joking and teasing. He enjoyed Jade's frequent teasing.

They fell silent for a while.

Zhou suddenly said, "Jade, show me the building where Carlos planned to create the after-school center for the children."

"Okay, but it's not much to see now. They turned it into an auto body shop to repair and repaint damaged cars." She directed him to the area south of downtown Tucson. Ten minutes later, they pulled up to the auto body shop.

"What about the storage units next door?" He gestured to a commercial outfit with several rows of metal storage containers. The majority were about fifteen feet wide and ten feet tall. The front of each unit was a metal door that slid up to open and that could be locked when down.

"Letty checked all that out after Carlos disappeared. She said no one working there had talked to Carlos. She said she talked to the owner, who is also the manager, and to a maintenance man on duty."

"Did she ask about any Chinese people?"

"We didn't know about the Chinese back then. Letty didn't know to ask."

Zhou got out of the car and walked toward the storage units. Jade followed.

In the open space between two of the long rows of metal storage units, they could see an older man with a broom sweeping the concrete drive.

"Hello," Zhou said to the man.

"Hello," the old man answered in heavily-accented English.

"I am investigating the disappearance of the man who rented the building next door about one year ago." Zhou gestured to the building.

"I sorry. No speak English good."

Jade stepped up to translate between English and Spanish.

They exchanged names and handshakes. The old man was known as Jesús Sánchez. Jade referred to him as Señor Sánchez after that.

Zhou continued. "Did you work here one year ago?"

"No, I went to my sister's home in Hermosillo for about two months in the winter. When I returned, there was no job for me. I did other work, but then in May, the owner lost his new employee, and he hired me again."

"Did you know Carlos Lopez?"

"Ah, yes. Carlos is a very friendly man. I have not seen him for a long time."

"I am his wife. He disappeared about one year ago," Jade explained.

No need to translate. Zhou could hear the sadness in her voice and the shocked and sad expression in the old man's face.

"Señor Sánchez, we hope to find Carlos. We have only one possible clue now," Zhou looked directly into the eyes of the old man. "Did you see any Chinese people visiting Carlos?"

"No, not visiting. But there was a group of them, maybe ten or twelve men. They rented a big storage unit here. The biggest unit. Then they rented a second unit. But they moved everything before I left for Mexico to visit my sister."

"Do you know where they went?" Zhou felt that tingle in his spine that came when he was making progress on a case.

"They gave me a big tip of money which made me very happy. I asked where they were going, and I asked if they could use me to work at the new location. They said they were moving to a bigger place, a warehouse in northwest Tucson near a dog rescue organization. They said maybe they would hire me later. They also were friendly. But their Spanish…not so good."

Zhou nodded. He looked again into Señor Sánchez's eyes.

"Thank you very much for the help."

Señor Sánchez looked at Jade. "Can you find Carlos? He is a good man."

Jade smiled faintly. "Everyone seems to think he is dead."

Señor Sánchez crossed himself in the Catholic way. "If this is true, then may he go with God."

Jade was quiet on the drive back to her house. Suddenly she squealed delightedly.

"Look!"

"Shénme?" She had startled Zhou.

Jade pointed to a lot on the corner filled with conifer trees. "Christmas trees! Let's stop and buy one."

She had such a childlike look of happiness on her face. He pulled the car into the lot. For the next twenty minutes, Jade led him on the search for a Christmas tree. Finally they found one which Jade pronounced "perfect." With the help of the vendor, they roped it to the roof of Jade's little sedan.

Off they went again. Half an hour later they were back at Jade's house.

Before they exited the car, Jade turned to Zhou and said, "What does "shénme" mean?"

Zhou smiled. "It is the same as 'what?' in English. If you don't understand something, you ask 'what?' I did not understand when you said, 'Look!'"

"Ah," said Jade. "Maybe you can teach me some Chinese."

The words "pillow talk" popped into Zhou's head. He smiled and said, "With pleasure."

They unloaded the tree and placed it in a bucket of water on Jade's patio.

"Later we'll decorate this," she said with satisfaction.

"Now let's look at your computer and find the warehouse next to the dog rescue place," Zhou reminded her.

The search didn't take long at all, thanks to Google, Google Maps, and Google Earth. They found the dog rescue organization on Marigold Street in northwest Tucson but still east of the interstate highway. Using the Earth function, they were able to follow the view on the street in a 360-degree circle. A large building was under construction across the street from the dog rescue organization. Zhou could see more than one building that might be a warehouse.

"Tomorrow we will go to visit this street and find the warehouse. Perhaps the triad gang is still renting it." He paused. "Maybe I will go with Miss Letty. Too dangerous for you."

Jade sighed. "I'm not a precious little thing. I think it will be okay. You *can* take me with you. If we see any Chinese people, we'll run the other way."

Zhou shook his head. She *was* precious as far as he was concerned. And it wasn't so easy to run away from the triad gangsters.

"Let's eat now. I'm going to fix us some supper." Jade left for the kitchen.

Later after supper, Jade invited Zhou to go up on the roof with her.

Zhou refused the offer of a beer but agreed to climb up on the roof. He understood immediately why she liked it there. It was quiet and they could see the stars beginning to appear in the night sky. He thought maybe the roof would be a good place to hide Jade if Chong Ma or one of his 49ers showed up.

They were soon joined by Zorro and Don Diego, Jade's cats. The four sat in silence for a while.

"What do neighbors think of Jade and cats on roof?"

"I doubt if they've ever noticed. From the street, it's not that easy to see what's going on up here."

Good, Zhou thought. The gangsters would be less likely to see Jade if she were on the roof.

More gentle silence rested between them.

Finally, Zhou spoke again, "Tell me about the one called Ricardo."

"You mean at Maria's house? Ricardo is Carlos's little brother. Carlos has three older sisters. They are Mercedes, Sylvia, and Maria. They are the mothers of most of those kids you were playing with. They are my nieces and nephews. Then came Carlos, then Ricardo, then Daniela, the baby. Daniela wasn't there today. She's seventeen, a very pretty girl and very sweet. She's with her boyfriend a lot."

Jade paused for a moment, "Ricardo is, I guess, about twenty-two or twenty-three now. He really idolized Carlos. I don't know what he's doing these days. I don't know if he has a job. He's not in school. He seems to sort of drift around. That was him playing the guitar. Why do you ask about him?"

As each person took the book of photos in their hands that afternoon, Zhou carefully watched their faces. There was no response from any of them until Ricardo took the book. He looked very uncomfortable and turned the pages as if there might be a scorpion under the next leaf.

"I think Ricardo recognized someone in the book, maybe Bao or Chong Ma."

Jade was shocked.

"You see that he has a shirt with long sleeves buttoned." Zhou continued.

"Yes. Why is that important?"

"Ricardo may be a drug addict. Maybe he hides needle marks on his arm. I want to talk to him."

They fell silent again.

Finally Jade said, "Want to go decorate the Christmas tree?"

"Yes. This is my first time to do this holiday task."

Jade laughed. "It's not hard work. I'll show you."

They descended and went directly to the garage. Zhou helped Jade bring in a stand for the tree and a box of decorations.

As they worked, Jade explained the meaning of each ornament. There were the shining balls in different colors and a long string of electric lights. They started with the lights. What surprised him were the religious-themed ornaments. Wise Men. Angels. The Manger and the Baby Jesus. Shepherds. Sheep. Snowflakes. Tinsel. Zhou came to understand that religion was an important part of Christmas for Jade. He had learned when living in France that religion was more important in America than in many other countries. In China and in France, Christmas was a time to visit friends, eat, and exchange gifts. Not all Frenchmen went to Catholic Mass on a regular basis or at all. Most Chinese had no idea that Christmas had its origin in religious beliefs, or that many of the symbols were religious. In China, Christmas was an intensely-commercial holiday only recently adopted, mostly by urban Chinese.

Zhou placed the angel on top of the tree and said casually, "Jade, your beautiful hair is a problem. Everyone can see you first."

"Tell me about it," she said ruefully. "I've hated this hair since I was a kid." She pulled at the curls. "I mean, I like it okay...it's just that it attracts so much attention! It's kind of hard to blend into a crowd with this carrot top. When Seri and I were in China, everyone stared at me."

"Carrot top," he repeated with a smile. Good words to describe her. He had not heard this phrase before now.

"Perhaps it is time now to cover your head with a hat or scarf when we go out."

"I could cut my hair short and dye it black," Jade said agreeably. "I have got some of that black hair dye left over from Halloween. I was a witch at the Halloween party. My students loved my costume! I dyed my hair black. I could do it again."

"Change hair to black!" Zhou was dismayed. "No!"

"It's that wash-out kind of dye. It won't last. I have some purple dye, too."

"Purple hair!" Zhou laughed.

They fell into a companionable silence again.

"Tell me about your wife…I mean your ex-wife."

"Chen Siu Lin is an administrator in a big business. Initially, she found me interesting and exciting. She thought my job was romantic. The idea of fighting crime and of traveling around the world was very romantic to her. She wanted to live in the West. She discovered later that her husband's investigator job is not so romantic. My work is hard work and dangerous, and it does not pay well. She came to be unhappy. She became very disappointed with me. She thought I had little ambition. No desire to be wealthy.

She wanted a divorce so I gave it to her. No gun necessary," Zhou grinned at Jade. "She married a rich entrepreneur soon after."

"I still think you dodged a bullet, Zhou."

"Thank you. I came to understand later that I married her because it was time to marry, not because I felt strong love. The next time I marry, I marry for love."

Jade beamed and nodded.

They were almost finished now.

"Tomorrow we talk to Miss Letty and tell her what we have learned," Zhou said.

"Yes, let's invite Letty here and we'll tell her everything. I bet she has some things to tell us, too."

As with the previous night, Zhou slept on the living room couch, and Jade went to her room.

CHAPTER 14

Monday morning. Letty hadn't slept well because of worrying about everything she'd learned from her Tío Miguel at the café in Nogales, Sonora. She forced herself to leave her warm bed and quickly dress. She tiptoed past Will's room where he was sleeping peacefully. Millie went out the back door, and Letty quietly made herself a cup of coffee. Sitting at the kitchen table, she reviewed her next steps. She wanted to talk to Zhou, of course, and tell him what she'd learned in Nogales about the Chinese activities there and on the O'odham reservation.

She also wanted to talk to Marv Iverson. Even though he was retired, he liked knowing what was going on, and Letty considered his insights and contacts invaluable. She and Zhou must bring federal law enforcement into this now, and she wanted to know if Marv could recommend someone to contact first, preferably in the Border Patrol or ICE. Maybe Marv knew someone in ICE who could connect her to the Shadow Wolves. She wanted someone who would be sensitive to the fact that several innocent people could get hurt if the feds were too heavy-handed.

Both ICE and the Border Patrol eventually had to answer to the Department of Homeland Security. That meant Sam Lambert, who worked for Homeland Security, could and would take control of this investigation if he found out about it first. If Letty could avoid dealing with Sam Lambert, she would. He wasn't that knowledgeable about local affairs, he wasn't directly involved in what was going on day-by-day on the border, plus he had told her to stay out of this. Handing the investigation over to Lambert seemed to Letty like jumping to the top when she preferred to start at the ground level. She figured that Border Patrol and ICE agents who were out in the desert every day, boots on the ground, would be the best people to bring into this dicey situation. Letty didn't want to antagonize Lambert because she considered him unpredictable. Avoidance was the best route. Letty knew, too, that her real problem was with Lambert's arrogant attitude. He could screw everything up.

Beyond the overriding concern for the safety of her two brothers, Letty's attention now was on the location and status of the two missing young women. She thought it quite likely that the gangsters had hidden the kidnapped Hong Kong official's daughter as well as the peasant migrant Esperanza whom Eduardo so wanted to find. Her gut feeling was that if she could find where the Chinese were headquartered and figure out what they were up to, she might very well find the two girls. Lambert would not prioritize them or her brothers' safety. He would simply be looking to bring down the triad gangsters' smuggling operations and enhance his own reputation in the process. If innocents got caught in the crossfire, it would be of secondary concern to him.

Then there was José Gomez, the nephew of Sylvia Baird. Letty was fully aware of her responsibility to Mrs. Baird. She intended to give full attention to José's arrest for the murder of Barbara Lyle. Again, her gut feeling was that there was a connection to the Chinese. She could think of no other reason that Gomez had blurted out his anger about those Chinese girls to Barbara Lyle's son. She had to find what that connection might be. Letty would meet with the lawyer, Jessica Cameron, in just a couple of hours. She also wanted to talk to her Tucson detective pal, Adelita García.

But first, something had been nagging at Letty since Friday. Her first call of the day was to her little sister, Elena. She wanted to make sure Elena was safe and that she stayed that way.

"Hello, Elena. Did I wake you up?"

"No, Letty. I'm going out now with some co-workers to collect samples in Sabino Creek."

"Samples of what?"

"I'm not exactly sure. Our prof said he'd explain it to us in detail later. Something about the water quality of snowmelt flowing into the creek from Mt. Lemmon. Microbial life now may be different than at other times of the year."

"Sounds like fun."

Elena laughed. "Hey, I'm glad you called. I have some great news!"

"Good. What is it?"

"My professor won a grant to take his lab assistants and students to attend a conference in Washington, D.C. We're leaving Wednesday for a week. I'm sorry I haven't told you about this, but we just found out yesterday that we won the grant. We'll go to the conference and do some sightseeing, too. They are paying for everything – our plane tickets and our hotel rooms, and even our meals."

Letty breathed a sigh of relief. Elena in Washington, D.C., out of the reach of Chinese gangsters was just about the best news she'd received in days.

"That is great news! Do you need me to give you some spending money?"

"Nah, Letty. You do enough for me already. I have some money saved. I'll use it for snacks and maybe get a souvenir. No problem! I'm so excited."

Elena asked about her brothers. Letty decided to avoid the topic of Will's shoulder dislocation. Instead she said, "Eduardo is fine. I talked to him yesterday. And little brother Will has a girlfriend."

"Really!" Elena squealed. "Awesome! What she like?"

"She's smart and pretty and her name is Clarice. She's in his bicycling club. You should see the way they look at each other. She kissed him on the cheek, and he turned beet red…well, as red as a full-blood O'odham can get. He's been in the sun a lot lately, and he's even darker than usual. He told me that he really likes her, and he emphasized the word 'like.' You can meet her when you come home."

Elena giggled. "I can't wait. I know I'm going to like her, too."

They chatted a few more minutes, then said their goodbyes.

Marv was next. Letty told him what had happened with Will and all the information that came from her Uncle Miguel, although she didn't mention that Miguel was the source. She had to wait for Marv to get paper and pen. He took extensive notes on Letty's description of the isolated desert location where the smugglers had been seen.

"I'm going to contact a friend in ICE," Marv said. "This is serious. You can't do this by yourself. Since it's on the reservation and way in the back country, maybe they'll want to call on the Shadow Wolves."

"That's what I was thinking, too, Marv. Let me know when you have a name and number I can call. I really appreciate your help."

"No problem." They said their goodbyes.

By that time, Millie indicated that she was hungry, so Letty stopped long enough to feed her and give her bowl of fresh water. As usual, Millie ate like she would never have the opportunity to eat again for the rest of her life. The food was gone in about sixty seconds.

"Don't eat so fast! You're going to choke, you goof ball," Letty said. Millie wagged her tail amicably.

Adelita was next. She and Letty had an off-the-record relationship that no one official knew about. They had helped each other by sharing key information for nearly the entire time that Letty had worked as a private investigator and during the time Adelita worked her way up to the job of detective in the Tucson Police Department. Letty considered her relationship with Adelita to be professionally invaluable. And they were friends and had been for many years. A true friendship was valuable beyond all measure. Letty knew that for certain.

Letty filled Adelita in on almost everything. She told Adelita about being hired by Sylvia Baird.

"What can you tell me about the arrest of José Gomez?" Letty asked.

"There was a report about a fight between two groups of boys, one led by Gomez and the other by the dead woman's son, Travis Lyle. Instead of going home like the police officer told him, Gomez went to the Lyle home. He and Travis Lyle were seen arguing loudly in the Lyles' front yard. Gomez was seen later getting in his car and driving away. We don't have an exact time on that because the neighbor wasn't sure. Around the same time, a 911 call came in from the husband of the dead woman. We do have the exact time that the call came in. An ambulance was sent, but she was already dead when they arrived."

"We set up a crime scene. One of our officers found a gun in the hedge outside the wall around the Lyles' back yard. There's a wrought-iron gate in the wall that leads to the back yard. You can't see the gate from the street because of an oleander hedge that is nearly fifteen feet high. We found the gun between the wall and the oleander bushes about ten feet from the gate. Looks like someone shot through the gate then tossed the gun into the hedge. The gun is being tested now for fingerprints and ballistics. The dead woman is at the morgue. They'll do an autopsy on her this week. Retrieving the bullet from her brain is a priority. We want to see if it matches the gun. We interviewed both the husband and the son. They said pretty much the same thing. A shot came from the street and killed the woman. Not much to add although the son, Travis, did say he thought it was Gomez who shot her. Travis didn't see Gomez fire the shot, though. Gomez did not have gunshot residue on his hands."

"Adelita, it looks like there's a connection to the Chinese triads I told you about."

"What! That's crazy! Tell me more!"

Letty explained what she'd learned from her interview with José's girlfriend Emily Castro. "I'm looking into this now," Letty said. "It's a real possibility that there's way more to this than some teenager getting pissed off and trying to kill another teenager over a girl. Also, I have a source that tells me the Chinese are smuggling, but not going north. They are taking contraband south into Mexico."

"Wow! Maybe weapons smuggling? This is getting nasty. Let me know as soon as you learn more. We'll figure this out together. Meanwhile, you be careful, Letty. Watch your back."

"I am watching. I'll check with you tomorrow."

Letty decided to wait on contacting Zhou. She wanted to gather as much information as possible before she saw him again. That meant meeting with Jessica Cameron first and seeing if she could interview the Lyles, both father and son. She decided that she preferred to go to Jade's house and talk to Zhou in person. Letty took a quick shower, dressed, and headed for Jessica Cameron's office.

* * *

Jessica Cameron's office was in a large law firm on the tenth story of a high-rise building in downtown Tucson. Letty didn't much like having to go downtown. Parking was always a problem, and a parking place always cost her money. She found the cheapest option – the lower level of the multistory main library. First hour free. Two dollars for every hour after that.

Letty walked the short distance to the office building and took the elevator to the Clark law firm. She introduced herself and gave her card to the receptionist who disappeared for a few minutes. Jessica Cameron appeared soon after with a faint smile on her face.

"Welcome, Ms. Valdez. Please come into my office."

Letty noticed that Jessica Cameron didn't look that old – maybe mid-thirties – but she had a spacious office with a great view of the Tucson Mountains to the west. Cameron is either well-connected, or she's doing a very good job for the firm, Letty thought to herself. Maybe she knows how to bring in wealthy clients, or maybe she's just good at winning cases.

Cameron gestured to a chair and said, "I'll get to the point so we don't waste each other's time. I want us to keep each other informed and work together as a team. Are you on board with that?"

Letty nodded yes.

"You are familiar with the outlines of the case. Two groups of teenage boys got into a conflict that was broken up by police. Our client, José Gomez, follows Travis Lyle to his home in the Sam Hughes neighborhood, Gomez and Lyle get into a shouting match, then Gomez is seen driving away from the Lyle home about the same time that Barbara Lyle is shot. A gun was found nearby, but so far, we have no link between the gun and our client. We're waiting on forensics. At this point there is no direct proof that our client shot Mrs. Lyle. But the fact that he followed Travis Lyle home, they got into it again, and then Mrs. Lyle was killed while standing next to her son makes it look really bad for José Gomez. He had motive and opportunity. If the gun turns out to have his fingerprints on it, then he had means. There was no gunshot residue on his hands, but the prosecution can just argue that he had gloves on. Circumstantial evidence against him is strong. There appears to be no other suspect."

Cameron paused. "Do you need water or coffee or anything?"

"No, thank you."

"Okay. So what do you have so far?" she asked Letty.

"Ms. Cameron, I want to make clear that, if we are on the same team, the information I give you is to be kept between us until the right time to make it public. Lives may depend on your discretion."

Cameron's eyebrows went up in surprise. "Well….I didn't expect this. Yes, of course. You can count on me."

"This case appears to be much more complicated that what is in the police report. I interviewed Gomez, and I'm fairly certain that he's hiding something. He simply made no attempt to defend himself. He may be trying to protect someone."

Cameron nodded. "I see. Go on."

"I also interviewed his mother and his girlfriend Emily Castro. Emily told me that the fight – the one the boys got into that the cops broke up – may have been about her. She said José was furious that Travis Lyle had been hitting on her. Then she said something very interesting."

Letty paused. "Emily said she heard Gomez say to Travis, 'Why are you hitting on my girlfriend when you have all those Chinese girls?'"

Cameron shook her head. "I don't understand. What Chinese girls? Why is that important to this case?"

Letty launched into the tale of Interpol, Chinese triad gangsters, human and drug trafficking, Homeland Security, her friend Jade Lopez, and a Beijing cop named Zhou Liang Wei.

"Wow!" Jessica Cameron said. "So you think Travis Lyle is mixed up in the trafficking, and José knew about it somehow?"

"That's correct. No proof yet, but the comment about Chinese girls says a lot to me. Emily Castro said it wasn't about any Chinese-American girls at school. She didn't know what Gomez was talking about. He won't say."

Jessica Cameron leaned back in her chair. "That's quite a story."

"There's more. I learned from two other sources that this Chinese criminal gang had been smuggling Chinese girls into the U.S. from Mexico. About a year ago, they changed their business, cut back on the girls, and started smuggling something from the U.S. into Mexico. First south to north. Now north to south. My sources say that that they had – or still have – a drop-off location in Tucson, then they take the contraband out to a rather isolated area on the reservation to move it across the border. The Sinaloa Cartel may be involved, too, although I have no confirmation of that. In Tucson, there is a Mexican-American man, a coyote, whom we think was moving the girls north, and is now helping move the contraband to the south. An Anglo man was seen at least once at the coyote's drop-off in Tucson."

"That could be Travis?"

"Yes, or more likely his dad. Or some other player that we haven't come across yet. There's a possibility that Mrs. Lyle was involved, or maybe she just got caught in the crossfire."

"What do you think they are smuggling?"

"The Beijing cop shared with me a long list of contraband that the triad gangs are known to smuggle in various locations in the world. But I think guns are the most likely. They started off smuggling girls and probably drugs, too, into the U.S., but then moved into weapons smuggling. There's a lot of money in guns. They are easy to get in the U.S. Guns are a lot less trouble to deal with than a bunch of terrified Chinese teenage peasant girls who thought they were going to get a job and instead found themselves brutalized by gangsters and turned into unpaid prostitutes."

"So circumstantial evidence makes the case for my client look really bad unless we can prove that Mrs. Lyle got caught up in something far more complicated and nefarious than any of us thought," Jessica Cameron concluded.

"Exactly. I'm following up on my leads. I'm hoping to figure out what is being smuggled, and by whom, and what that has to do with the Lyle family. Finding the answers to these questions will shift suspicion from José Gomez to the real culprits."

Letty paused. "There's more, too. The coyote here in Tucson may have turned over to the Chinese a Mexican girl who had just come across the border illegally. He probably sold her to the Chinese. And the Beijing cop is also looking for the daughter of a Hong Kong official who was kidnapped. We think the gangsters have her, too. My view of this is based on an incident which occurred a couple of nights ago in Himmel Park. A Chinese girl was seen attempting to run away from a bunch of Chinese men. They caught her and hauled her off in a van. And for some reason, these Chinese gangsters are very interested in Jade Lopez. She's an elementary school teacher here in Tucson. Perhaps you remember her husband, Carlos Lopez, who disappeared about a year ago. The gangsters have searched her house twice for something. We don't know what they are looking for. So these three women are in danger. It's possible that Emily Castro might be in danger of kidnapping and human trafficking, too, although I'm not sure about that. That's why we have to proceed carefully."

"What do you need from me?" Cameron asked intensely.

"I'm going to attempt to interview father and son Lyle, but I'm going to try to talk to them separately. I don't expect that they will be very cooperative. Also I'm going to be doing some serious research on both Barbara and Fred Lyle. The comment that José made to Travis about the Chinese girls suggests to me that Travis found out about the smuggling of Chinese girls, and he probably bragged about it to the other boys. It's very likely that Travis took advantage of them sexually. That's a nice way of saying that he may have been raping those girls. But it's unlikely that a teenage boy would be able to form a cooperative business relationship with Chinese gangsters. My guess is that one or both parents were involved. We need to know as much as possible about the Lyles. I suggest you start with doing some research on them, and I will, too."

Jessica Cameron was grinning now. "This is the most interesting case I've been handed for ages! Thank you so much."

Letty snorted. "Interesting, yes, but not so much fun if a Hong Kong gangster is after you with a hatchet. You should watch your back. Be more careful about security. We don't know how much they know about you and about me. They will become aware of you at some point."

"Okay. I'll take your advice," Cameron said seriously. "But I must tell you. This has a lot of potential for making some money and also enhancing the reputation of the firm. I just want to say that I am very, very pleased to have you on our team, Letty Valdez. I am very impressed with what you've learned so far."

Letty stood. "Time for me to get back to work. Let's stay in touch."

The two women shook hands. Letty made it back to the library parking garage within the sixty minutes allowed. She did not have to pay for parking.

* * *

The neighborhood where the Lyles lived was named after Welsh immigrant Sam Hughes, who came to Tucson in 1858. The neighborhood was graced with many beautiful older homes in various architectural styles, yet almost always with a Spanish influence. Large trees in elegantly-landscaped yards provided more shade than many Tucson neighborhoods. Bicycles and walkers abounded. Many University of Arizona professors owned homes and lived in Sam

Hughes. Jade also lived in this neighborhood in a much smaller and more modest home than many of the residents.

Letty parked a block away and watched the Lyle residence. The best thing would be to interview them separately. Travis Lyle at age 18 was old enough to be interviewed without a parent present.

She waited, and after a while, she saw a wide metal gate at the rear of the Lyle property slide open onto the alley. Travis drove out into the street. The gate closed behind him automatically. It was around lunchtime by now so she figured he'd come home from school for lunch, or maybe he'd never gone to school at all that morning. She followed him from a discreet distance. He showed no indication that he knew he was being followed.

Letty noticed that Travis was tall and well-built, with very blonde hair cut stylishly. He was wearing well-tailored clothing and expensive running shoes.

Lyle drove to a Chinese restaurant on Speedway Boulevard, parked and went in. She could see him ordering at the counter. He was sitting at a booth waiting for his lunch when Letty slipped into the booth opposite him.

"Hi, Travis. My name is Letty Valdez, and I'm a private investigator. I'm looking into the death of your mother. I'm very sorry to hear that she died and in such an awful way." Letty tried her best to look sympathetic.

"Yeah," Travis said. "It was bad. But they already caught the guy who killed her. His name is José Gomez."

"Right. That's what I'm doing. Trying to build a case." She didn't say that she was trying to build a case for the defense.

"I'd like to ask you a few questions. I promise I won't take much time."

"I'm not sure my dad would think this is okay," he said. He looked around furtively as if he were guilty of something. His eyes were very blue.

"Your dad is committed to seeing your mother's killer go to jail, and if you can help us, that would be great."

"Okay. What do you want to know?"

"Please describe what happened that afternoon."

"We were sitting on the back patio – my dad and my mom and me – and they were drinking margaritas. I had a beer."

Underage and his parents let him drink, Letty noted.

"What were you talking about?"

Travis immediately began to look uncomfortable. He turned his head away from Letty and said, "Nothing. I don't remember."

"Then what happened?"

"Gomez shot my mother."

"Where was she sitting?"

"Next to me."

"Where was your dad sitting?"

"He wasn't there. He'd gone into the house to get something, some snacks, I think."

"Okay. So you and your mom were sitting there and then what happened?"

"This bullet came from the direction of the street and hit my mom in her forehead. She fell over backward onto the patio."

"You live on a corner. When you say the direction of the street, do you mean the south or the east?"

"South."

"There's a gate there."

"Yeah, I think Gomez was standing there at the gate, and he shot through the iron railings. There are spaces between them that you can see through."

"Why do you think Gomez shot your mom?"

"I think he was trying to shoot me!"

"Why?"

"He's an asshole. He just doesn't like me. I tried to date this girl he likes, and that pissed him off."

"What's the girl's name?"

"Emily something. I don't remember."

"What happened after you mom fell over?"

"I was so shocked. I don't know what I did."

"How about your dad?"

"He came from the house. He ran to my mom when he saw her there. Then he called 911 on his phone."

Letty sat back.

"Have you had any contact with anyone else about this?

"The police interviewed me and my dad. That's all."

"One more thing. In the report, it says that Gomez said something to you about Chinese girls. What was that about?" Letty was told this by Emily Castro, but implied that it was in the police report.

Travis couldn't hide his shock and dismay at this question. He shook his head from side to side.

"No," he said vehemently. "Nobody said anything about Chinese girls. I don't know anything about that. No."

Letty was sure he was lying.

The waiter came with Travis's meal.

Letty stood up. "Thank you, Travis. Your information has been helpful. Again, I want to say how sorry I am that you lost your mother."

Travis mumbled and looked down.

Letty headed back to the Lyle home in the Sam Hughes district. First she drove around the block and through the alley, carefully observing the neighbors' potential views of the Lyle property. She noticed, too, that there was a side door into the Lyle house quite near the wrought-iron gate and hedge. The door was not mentioned in the police report.

Letty knocked on the Lyles' front door. Fred Lyle answered.

"Mr. Lyle?"

"Yes," Lyle said abruptly. He looked a lot like his son except for carrying a few more pounds and a scowl on his face.

"My name is Letty Valdez, and I'm a private investigator. I'm looking into the death of your wife. I'm very sorry to hear about her death. I was wondering if you could talk with me for a few minutes and answer a few questions."

"I already talked to the police."

"Yes, but we're hoping to gain more information to make a stronger case."

"Who did you say you work for?"

"I didn't. My client wants to remain anonymous."

Lyle stepped back and slammed the door in Letty's face.

Chapter 15

Back in her office, Letty first called home. Will was fine. Clarice was with him. Bring home some pizza was their urgent request.

She turned on her desktop computer and immersed herself for over an hour. She looked first to see what she could find on Kevin Kwok. The triad 49er Bao had rented a car at the airport under Kwok's name, and Zhou wanted to know if Letty could find out more about him.

Kwok's case was similar to Carlos Lopez's, but without any mention of missing money as in the case of Carlos. Kwok had been a moderately-successful real estate agent at the time of his disappearance, which was around the same time that Carlos had disappeared. Letty ran through those personal and financial records that she could legally access. No police record, only one speeding ticket. His bank account was still open but had seen no activity on it for nearly a year. His Facebook page was still there, but there hadn't been any postings for the same length of time. His parents had reported him a missing person, but despite police efforts, there had been no sign of him at all. Letty looked for credit-card use, typically a real giveaway of where a person was living. There had been no charges made at all since Kwok's disappearance. Same with his cell phone. No calls out, and since his bill wasn't paid, the service had been cancelled.

Looks like Kevin Kwok may have met the same fate at Carlos, Letty thought to herself. Somehow he had crossed paths with the triad gang, and he had come out on the short end. Maybe he tried to rent or sell them some real estate. Then maybe he discovered what they were up to and threatened to report them, or maybe he tried to get in on their smuggling activities and take a cut. No way to know at this point. Maybe he or his remains would turn up at some point.

On a whim, Letty first looked for anything she could find about Barbara Lyle. The social aspect of Barbara's life was much stronger than any business or financial affairs. She appeared to be a socially well-connected Tucson matron with an affluent businessman for a husband. She was on the board of several charities and a local arts organization. Her Facebook posts had frequent comments about these organizations and events she attended in their names.

Letty began looking for responses to Barbara Lyle's posts. If she could identify a close friend of Barbara Lyle's, she could talk to that person and determine if Lyle had revealed any secrets that pertained to the Chinese affair. She found a couple of potential names in Mrs. Lyle's Facebook postings, both women, and searched for them. They were both neighbors of the Lyles.

Next Letty took on Fred Lyle. She started by looking at public records about his business, social, and financial dealings. She decided to stick to the records available to anyone, and not try any tricks to get into databases that she technically wasn't supposed to access.

Nearly five years earlier, Letty learned that Fred Lyle had come perilously close to total financial ruin. He had been forced to file for bankruptcy and sell off many of his business assets as well as his home. His business empire had been rather extensive. He had owned a real estate company and a citywide chain of furniture and appliance stores, and he had operated a maintenance-and-repair business that provided services to numerous businesses in the city.

Letty thought that the loss of the Lyle home, a three-million-dollar estate in the Catalina Foothills above Skyline Drive, must have been particularly hard on a woman like Barbara Lyle. Despite the economic difficulties, Lyle was able to scrap together enough money to purchase a home in the Sam Hughes district that was so-cially acceptable if not as ostentatious as the Foothills estate. He was determined to recover his losses and maintain his social standing.

And recover Lyle did. Three years later, he was doing well finan-cially although exactly how he was making his money wasn't exactly clear. He had revived his maintenance operation, and it seemed to be doing well enough.

Connecting Lyle to weapons smuggling, or any other kind of smuggling, was going to be a much more difficult task. Finding information about a person's gun purchase and ownership was vir-tually impossible. Privacy laws protected the gun owners. Finding information on gun vendors was somewhat easier. Gun shop own-ers, even those with a "shop" in their home, were required to have a Federal Firearms License. These vendors were required by law to keep a registry of firearms sales, and a copy of Form 4473, "Firearms Transaction Record," that documented each gun purchase. The buyer had to give his name and other personal data on the form. This information was not made public. However, the law enforce-ment agency Bureau of Alcohol, Tobacco, Firearms, and Explosives – known commonly as ATF – was allowed access to these records in the course of an investigation. Sale of a gun by a private citizen to a private citizen required no records whatsoever.

This meant that, if Lyle had been purchasing guns from vendors with a Federal Firearms License, there would records available – but not to Letty. She would have to turn this over to Lawyer Cameron and her friend Detective Adelita García to open the records. Letty needed some crumb Lyle might have left behind in a trail that would tell her if he was involved in weapons purchases or sales.

Letty took another approach in her research. Facebook again. The giant social media platform had made it clear that gun sales and trade were not allowed. And yet there were numerous "pages" and "groups" devoted to various topics like "gun photography" and "recreational guns." There were designated "places" such as Steve's Gun Shop located about a ten-minute drive from Letty's office. Steve was telling the Facebook world that he had some new Ruger

Precision Rifles in stock, and he invited everyone to come by and check them out. It was just an invitation, not a direct attempt to sell. Yeah, right, Letty thought cynically.

Most of the pages, groups and places had comments made by individual Facebook users. She found Fred Lyle's personal page, then did a search to see if he had made any comments on the gun pages. Yes. Letty quickly began to feel as if she'd stumbled into a huge spider web that connected Lyle to weapons. He had made occasional comments on several of these pages, and even left a review or two. However, most comments were over a year old.

Of course, Letty thought to herself. If he had been smuggling girls and drugs to the north with the Chinese, he wouldn't have been concerned about being associated with guns and gun sales. But if he had begun smuggling guns south with his Chinese pals, he would have become much more circumspect about associating the name Lyle with the word "gun."

There was more work to do, but Letty would need help. She made quick calls to both Jessica Cameron and Adelita García. She asked them to meet her early the next morning at Jade's home. She told them that she had made some progress, and now it was time to bring them in. She called Zhou and told him that they would all meet and share information the following morning.

Then Letty turned off her computer, locked her office, and headed back to the Lyle neighborhood. She parked in a place that could not be seen from the Lyle house. She knocked on the door of one of the Facebook friends of Barbara Lyle.

An older woman wrapped in a sweater answered. She opened the front door but not the metal security screen. She had a combination of fear and suspicion on her face.

"Hello, my name is Letty Valdez. I'm a private investigator seeking information about the recent death of Mrs. Barbara Lyle. I was wondering if you could answer a few questions." Letty held up her private investigator's license with her photo. Letty knew the woman's name, Rita Benton, but did not want to have to explain how she knew this.

"What do you want to know?" Mrs. Benton asked.

"Did you see anyone in the street around the time Mrs. Lyle was killed?"

"No, in fact, I wasn't home at that time."

"Did you know Mrs. Lyle at all?"

"Yes, I considered her a good friend."

"Did she happen to say anything to you that indicated someone was bothering her or that she was fearful of anyone?"

Rita Benton fell silent. "I don't know if I should talk about this."

"We're trying to find a killer. We want justice for Mrs. Lyle."

"Then you should look at her husband," Rita Benton spit out. "He's a disreputable person. Barbara was afraid of him. He occasionally hit her. I tried to get her to seek help or report him, but she wouldn't."

"I see," said Letty. "Did she ever complain about any specific thing her husband did that upset her?"

"A couple of weeks or so ago, she told me that she was sick with worry. She found out that her husband was involved in something. I don't know what he was doing. Barbara just said it was unethical, but she didn't say any more than that. She asked him to stop, and he ignored her. She didn't know what to do."

"Was this the only time she talked about this?"

"Yes. She had changed quite recently. She used to be a happy and self-confident person. But lately, she had become depressed and very worried about something. She never told me exactly what was going on over there."

"Anything else you can think of?"

"No, but please don't tell Fred Lyle that I told you this."

"I most definitely will not tell him. You can trust me."

"I have to go now." She closed the door.

Letty went back to her pickup truck and headed straight for the nearest pizza shop. Will and Clarice would just have to deal with the fact that the pizzas Letty chose for supper had spinach on them.

* * *

Not far away, while Letty was researching Fred Lyle, Zhou and Jade were intensely involved in a search of Jade's property.

"They have been here twice," Zhou said, "both Bao and Chong Ma. There is something they are looking for here. They must think it very important to come here after Carlos disappeared, and then return a year later. You have no idea what it could be?"

"No, Zhou. Carlos was usually pretty open with me about everything. We didn't keep secrets. Or I thought that until all this came up. Carlos never mentioned Chinese people, not even once."

"Let's go in the opposite direction. We will start with your outdoor property, move to garage, then go indoors. Perhaps a new view will help us begin to see."

They worked together. They started in the front of the house, moved to the side, then into the back yard. They looked under pots, into tree branches and bushes, and looked for signs of disturbance in patio pavers, stones, and bare ground. They checked out the eaves and the roof. They even went into the alley. Nothing.

Next they went into the garage and the space that was Jade's pottery studio. Zhou had been through some of this space earlier, but this time, he went inch by inch. He knocked on walls to see if there were compartments behind them. He ran his fingers along the rafters. He looked behind and under and around and inside everything. He spent longer than usual going through the box of clothing and personal items that had belonged to Carlos. Jade watched but said very little.

Next Zhou came to the area where she created pots. He lifted the wheel from its stand and took apart the splash pans to see if anything was hidden there. Nothing. He moved onto the cabinet that had Jade's pottery supplies. As he had done earlier, he looked behind everything to make sure nothing was hidden there. Then he began picking up each individual item in the cabinets. As he went, he asked Jade to explain what the function of each item was.

There were various kinds of tools in a wooden tool carrier that were used to cut and shape the clay. There were safety masks and gloves. There were plastic and wood circles that Jade called "bats."

She said they were used to safely move a wet clay pot. There were sponges, a sander, a scrubber, and thick wooden dowels she used as slab rollers. Zhou removed from the shelf the wooden carrier that held these tools and set it on the work table.

Zhou looked confused. "I do not understand how pottery is created."

"Okay. You start with wet clay. I won't go into detail about the different kinds of clay. That's another whole thing in itself. You can either hand-build a pot or something else like a clay sculpture. Or you can throw the clay on the wheel to create a round object like a bowl or cup. Then you put everything in a kiln. I don't have a kiln actually. I let my pots dry, then I take them to a potter's cooperative. I'm a member, and I get to use their kiln. The kiln is like a really hot oven, and it bakes the clay. The first firing – that's what you call it when you put it in the kiln and heat it up – you "fire" the pots. The first firing is called bisque firing, which is at a lower temperature. Then you glaze the pot with these glazes and fire them again and the glaze changes chemical composition and sort of melts onto the pot. We determine the temperature with "cones." There are variations of all this, too. For example, you can pit fire pottery and the smoke makes interesting patterns on the pots."

"Complicated," was his response.

Under the tool carrier and pushed back into the shadows was a wooden box that Zhou had not noticed earlier. It was about eight inches wide, six inches deep, and four inches high. It was locked. He put it on the work table next to the tool carrier.

"What about this wooden box?"

"I don't know, Zhou. I don't remember that. We may have to break it open to see what is inside."

"What are these?" Zhou picked up a small plastic sack with a pink-tan colored powder inside.

"That's cobalt carbonate. You add it to the glaze and when it's fired, the pot comes out this lovely blue color." Jade pointed to other small plastic sacks with different colored powders. That one makes copper red although sometimes it can come out a blue-green in firing. That one is kind of a gray-white, and that one is for black. This one is brown, and that one is a red oxide color."

Jade smiled and said teasingly. "If you are interested, you should visit China sometime. The Chinese made gorgeous pottery, especially porcelain works in the Ming Dynasty. Have you heard of the Ming Dynasty? I could give you a book to read about the Ming Dynasty and its porcelain."

Zhou grinned. "So now you teach me about China? Such a good teacher you are. I do believe I know the Ming."

He held two of the small sacks full of powder, one in each hand. "Why is one slightly heavier than the other?"

"It shouldn't be heavier. They have the same amounts in each sack."

Zhou sat the two sacks down on Jade's work bench and carefully opened one. He spread it flat so that the air was expelled, and the power extended to the edge of the opening but did not fall out. A metal key was clearly visible in the power. Jade handled him a pair of needle-nose pliers, and he removed it from the sack.

"This is a key to what?" he asked.

"I have no idea. Do you think Carlos hid it here?"

"Yes, I do think this," he responded. "You did not leave it there?"

"No. And I know the key wasn't in the sack at the store. I watched the clerk put the powder into each sack."

Zhou wiped the key clean and inserted it into the lock of the wooden box. The lock opened easily.

"Wah!" Zhou said.

Jade's eyes were opened wide. "What's inside?"

"Papers. Two papers. Two pages, I mean. Let's go inside and have a look."

They returned to the kitchen, sat at the table, and carefully opened the folded sheets of paper. Zhou pulled them apart and set them side by side.

The first page had only numbers in two columns. The second page had a column with names on the left, then three columns with numbers.

"What is this?" Jade asked.

"I do not know, but I think this is very important. We must show Miss Letty. I think she will know."

Zhou's phone rang. It was Letty.

"Hey, Zhou. I've arranged a meeting between you, me, a Tucson police detective who is also my friend, and the lawyer of my client …and Jade, of course. I have a lot to tell you. I've made a lot of progress. It's time to get some help from law enforcement.

"I also have many things to tell you. I believe Jade and I found what Chong Ma and Bao were looking for at Jade's house. We found papers in a box, and we found the key to open the box. I want you to see them."

"That's good news. The puzzle pieces are starting to come together."

"So it seems."

"I'm off now to get some pizza for a couple of hungry teenagers. Tell Jade it's time for her to feed you."

Zhou laughed. "I will see you tomorrow."

"Adios, amigo."

Zhou turned to Jade. "Please translate 'Adios, amigo.' Letty said this to me."

Jade smiled. "She must like you. That's the Spanish way to say goodbye. 'Amigo' means friend. So she was saying 'Goodbye, friend.' Now you translate for me. What does 'wah!' mean?"

Zhou laughed. "Nothing. It means nothing. It's like your 'wow!' You say 'wow!' when you are surprised. I say, 'wah!'"

"Wah!" Jade repeated.

"I have more," Zhou added. "Miss Letty says to tell Jade that she should feed Letty's amigo Zhou."

Jade laughed. "Coming right up!"

* * *

Later that evening, Letty received another call. It was Marv Iverson.

"My friends at ICE were very interested in your story, Letty. Seems that they also had heard reports of some smuggling going on, but they didn't know where or what or when. Your description of the location was the best information they'd received. They called in Johnny Chiago. He's the Shadow Wolves' lead officer now. He sent a couple of his Wolves out there today to look for the wash where the contraband is being carried down from the road as well as where the smugglers are crossing the border. They think they found the wash where the goods are being transported. While they were looking for the wash, Johnny went on horseback with your Uncle Mando to see if they could find the abandoned drop-off house. They think they found it, too."

"My Uncle Mando? He usually tries to stay out of all that border stuff."

"Yeah, turns out he and Chiago went to school together at Sells when they were kids. They were best buds back then. Chiago left for several years to serve in the military. Then he lived in California for a while. He came back to Arizona to join the Shadow Wolves. It was a reunion for those two. They both said they really enjoyed themselves wandering around out there. And they found the house. No one was there, but there were signs that several people had been there. Chiago and your uncle found carpet booties." Marv referred to the scraps of carpet attached to shoes to erase footprints on dirt and sand paths.

"That's a sure sign of smuggling," Letty pointed out.

"Right. So now it's a matter of waiting for them to bring in more contraband. The Border Patrol is setting up a nighttime surveillance so they can see who comes and goes at the abandoned house."

"Oh, Marv. You're a wonder. Thank you so much!"

"My pleasure, Letty. I quite enjoyed myself today. Sometimes I get tired of being retired, and there's only so much football a person can watch."

Letty laughed. "I never thought I'd hear you say that, Marv. It will be our secret. I won't tell the Wildcats."

CHAPTER 16

Another morning began very early for Letty, and it would have to be another morning without a run. She needed her daily jog around the neighborhood because it was the best way to clear her head after a rough night. There were plenty of rough nights full of Iraq nightmares. As usual, she started by putting Millie out and making herself a cup of coffee.

By eight a.m., Letty was at Jade's house. Adelita pulled up at the same time in her own car, not a Tucson police unit. Two minutes later, Jessica Cameron's Mini-Cooper pulled in behind Letty's pickup.

Inside they found Zhou and Jade at the computer trying to identify any of the names on the second paper found in the pottery studio the day before.

Letty introduced everyone.

"I have called you all together because we're at a point in this investigation that we need to work together. No single one of us can pull this off. Our first priority is to maintain safety. We know these triad gangsters are killers. We want to find and rescue the two missing girls – one from Hong Kong and the other from southern Mexico. And then we want to stop this smuggling ring.

"Zhou, you go first. What have you found since we last talked?"

Zhou explained that he and Jade had spoken to Señor Sanchez at the storage units next to where Carlos had worked.

"He wasn't there when you investigated, Letty," Jade interrupted. "He was in Hermosillo for the winter. That's why you didn't find him."

Zhou continued. "Mr. Sanchez told us that the triad gang moved cargo to a warehouse in northwest Tucson over a year ago. We found it on Google Earth. I want to go there and find the correct warehouse and determine what is being stored there. Also, I believe that the brother of Carlos knows something. He seemed to recognize photos in my mugshot book. I want to talk to him."

He paused for dramatic effect.

"Best find," Zhou continued, "is this." He pulled out the two sheets of paper. Letty, Adelita, and Jessica leaned forward.

Letty said, "This first page with all numbers looks like bank routing numbers and account numbers. Please put this first number into the search box."

Sure enough, the number led to the Pima National Bank, Tucson, Arizona. Further searches led to identification of banks in Phoenix and San Diego, as well as Tucson.

"I can get a subpoena to look at these accounts," said Adelita.

"Right!" Jessica Cameron said with enthusiasm. It was clear that she was very excited. Letty thought to herself that Lawyer Cameron must get tired of the same dull corporate cases she usually handled. Maybe she should take on more criminal law cases.

"In the second page, we are looking at these names. Some we find are local residents," Zhou continued.

Letty looked at the columns of numbers next to the names. "This will have to be determined, but it looks like the kind of information we find in Form 4473."

"What is Form 4473?" Zhou asked.

"When someone purchases a gun from a federally-licensed weapons vendor, like at a gun show, the buyer has to fill out Form 4473. The numbers will be the buyer's date of birth, whether or not they passed the criminal background check system, and this last column could be the serial number of the gun that was purchased."

"This is helpful information, yes?" Zhou asked.

"Oh, yes. Very helpful. Well done, Zhou," Letty added. The other three women nodded their heads.

Zhou said quietly, "Well done, Carlos."

Silence. Again, the women solemnly nodded their heads.

"Any idea how Carlos acquired this information?" Letty looked at Jade.

Jade jumped up. "Give me a minute."

She moved toward a filing cabinet, and opened one of the drawers. Pulling a folder from the cabinet, she opened it and began scanning the papers inside. Suddenly, she stopped and held up one of the papers. "Before Carlos won the big grant, he worked hard to get donations from community organizations and individuals. This is a list of contributors. Barbara Lyle's name is on the list." She handed the folder to Letty.

"So that must be the connection," Letty said, taking the folder. "We may never know what happened between them."

"In any case, we can't leave these papers here," said Adelita.

"Jade, these papers are in your possession and apparently, they belonged to Carlos before he disappeared," Letty said. "But clearly it's not safe to leave them here at your house."

Jessica Cameron intervened. "Jade, I'd like for my firm to represent you. If it turns out that we find the persons responsible for your husband's disappearance, you will need legal representation to assure that your interests are protected. In that capacity, this box, key, and papers will become very relevant. They can go into my office safe until we know more. We have security personnel present in the building 24-7. If it turns out that the papers refer to bank accounts and Form 4473 relevant to the Lyle murder case, then I can turn everything over to TPD as evidence. As you know, I am representing the person who is being accused of the Lyle murder, unfairly I believe, so I have a role in that as well."

Adelita added. "It's not safe here, and if it goes into our evidence department, it won't get the attention it deserves right now. Going to Jessica's secure office where it is locked up is the best idea for the moment. Also it would be good if you could start working on figuring out what those numbers mean." She looked directly at Jessica Cameron.

Jessica nodded. "Will do."

"Okay," Jade said. "So you will be my lawyer now? Is this going to cost me anything?"

Jessica smiled. "No charge. If it turns out that I can make some money out of this for you, then you can give me a share. That's how it works typically."

Jade sighed. "What do you think, Zhou?"

"Agreed that it is not safe to leave the papers here. We need time to determine what the numbers mean. I like the idea of the papers in a strong safe in a secure lawyer's office."

"Then consider it done," Jade said. "Jessica, take this with you today and keep it safe."

Then Letty said, "Okay, it's my turn."

She described again her brother's encounter with the triad members in the park, his shoulder injury, and the abduction of the Chinese girl. She went over what she had learned in Nogales about the movement of Chinese smugglers across the border at an especially-isolated part of the Tohono O'odham reservation. She did not mention her Uncle Miguel from whom she received this information. She followed up by saying that her retired former boss, Marv Iverson, had made contact with the Shadow Wolves.

"Marv called a friend in ICE – that's the Immigration and Customs Enforcement. ICE is the agency that the Shadow Wolves report to. They are an elite tracking team. All the members are Native Americans. Marv reports the Shadow Wolves have already found the smugglers' route in the desert and the crossing they are using. Next Border Patrol set up surveillance. We just have to wait for the smugglers to show up with their next shipment. I'll try to find out when that shipment is going to happen."

Then Letty recounted her interviews with José Gomez, Emily Castro, Travis Lyle, Fred Lyle, and Barbara Lyle's friend, Rita Benton. She gave an overview of her Internet searches. Results of these searches suggested that Fred Lyle might have been an enthusiastic and frequent gun purchaser until a year ago when he stopped posting on social media altogether. Letty speculated that his gun purchases had increased in number at that time, and Lyle didn't want to draw attention to himself.

"More subpoenas," Jessica Cameron said, and Adelita García shook her head yes. "Maybe we'll find Fred Lyle on the other end of those numbers on these papers. Or maybe some Chinese gangsters."

"I also want to make note of something that has not been previously reported," Letty continued. "There is a side door at the Lyle residence quite near a gate. Travis said that his dad was not present when his mother was shot. It is possible that Lyle went inside the house, exited the side door, and shot his wife from that gate. It is possible that he quickly ran back inside to emerge from the back of the house onto the patio where his wife's body had fallen. Travis was in a state of shock and was looking only at his mother's body. He would not have noticed his father's delay in returning to the patio."

"Makes sense, Letty," said Adelita. "Means, motive, and opportunity. Opportunity? Yes, with the side door there. Means? Maybe we can link the gun to Lyle. It's too late to find gun residue on his hands, but we may find some on his clothing if he hasn't done his laundry. And he doesn't seem like the kind of man who would do his own laundry. The motive could very well be that his wife was about to go to the authorities and tell them that her husband was a weapons smuggler. Your interview with the neighbor may indicate that."

Jessica Cameron said approvingly, "No better way to prove our client innocent than to find the real killer."

Letty sat back. "We've got a lot of work to do. Zhou, I think you and I should go talk to Carlos's brother. I also think we should see if we can find this coyote that my brother Eduardo talked to and have a little chat with him. We can also check out the warehouse where the triad gang is operating out of now. Maybe we can find out when the next shipment goes out."

Zhou interjected. "I want to do this work, but I fear leaving Jade alone here."

"I'll stay with her," Adelita said. "I'm off work today. She can catch me up on what's been going on. I'll bring my gun in from my car."

"I'm off to work," Jessica Cameron said. "I can't wait to hear from you again, Letty, and you, too, Mr. Zhou."

* * *

Ten minutes later, Jessica Cameron was headed downtown, Adelita and Jade were chatting away at Jade's house, and Zhou and Letty were in her pickup headed to the Sixth Avenue and Sixth Street intersection near downtown. Jade had already called ahead to Maria Lopez's home and learned from his sister that Ricardo Lopez was at a coffee house on Sixth Street.

When Letty and Zhou entered the coffee house, Ricardo looked up and became instantly alarmed. He rose, grabbed his hoodie, and headed for the rear exit.

Zhou put a hand on Ricardo's shoulder and pushed him back down into the chair.

"We come here to talk to you. Do you know Ms. Letty Valdez?"

"Yes, she's a friend of my sister-in-law's. She's also a private investigator."

"When I showed you the book of photos at your mother's home, you looked nervous. I think you recognized someone. Who was it?" Zhou asked.

Letty interjected. "Ricardo, you might as well tell the truth because we're going to find out sooner or later anyway. There are a couple of young women whose lives are at risk right now, and we're trying to help them."

Zhou continued, "We believe there is a gang of Chinese criminals operating in this area. We think they may be involved in smuggling guns, drugs, and young women. Many of the women are forced into sexual slavery in America."

Ricardo turned pale and stared at his hands. "I didn't know about the sex trade. But drug smuggling, yes," he spoke barely above a whisper.

"Can you help us find them? We understand they have a warehouse in Tucson, and maybe there's a hiding place on the reservation. What do you know?" Letty asked.

"I don't know for sure but I think maybe they were in Nogales. I never went looking for them. They always found me. What's this got to do with Carlos?" Ricardo turned toward Zhou.

"We are investigating this now. How do you know these Chinese gangsters?"

Ricardo sighed deeply. "Heroin. I've been addicted since I was 15." He saw Zhou glance down at his arms. "Yeah, I keep my arms covered so no one will see the needle tracks. I got my fix from them. Then they started asking me to do little jobs for them. If you want to know the truth, I became like a slave. I'm in a rehab program now trying to get off the heroin. I don't want anything to do with those Chinese dudes. They're scary."

"Twice now, they have entered Jade's home looking for something. She is in danger." Zhou added.

Ricardo looked terrified. "They are after Jade?"

"Yes. They think she knows something that will disrupt their operations."

Ricardo frowned, "Carlos called me on his cell phone right before he disappeared. He told me that he had evidence on the Chinese dudes that would bring them down. He said he was going to meet them and tell them that if they didn't leave him and Jade alone, he was going to the police. Carlos told me that he had some incriminating papers in a locked box at his house. I think maybe that's what they're looking for."

"What else?" Letty asked.

Ricardo began to cry. "I think they killed my brother."

"Why did they go after Carlos? Was it only that he threatened to go to the police? Was there more?" Letty asked.

"They wanted that money he had for the barrio social program. They needed to buy a big shipment of heroin. It was easier threatening him than waiting for the money to come from Hong Kong, or robbing a bank, or whatever they do to get cash. Carlos told me that they threatened to kill me and to kidnap my little sister Daniela and Jade, too. Now I know from you that they probably would turned over my little sister and Jade and forced them to be sex slaves. Carlos intended to save his family and the money by threatening to expose them."

Zhou was filling in the picture now. Carlos was an honorable man in an impossible situation. He had been drawn into the triad trouble by his drug-addicted little brother. Carlos's access to the one hundred thousand dollars captured the triad gang's attention. Threatening to kidnap and enslave his beloved wife and sister and kill his baby brother meant that the gangsters could demand money and his silence. Or maybe they just decided to take the money and get rid of Carlos because he was in their way.

"How did they find out about the key with the incriminating papers?" Letty asked.

"I didn't mean to tell them, really I didn't," Ricardo began to sob in earnest now. "I was really strung out one night on some really good shit they brought in from Asia. This was after Carlos disappeared. I told one of my compañeros who was shooting up with me that they would be brought down someday somehow. I told him that Carlos had given Jade some evidence against the triad gang, some papers that would incriminate them. I was just talking too much. What I didn't know was that later my drug compañero sold that information to the gangsters. He turned up dead not long after that. One of the photos in your book is of a man named Chong Ma. He's the killer. He called me a waste of skin. He's right, too."

"Why hasn't he killed you yet?" Letty again.

"I don't know." Ricardo's voice cracked. "Maybe they don't want Jade to suspect anything until they figure out what she has and where it is. I don't know. I don't know. I don't know." Ricardo sat in his chair and said nothing more. Grief overwhelmed his features.

Letty and Zhou rose from the table at the same time. They left the coffee house and didn't look back.

"They killed Carlos before they knew about papers," Zhou said.

"Yes, then they learned from Ricardo that Carlos had left behind some incriminating evidence that would ruin them. That's when they went to Jade's house and started looking."

"Where is Carlos?"

"Somewhere out in the desert," Letty responded. "We may never find his bones."

* * *

Ten minutes later, Zhou and Letty pulled up in front of the coyote's house. They got out of the pickup, strode up the front walk, and knocked forcefully on the front door.

A thin, rough-looking Hispanic man in a t-shirt and jeans opened the door. He took one look at them then immediately attempted to slam the door shut.

Zhou pushed the man back into the squalid living room of the house, grabbed the coyote's arm and pulled it behind him. He shoved the man up against the wall.

"What do you want? I did what you asked."

Zhou glanced at Letty. He thinks I'm a triad member. Letty nodded.

"First, I'd like to know your name." Letty said.

"None of your business." Zhou tightened his grip on the man's arm. He groaned and began panting.

"Okay. Okay. I'm Paco."

"Paco what?"

"Paco Frijoles."

Letty shook her head. Zhou bounced the coyote's face against the wall, causing his nose to bleed.

"Very funny, Mister Beans. Want to try again?"

"My name is Paco Valenzuela. I didn't do nothin'," He sighed heavily.

"Mr. Valenzuela. Let me make this clear. My friend and I are private investigators. We're not associated with your Chinese colleagues. We're not associated with the Tucson police or the Sheriff's Department, or ICE or the Border Patrol. We work for a private client who wants some answers, and he doesn't care what we have to do to you to get those answers. He said if we have to get rough, that's okay with him. Understand?"

"Got it."

"What did your Chinese pals ask you to do?"

"They wanted me to give them that little Mexican girl. I did that, but I didn't want to. She was worth a lot of money 'cause she's young and really pretty. I just gave her to them for nothing. I was scared not to." He couldn't help but sound annoyed. "And I helped them load their shit into that truck."

"When and where did this happen?"

"I gave them the girl here at my house a few days ago. I helped them load their boxes at the warehouse up north on Marigold Street. They took the girl with them."

Zhou nodded. Correct answer.

"They are planning another shipment?"

"Yes. They said they are going out sometime later today, just before sunset."

"Hmmm…very interesting," Letty said. "And where will they take their shipment?"

"They have a place out on the reservation southwest of Topawa somewhere in the desert. They take the stuff in a truck, almost always early in the evening. Then before morning under cover of darkness, they smuggle the stuff across the border."

"You know where?"

"No. I never went there. I'm like a middle man here in town. I have nothing to do with buying the stuff or getting it across the border. I just help store it and move it around. The less I have to do with those Chinese dudes, the better it is for me."

Zhou let go of Valenzuela's arm. Both men turned and looked at Letty.

"Anything else you can tell us?" she asked.

"No! You've totally screwed me now. They'll find out you were here, and they will kill me."

"Maybe that's your karma, Mr. Valenzuela, for playing with the bad guys."

Letty and Zhou turned and walked back to the pickup. They got in and drove away. A couple of blocks passed, and then Letty pulled over.

"You are good, Miss Letty," Zhou said. "You would be good with Interpol for seeking information."

"I don't like dealing with that kind of man. He exploits poor people by charging a high fee to smuggle them across the border and then he abandons them in the desert. Too many have died out there. He's the kind of man who smuggles drugs, too, and what he does to women is unconscionable. He deserves bad things to happen to him. I don't think he'll stick around in Tucson. In fact, I bet he's throwing together a few possessions right now. He'll be on the road within an hour. But I'll report him when this is over, and let's hope they catch him."

"We can go to the warehouse now but maybe that is not so good an idea," Zhou said thoughtfully. "If we confront them, then maybe we will not find the Hong Kong official's daughter or the Mexican girl. What do you suggest?"

"Maybe we can watch from a distance, identify their truck and see where it goes."

Letty pulled her phone out of her back pocket. "I'll check my messages first."

The first message was from Jessica Cameron, "I'm at my office now, and the items are safe and secure."

The second message was from Adelita García.

"Oh, no," Letty looked at Zhou. "Adelita was called into work. There was a home invasion and two murders on the southwest side. She says she took Jade to my house. She called Will, and Will said to bring Jade to stay with him and Clarice. This message was sent more than hour ago."

Zhou looked very worried. "Do triad members know about you and your home? Your brother is hurt. He cannot protect Jade."

"I don't know if they know about me or where I live. We'd better get over there fast."

Letty quickly drove a few blocks south and east, and then turned north onto the express Kino Parkway.

Two minutes later, a small gray sedan pulled up in the left lane even with Letty's pickup truck. Zhou looked over and saw Chong Ma in the passenger seat pointing a gun at Letty's head. He was looking at Zhou. He had a big smile on his face. Letty saw the gun and the dead eyes behind it at the same time Zhou saw it. She braked and jerked the pickup truck to the right and off the expressway into an empty parking lot. She pulled her gun from her truck's glove compartment. Luckily no one was behind them to rear-end them at the sudden braking. The gray sedan sped off. No shot was fired.

"Not good," Letty said. "They definitely know who I am and that I know you."

"We must go to your house quickly," was Zhou's response.

Twelve minutes later they pulled up in front of Letty's house and got out of her pickup. Letty noticed immediately that Millie was barking furiously in the backyard. At the same time, she was running full speed toward the backdoor, then back again to the side gate. She repeated this three times before Letty could get to the gate. Letty unlocked it, led Zhou through the gate and locked it behind her. They entered the back door. Millie was right behind them.

"Will, where are you?" Letty called.

All she could hear was some muffled voices.

In the living room, Letty and Zhou found Will and Clarice with bound hands and feet. Both were side by side, tied to chairs. Duct tape covered their mouths.

Letty pulled the tape off Will's mouth. "What happened?"

Will growled. "They took Jade. I couldn't do anything." He looked over at Clarice. Zhou pulled the tape off her mouth.

"They hurt Will. Let me help. I want to bring those bastards down," Clarice growled, too.

"Who took her?" Letty asked urgently.

Will grimaced. "Same Chinese dudes who grabbed that girl in the park."

Zhou looked at Letty. "We must find her. We must find Jade. They will kill her."

CHAPTER 17

"WILL, are you okay?" Letty couldn't help but notice the pained expression on her little brother's face.

"They hit Will in the face! Then they pulled his arm behind his back to tie him up!" Clarice said angrily. "I mean the arm with the dislocated shoulder. They really hurt him. Bastards!"

The Army medic kicked in. Letty said, "Let me look." She quickly examined Will. "You're going to have a black eye. Your shoulder was not dislocated again. There may be some tendon and ligament damage. It's hurting, right?"

"Yeah, it hurts. I'll take some pain pills. Let's go find Jade. Who is this? The one you call Zhou?"

Letty made a gesture toward Zhou. "Yes, Zhou, this is my brother Will and his friend Clarice." She turned again to Will. "You and Clarice should stay here."

"No!" Will and Clarice said together. "We can all go together," Will argued, "Clarice and I can be lookouts and call the cops and flag them down when they come. You and Zhou go into the warehouse and try to find Jade. There are several of these Chinese dudes. You need us."

"How many?" Zhou asked quietly.

"Three came in the house. At least one was in the car outside. Maybe more. It was a big black limousine. I couldn't see how many were in it."

Clarice went into the kitchen and came back with a bottle of pills and a bottle of water. She gave two pills and the water to Will.

"I agree with Will," Zhou spoke to Letty. "They can watch outside. See who comes and goes. Determine how many there are. They can call police. You and I will go inside."

"Okay, okay," Letty said. "But I don't like this."

Will and Clarice were headed for the door. "Come on. You're wasting time." Will urged her.

"We'll go in my car. More room and they won't be expecting it. They'll be looking for your pickup and maybe they won't notice my car," Clarice added.

"I'm driving," insisted Letty.

Clarice handed her the keys. They all exited the house, Letty locked the door and went first to her pickup and retrieved her handgun and its holster from the glove compartment. She was the last to get into Clarice's car. She slipped the gun under the driver's seat. Zhou saw this and nodded approvingly, but Will and Clarice were too distracted to notice.

As Letty had noted earlier, Clarice's car was a Volkswagen. Much to Letty's surprise and approval, Clarice's VW Golf-All Track had four-wheel drive and a manual transmission. Letty preferred driving a stick shift. Always had. Always would.

No one noticed until a few blocks later that they had a fifth passenger with them. Millie the rescue pit bull was lying quietly in the back. She had jumped into the car along with everyone else, withdrawn to the back behind the rear seats, and settled down quietly.

Zhou directed Letty west on River Road, then farther west onto Ruthrauff Road. He told her to turn south until they found a turnoff to the much smaller Marigold Street. At this point, they were very close to Interstate 10. Marigold Street was a rough street with no curbs and lots of potholes. There were several warehouses with unpaved drives and gravel parking lots on both sides of the street. Ahead, Letty could see the dog rescue center on the south side of Marigold.

She drove slowly down the street. Suddenly Zhou said, "There!" He pointed to a nondescript metal building on the north side of Marigold Street. A faded sign promising Plumbing Supplies was off to the side and hanging by one corner on its rusty metal frame. The little gray sedan that Zhou and Letty had seen earlier was parked outside this warehouse. Letty parked across the street in the shade of a mesquite tree. She made sure that a big dumpster partially blocked the view from the warehouse of Clarice's parked car.

"Okay. Will, call Adelita García and explain to her what has happened. We're going to need patrol cars out here, and we may need EMTs and an ambulance. Clarice, you take care of Will. Don't let him do anything dangerous. Stay here, Will." Clarice nodded seriously.

Zhou was halfway out of the car when Letty said to him, "Let's go."

She retrieved the gun and holster from under the seat and joined Zhou. As they hurried toward the warehouse, she fastened the holster belt around her with the gun inserted into the leather holster, grip facing up, at the small of her back. She knew from experience that she could draw the gun from its holster and have it pointed at someone within three seconds. She hoped it didn't come to that.

Letty and Zhou approached the door of the warehouse building. There were windows on each side of the door. They peeked in and saw that the door led to a small office-reception room. At the rear of this room was another door that was wide open. Through this open door, they could see a much larger warehouse space, two stories high, with a concrete floor. At the back of this much larger room and on the side wall to the right, almost in the back corner, was a fifteen-foot- wide, twelve-foot-high garage-like doorway. To the left, the view was blocked. No Chinese gangsters were visible anywhere.

The warehouse was almost entirely empty.

Letty whispered to Zhou. "Looks like they've already moved the contraband out. That garage door is big enough for a large van or even a ten-foot-high truck." Zhou nodded his agreement. They moved carefully into the smaller office room, then stepped quietly into the larger room.

On their left was a temporary wall of plywood that extended about ten feet into the room. They couldn't see what was on the other side of this temporary wall. Both moved close to the wall and crept toward its end.

Suddenly three Chinese men dressed in black suits appeared from the other side of the temporary wall. They stood side by side about fifteen feet away. They glared at Zhou. Zhou glanced at Letty. He stepped forward toward the three men. As he moved forward, Zhou looked to his left. He gasped. He could see Jade tied to a chair. A large black limousine was parked about ten feet behind her. A triad driver was behind the wheel of the limo.

Chong Ma was standing next to Jade. He did not acknowledge Zhou and Letty's appearance. He raised his fist and in a low, guttural voice demanded of Jade, "I ask you. Last time. Where is it?" Jade raised her head. Both Letty and Zhou could see that she had a black eye and a bruised jaw. Blood oozed down her face from a cut near her hairline.

"I don't know." She whispered. She looked over and saw Zhou and Letty. "Zhou," she cried softly.

The three men moved toward Zhou menacingly. Rather than retreat, Zhou moved forward quickly, blocked the first man's attempt at a punch, then kicked him viciously in his stomach, then his knee. The man cried out in pain and fell back unable to stand. The other two came at Zhou at the same time. Zhou feinted in one direction, then the next, to avoid their punches. Then he attacked. In only a couple of seconds, one of the men found himself with one of his arms crossed under his other arm. The arms suddenly had excruciating tension on them. Letty heard a bone crack. Meanwhile, Zhou danced around the third man. A couple of kicks later, Zhou had the man on the floor face down. Zhou stood over him and grabbed his hair. He smashed the man's head into the floor. Letty could see the attacker lose consciousness and go limp. The other two men were groaning in pain.

Amazing. Letty had seen some martial arts experts in her time in the military, but nothing like this. She had never seen one man take on three at the same time and emerge completely unscathed. And so fast. The thought crossed her mind that if they got out of this alive, she was going to ask Zhou to teach her.

Just as Zhou stood and looked toward Chong Ma, Letty realized that yet another 49er was coming toward them, but this time, she was the target. She stood straight, legs slightly apart, balanced. Her teacher told her to find her balance first. Then she heard her teacher's voice in her mind: "element of surprise."

Just as the triad 49er got within striking range, instead of backing up or running, Letty moved aggressively toward him. The smirk on his face instantly disappeared. He had not expected this woman to come at him.

Letty grabbed his right arm and pulled him toward her violently. As his body passed hers, she turned to the right to pull him even farther. As he went past, her left foot kicked out into the back of his knees. He went down. She still had control of his right arm. She twisted it violently backwards and up. She could feel the elbow dislocate. Then a vengeful thought crossed her mind. She wished that this man was the one who had dislocated her little brother's shoulder, although she knew that it was Bao who had hurt Will. She could feel the triad 49er's tendons, ligaments and muscles giving way. The man cried out in pain and ended up rolling on the floor and whimpering.

She looked up and saw Zhou standing deadly still, staring at Jade. Chong Ma had his hand on Jade's shoulder. Then he began stroking Jade's red curls. He said something in Chinese to Zhou. Letty could see the muscles in Zhou's jaw twitch. Zhou said nothing.

Suddenly to her right behind her, she heard a noise. She looked back and saw Will running into the warehouse toward her. Her heart sank. At the same time, yet another 49er appeared in front of them both. Letty thought maybe he was the driver in the limousine, but she wasn't sure. The 49er stopped about ten feet away. He pulled a gun from his jacket. Will had come to a stop. The 49er pointed his gun directly at Will's head.

Everything froze. Time stopped. Letty was paralyzed in horror. She felt this sudden fire of rage flow through her. She knew if her baby brother was hurt, or god forbid, killed, she would kill every triad gangster in the room with her bare hands, starting with the shooter. Then she would go looking for more to kill. She also knew she would never recover if Will died. Not after seeing so much blood and death in Iraq. Not after losing Chava. She would never recover. She would never forgive herself for allowing her little brother to get hurt.

Letty cried out, "No! Will!"

Suddenly a ball of fur flew past her. Millie! Millie had followed Will to the warehouse. Somehow this gentle runt of a sweetheart pit bull knew that her master was in danger. Her brawny, muscular hind legs propelled her toward the man with the gun. Millie's powerful jaws clamped down on his wrist before he could react. The 49er screamed in pain and terror. He dropped the gun. Letty immediately moved to kick the gun out of reach. Millie held on, even when the man attempted to retreat, to run away, to escape this canine fury. The dog's fangs sank deep into his flesh.

"Okay, Millie. You can let go now." Letty said in the calmest voice she could muster. Millie let go of the man's wrist, dropped down to the floor, and came to stand politely at Letty's side. Her tail was wagging.

Chong Ma yelled at all the 49ers. The two that Zhou had attacked pulled the third still-unconscious man toward the limousine. They all got in, as did the driver who was crying and nursing his bleeding and fang-punctured wrist.

Another frozen moment followed. Letty became aware that Clarice was behind her now. Will stood still, not sure what to do.

Chong Ma pulled a gun from a pocket in his suit jacket. He never took his eyes off Zhou. He pointed the gun at Jade's head.

Letty reached behind her and pulled her gun from its holster. She stepped forward to stand beside Zhou. Her gun was pointed at Chong Ma's head. "Tell him to put the gun down. Tell him he better not hurt her. Tell him I'm a very good shot."

Chong Ma looked at her, and smiled.

"I speak English, Miss Valdez," Chong said quietly.

He called to one of his 49ers. The least injured man reappeared limping and stood next to him. Chong Ma issued a brief command and the 49er began untying Jade. All the while, Chong Ma held the gun to her head.

The 49er pulled Jade up and shoved her into the limousine.

"Until we meet again," Chong Ma said.

He moved around to the other side of the limo, got into the driver's seat, and started the engine. Zhou ran toward the limo, but it was too late. The limousine, tires squealing, exited the open warehouse door and drove rapidly down Marigold Street toward the interstate highway.

Letty could hear police sirens approaching, but she could tell from the volume that they were at least two, maybe three blocks away. Too far away to catch the limo. Letty had no license plate number to help track the limo down. She knew that as soon as Chong Ma got on the interstate, he would drive fast, find a safe place to exit, and hide out for a while. She didn't know if he cared enough about his 49ers to get medical treatment for them. They definitely needed medical treatment.

* * *

For what seemed like an eternity, Letty, Zhou, Will and even Clarice had to give statements to the police, who had arrived too late to stop the black limousine. An ambulance came, but no one needed medical help.

Letty gave a good description of the limousine although she did not have its license plate number. She was glad to learn the cops had already issued a BOLO (be on the lookout) alert. Law enforcement at every level was watching for the limo.

While the police were getting statements from Will and Clarice, Letty and Zhou stood close together. To say that Zhou looked distressed was a great understatement.

"Letty, I cannot allow them to hurt Jade even more. Please help me find her."

"Zhou, I think it's possible that they will go to the hideout in the back country on the reservation. It will cause way too much attention to go through the international border crossing at Nogales to enter Mexico. Even the slightest glance into that limo is going to reveal to the agents that something has happened. A limo full of injured Chinese men, and one obviously-hurt white woman is going to attract a lot of attention. They need to become invisible now. Law enforcement has been notified. That includes tribal police and the Sheriff's Department. If they make it to the desert hideout, they may think that they can go across the border with their contraband. They don't know that the Border Patrol is waiting for them."

Letty paused. "But I can't be sure. We don't really know what they will do."

Will and Clarice approached. They both had very sheepish looks on their young faces.

"You two get in the car and put Millie in there with you," Letty spoke to them roughly. "We're going to my house now."

Zhou nodded his agreement. He felt like he might fly apart from his concern for Jade, but that wasn't going to help find her. He knew that he was in very foreign territory and needed all the help he could get. Letty had proved herself to be a warrior. He would follow her lead.

* * *

No one said anything on the drive back to Letty's house. When they arrived, they all went into the living room. Letty confronted Will and Clarice.

"Will, what the hell were you thinking? I told you to stay put. How old are you?"

"Almost eighteen," Will looked really ashamed of himself. "Letty, I'm sorry…"

"Shut up! Almost eighteen and you act like an eight-year-old. You know those guys are dangerous. What the hell were you thinking? Never mind, I can answer that. You were *not* thinking!"

She turned her ire on Clarice.

"And you. Didn't I tell you to stop him from doing something stupid and dangerous?"

Clarice nodded yes. "He said the police wanted to talk to you on the phone. I should have stopped him. I'm so sorry, Letty. I let you down." Clarice's eyes filled with tears.

Letty turned back to Will. "You need to grow up, Little Brother. There's more going on here than you know. Lives are at stake. After all the blood and death I saw in Iraq, what do you think it's going to do to me to see you shot in the head in front of me?" Her voice cracked.

Zhou stepped forward and stood beside Letty.

Will shook his head in dismay. "Oh, Big Sister. I am so sorry. I've been a total idiot."

"Okay, you two morons go find us something to eat in the kitchen. And you damn sure better do what I say from here on out or there will be hell to pay."

Will and Clarice quickly nodded their heads in agreement.

"Don't just stand there. Go get us something to eat to take with us."

Will and Clarice went directly into the kitchen.

Letty sank down onto the couch. She felt old. She felt tired. She felt like she had to take care of everyone, and no one took care of her. She felt really alone.

Millie came to stand in front of Letty. Millie looked at Letty's eyes. Then Millie looked at the couch. Then Millie looked at Letty. Then at the couch. Then at Letty again.

"Okay," Letty sighed. "Any dog that saves my brother's life gets to sit on the couch." She patted the couch, and Millie jumped up to sit beside her. The dog settled down and put her head on Letty's thigh.

Zhou sat down next to Letty and Millie.

"What is your plan?

Letty's phone rang. It was Adelita.

"Hear you all are having some excitement."

"Yeah, you could say that."

"I'm still working this home invasion and murder case. I just want you to know that my colleagues tell me that they found a black limo at the Tucson International Airport with five injured Chinese dudes in it. They've all been taken to the hospital. After they are treated, they'll be taken directly to the Pima County Detention Center."

"What about Jade?"

"A witness in the airport parking lot saw another vehicle, a white van. It was driven by a Chinese man, young and in a white suit. The witness said he picked up a red-headed woman and a middle-aged Chinese man from very near a black limo that was parked in the parking lot. Law enforcement put out a BOLO on the van. The next report we got was that the van was spotted going south on I-19. That's all we have right now."

"Nogales! They're going to Nogales."

Letty relayed this info to Zhou after she said goodbye to Adelita.

"That is Bao and Chong Ma and Jade," he said. "Why they go to Nogales?"

"Chong Ma probably figures everything has gone to shit, and he needs to get across the border as soon as possible. He's making a run for it. He certainly is showing no loyalty to his 49ers. He's just abandoned them. My uncle told me about a house the gang has in Nogales on the American side. I'm almost certain that's where they are headed. We'll go there now."

Letty clasped her hands in front of her. "Zhou, I'm making a choice here. I don't know where the Hong Kong girl, Victoria, is. And I don't know where the Mexican girl is. I thought they were at the-drop-off house, but Marv says my uncle and the Shadow Wolf Chiago checked it out. There's no one there. There's no way to know where those two girls are for sure. But it's looking very likely that Chong Ma and Bao are taking Jade to Nogales. So I choose to go to Nogales and try to rescue Jade first. Then we'll look for the other two girls. Do you agree?"

Zhou nodded his heartfelt agreement.

Letty called to Will. "Zhou and I are going to Nogales and look for Jade."

"Take my car, Letty," Clarice said.

"That would be a great help, Clarice. I'll pay you for using it."

"No way, Letty. I want to help you find Jade and bring down those scumbags, too. I don't need the money anyway." She grinned and handed Letty the key to the Volkswagen.

"Will, you feed Millie. Give her some cooked chicken breast with the skin on it but no bone. She deserves a major treat after what she did. Clarice, see if you can get an appointment with our doctor and have Will's shoulder checked out, if not today, then tomorrow. They may want to X-ray him."

"Will, this means you have to do exactly what I say because Letty put me charge," Clarice said with a naughty smile. Her eyebrows jiggled up and down.

Will laughed.

Letty sighed. "And will you two please try to stay out of trouble!"

They both nodded seriously, then turned toward each other.

Letty said to Zhou. "Let's go find Jade."

CHAPTER 18

Letty zipped through the late afternoon traffic on Valencia heading west. By the time she reached Interstate 19 and turned south, the sun was low in the sky. Zhou sat quietly in the passenger seat. He was frowning, and the muscle in his jaw was twitching.

"Zhou, we don't know how this will turn out."

"I understand this."

"What's the best thing that can happen?"

"I find Jade safe and the other two safe also. I want to stop Chong Ma and Bao. For this, I must see Ting."

"Who is Ting?"

"She is the triad boss. They will do what she tells them to do. I must convince her to leave us alone. I do not want Chong Ma and Bao to see Jade again, to touch her again, to hurt her again."

"Then what will you do? Do you have a plan?" Letty had been wondering what the plan was for Zhou when he came to the end of this assignment.

"I will go to Hong Kong and try to meet with Ting. Next I go to Nanjing, visit my mother and aunties and uncles. Then I go to Beijing to report to my boss. There is a problem at the Ministry I must solve. Then I will resign my job. Then I return to Tucson."

"Return to Tucson? Really?"

"I hope to marry Jade. We will create a new life together. I will become a gong fu teacher in Tucson." He paused. "Do you think Jade will want me?"

Letty laughed. "Yes, indeed. She wants your ice cream."

For the first time in a couple of days, Zhou smiled, but only slightly.

"I will be your first gong fu student," Letty added. "I can take out only one at a time. You can take out three."

"More than three," Zhou said seriously.

Letty believed him.

They fell silent for a while.

"Zhou, what did Chong Ma say to you back in the warehouse? He spoke Chinese."

"Cantonese. Chong Ma spoke Cantonese, not Mandarin. He touched Jade's hair. He said she was beautiful, and her red hair would make it easy to sell her. She would service twelve to fifteen men each day. Chong Ma said he would be the first to enjoy her."

Letty groaned. "We'll find her. We have to find her."

Letty's phone rang. She handed it to Zhou.

"Hello, Miss García. I am Zhou. I answer this phone for Miss Letty. She is driving."

He listened quietly, said, "Okay. I will tell her."

"Your friend the police detective says to tell you this. The white van was seen by a deputy of Pima County Sheriff Department. The deputy followed the van, siren on, and tried to stop the van. Next, shots were fired from the van into the sheriff's deputy car tire. The deputy's car lost control and wrecked. The deputy is not badly hurt. The van and occupants escaped. They are driving fast, and they will arrive in Nogales very soon."

"We also will arrive soon, Zhou. We have an advantage. It's dark now."

Not long after, Letty entered the city limits of Nogales. She knew exactly where she was going because she had visited her Tío Miguel's house several times when he lived on the north side of the border. She turned off the main highway, took a couple of turns on side streets and soon they were in the familiar neighborhood. She drove past Tío Miguel's old house, and quickly identified the triad gang's house. It was the only white house on the block. All the others were painted Mexican-style in colors of blue, sage green, ochre yellow or the soft tan of adobe. Even in the dark, the houses glowed. She parked a block away, next to an empty lot in the dark shadows of a big mesquite tree.

"You can't carry a gun here in the U.S., correct?" Letty asked Zhou.

"True. No permit. But I have this." Zhou lifted a pant leg and Letty could see a very lethal-looking knife strapped to his calf.

"How long has that been there?"

"Since I arrive in Tucson."

Letty attached her holstered gun to her back waist again.

They quickly walked to the end of the block and turned onto Ironwood Street. The white house was only a couple of doors down. Letty and Zhou faded into the shadow of an adobe wall next to the house. Curtains were closed, but it was clear that lights were on in the house and there was activity inside. They could see shadows moving against the curtains.

"How many do you think there are?" Letty asked.

"Only Chong Ma and Bao. If there were others, we would see a guard here and more movement. Most of them are either in the desert at the drop-off house or they are in the Tucson hospital."

"I'm going around back just to make sure no one else is there." Letty disappeared for a few minutes. "Nothing. It's very dark back there. The van is parked in the back yard. It's empty."

"Nothing more here. I think only Chong Ma and Bao. I hope Jade is inside."

"Okay, shall we go in together?"

"Yes, together."

Letty suddenly felt that terror that she felt the first time she went out on a convoy with her unit. She was there to provide emergency medical aid if anything went wrong. For months, nothing serious happened. Her ministrations mostly had involved helping soldiers deal with sprains, pulled muscles, cuts and bruises, headaches, indigestion, constipation and diarrhea. Unofficially she offered a listening ear. They were lonely, missed home and family, and they couldn't talk about that in front of their male counterparts. But

Letty was a woman and a healer. Her listening was part of her healing. After a while, Letty's initial terror subsided. Then, one sunny day on a dusty desert road, an IED explosion brought the terror back forever. After that, it remained just under the surface, waiting for the next IED explosion or sniper fire or rocket screaming overhead or the sound of a bomb making contact with the earth and houses and human flesh.

In this moment on the front porch of a house in Nogales, Arizona, the terror was out in full force.

"I'm scared," Letty whispered.

"I also am scared."

"You get scared?" Letty was genuinely surprised.

"Always," was Zhou's quiet answer.

Letty and Zhou went up onto the porch very quietly.

They looked at each other. Letty pulled out her gun. She nodded to Zhou.

Zhou kicked in the door.

Chong Ma and Bao were busy stuffing U.S. currency into two duffle bags. Letty could see stacks of one-hundred-dollar bills wrapped neatly with currency straps. Both bags were nearly full. Letty wouldn't even try to guess the worth of those duffle bag contents.

Jade was tied to a chair against the wall. Next to her were two young women: Victoria, the Hong Kong official's daughter, and the Mexican teenage girl, Esperanza. All three were bound at hands and feet, mouths taped shut. All three began to squirm and whimper.

Letty pointed her gun at the two men and yelled, "On the floor!" Instead of resisting or following her directions, both men ignored her. They grabbed their duffle bags and ran down the hallway and into a bedroom. Zhou and Letty followed.

There wasn't much light in the bedroom, only a single bare bulb hanging from a socket in the middle of the ceiling. Chong Ma was in a closet pulling up a trap door in the floor. As soon as he managed to open it, he swung onto a ladder and disappeared into the tunnel below. Bao was right behind him. Bao pulled a gun from his front jacket pocket and shot randomly behind him. The shot missed both Letty and Zhou and went into the ceiling. Bao went down the tunnel ladder right behind Chong Ma. He pulled the tunnel door behind him.

Zhou attempted to pull the trap door open again.

"What is this?" Zhou demanded.

"No!" Letty yelled. "Don't go there. It's a tunnel, and it leads straight into Mexico. It's too dangerous for you to follow them. They'll shoot you." Then Letty couldn't help herself. She started laughing, and she couldn't stop. "They are running as fast as their little gangster feet can take them through the tunnel across the border into Mexico. It won't be very far either. We're really close to the border. We won't be seeing them again."

Zhou's eyes were wide. "You are saying that there are tunnels under the border?"

Letty giggled again. Maybe the release of tension made everything seem so funny.

"Oh, yeah. Smugglers buy these old houses and build a tunnel. They bring drugs into the U.S. this way. The Border Patrol finds the tunnels and closes them. The smugglers move to another house and build another tunnel. Then the Border Patrol finds it and closes it. It's common knowledge. Somehow the triad found a house with a functioning tunnel that had not yet been discovered."

Zhou shook his head. "I go to Jade now."

They returned to the living room. Zhou went directly to Jade. He untied her, removed the tape from her mouth very carefully, and held her gently in his arms. They whispered to each other. Jade began to cry softly.

Letty untied the other two women and removed the tape.

When Victoria was free, she said to Zhou in Cantonese. "You arrived just in time. One of them said that their last act would be to shoot us all in the head." She began to cry, too.

Zhou translated this for Letty.

Just in time. Letty let out a long sigh. Death and destruction. Why are so many humans so dedicated to death and destruction?

The Mexican girl spoke only in Spanish. She said to Letty, "Did the Angel send you?"

"The Angel? Who is the Angel?"

"He saved me in the desert."

"Ah, that's my brother Eduardo."

"Yes, that is his name. The Angel is called Eduardo. And you are his sister?"

"Yes, you must be Esperanza."

Esperanza smiled, and then she, too, began to cry.

Oh, my. Everyone is crying. We should be celebrating, Letty thought.

"I want to thank you for saving us," Esperanza said. "You also are an angel. Can I see Angelito now?"

"We'll call him. You can see him later tonight," Letty said reassuringly. "Are you hurt?"

"No," said Esperanza. "I was afraid."

Letty turned to Victoria. "Do you speak English?"

"Yes. I speak English."

"Are you hurt?"

"No, only bruises. They were rough with us. They were going to kill us. Thank you for coming to rescue us. I would like to call my father now."

"Yes, but later. We have to call the authorities first."

Letty called the Border Patrol, the Nogales police and the Pima County Sheriff's Department and told them about the tunnel and the two escaping triad gangsters. She knew that the chances of Chong Ma and Bao being caught were really low now. They had probably already disappeared into Nogales, Sonora. They would wait until things had cooled off and then make their move. Maybe it would be a bus trip to Guaymas and a berth on a ship sailing for Asia. Or more likely they would make their way to Hermosillo and get flights. They would likely separate, too. Chong Ma would go maybe to Vancouver, then to Seoul and on to Hong Kong, and

Bao to Mexico City, then on to Tokyo's Narita International Airport, then to Hong Kong. They would reunite there in their home territory.

Next, Letty called Will back at her house in Tucson.

"Everything is okay here. We have Jade now. Everything okay there?"

"That's really great news about Jade. Everything is fine here except that Clarice has turned into a tyrant. She's ordering me to do things." He laughed.

"What's she making you do?"

"I better not say." More laughter.

Oh dear, Letty thought. I hope one of them has sense enough to remember to use birth control.

"Will, I have something for you to do. Call Eduardo. He's either at Grandma's house or at Uncle Mando's. Tell him that he needs to come to our house tonight. I have a surprise for him."

"Eduardo is here. He came in about ten minutes ago. Want to talk to him?"

Letty waited until she heard Eduardo say hello. She handed the phone to Esperanza.

"Mi hermano," Letty said. My brother.

"Angelito?" Esperanza asked uncertainly.

"Esperanza! Is that you? Oh, my god!"

"Tu hermana es un ángel también," Esperanza giggled. She handed the phone to Letty.

"So, Little Brother, Esperanza says that you and I are both angels," Letty declared solemnly.

"Oh, Letty, you found her! That's so awesome! Where are you? I want to see her," Eduardo said impatiently.

"No, wait there. We're coming home very soon."

* * *

It was nearly midnight when they rolled into Letty's driveway in Tucson. Before all five could get out of Clarice's car, Eduardo was at the rear passenger door. He opened the door and pulled Esperanza from the car. She jumped into his arms, wound her legs around his waist and her arms around his neck, and began sobbing. Letty could hear Eduardo speaking softly to her in Spanish as he held her tight.

Zhou's phone rang. He answered briefly then handed the phone to Victoria. "Ba Ba!" she cried, and began chattering rapidly in Cantonese. Zhou lifted Jade gently from the car. "We take you to hospital now."

"No, Letty can fix me."

"I'll take a look, Jade, but you very well may need to go to the hospital. You should listen to Zhou."

"Yes," Zhou said severely. "You must do as I say."

"Okay, Jefe!" Jade saluted him.

Zhou looked at Letty.

"She's calling you Jefe, which means The Boss in Spanish."

"Yes. The Boss," Zhou said firmly, but his mouth twitched trying not to laugh. He couldn't remember ever being this happy.

"Come inside!" Will called out. Letty looked up and saw Will and Clarice on her front porch, their arms wrapped around each other. They were both grinning broadly.

Letty's phone rang again. It was Marv Iverson.

"Sorry to call so late, but I figured you'd want to know what happened out there on the reservation."

"I'm glad to hear from you. I have news for you, too."

"You start," Marv said.

"You know about us confronting the gangsters at the warehouse in north Tucson?"

"Yes, and some of them were caught at the airport and taken to the hospital. Wish I'd been there to see you kick their butts."

"Not me. I only brought down one of them. It was Zhou. He took out three of them in about ten seconds flat."

"I also heard two of them got away."

"That's right. We followed them to Nogales. We were able to rescue the three missing young women. One was abducted from Hong Kong, the other a Mexican migrant handed over to the triad gang by a coyote, and the third was Jade Lopez."

"Well done. And the two gangsters?"

"They did a runner. Turns out the house in Nogales has a tunnel with an opening in the bedroom closet. They disappeared into Mexico with two bags of U.S. currency, mainly one hundred-dollar bills. No doubt they are both on their way home to Hong Kong. Gone, gone, gone. Now what have you got?"

"Okay," Marv said efficiently. Letty realized again that he was enjoying himself. She was going to start bringing him in on more cases in the future – for his sake, not just hers.

"You know your Uncle Mando and the Shadow Wolf Johnny Chiago went out on horseback and found the old house out there that the gangsters were using for a drop-off. And you know Chiago's team of Shadow Wolves found the wash that led close to the border, the wash that the contraband was being hauled down. There are a bunch of washes and other arroyos and creek beds that all lead downhill toward the border. The Wolves found the right one. Surveillance was set up everywhere along the way – both ICE and Border Patrol. Early in the evening not long after sundown, a couple of vans pulled up on the Mexican side. Border Patrol agents used night goggle vision, and identified known Sinaloa Cartel operatives at one of the vans. The other van had a couple of Chinese dudes in charge. The vans were there to pick up the goods. One for Sinaloa. One for the triad gang."

Letty said. "So, as we suspected, the triad gang and Sinaloa were cooperating."

"Yep. Up above the wash on the ridge and back in a little more than a mile, a truck appeared at the abandoned house. You're not going to believe this. Guess who was driving it?"

"No idea. Not any Chinese triad members. They were all busy elsewhere."

"A white guy."

"Really? Has he been identified?"

"Yep. Remember that woman who was murdered recently? Barbara Lyle."

Letty gasped. She had guessed Lyle's involvement but had no proof. And never in a million years did she think he would make the delivery himself. He must have felt desperate.

"Her husband? Wow!"

"Yes, wow is right. His name is Fred Lyle. He got there, and he couldn't figure out where all his Chinese pals had gone. Just about that time, six Sinaloa guys showed up ready to unload and start carrying the goods down the wash to the border. The border there is just a series of posts closely arranged with wire between to stop vehicles from crossing over. It's pretty easy to just hand stuff over the posts. They're only about four or five feet tall.

"Anyway, Lyle couldn't get the stuff out of his truck fast enough," Marv continued. "It was clear that having no Chinese there was an unhappy surprise for him. He was acting really nervous. He wanted to empty the truck and get back to town ASAP."

"And Border Patrol and ICE screwed up his plans?"

"Big time. Oh, I forgot to mention. Tribal police and the Pima County Sheriff's Department were there, too."

"Everyone got arrested."

"Eventually. Lyle was arrested first before he could leave the scene. The Sinaloa guys had already been allowed to leave the house first and to carry the contraband down to the road that runs along the border. Border Patrol decided to save themselves the trouble of having to haul it themselves. As soon as the Sinaloa boys showed up at the bottom of the wash, they got arrested, too. Border Patrol had alerted Mexican authorities earlier, but they never showed. That means someone on the other side was likely bribed to look the other way, or maybe they were scared off."

"What was the contraband?"

"Guns, guns, guns – and lots of them."

"Did the Sinaloa and Chinese dudes on the Mexican side see all this?"

"We assume they did. It was dark, but night vision goggles are easily available for those with the money to buy them."

"This is all very good news. Now we just need to make sure Lyle is held responsible for his wife's murder as well as gun running. I think that's going to be easier now. Are all of our guys okay? How about my uncle?"

"Mando is fine. He told me the whole thing was really fun for him. It was for me, too. One of the best parts was seeing how Sam Lambert got his panties all in a twist about this. He didn't know what was going on until the last minute. He was livid." Marv laughed uproariously.

"Marv, you're the best. I'll call you tomorrow."

Letty went into her house. Millie was waiting for her by the door, tail wagging. Letty sank onto the couch. Millie joined her.

CHAPTER 19

Letty spent the next day at her office trying to catch up with phone calls, emails, and paperwork. She was exhausted and elated at the same time. The rescue of the three young women gave her a great sense of satisfaction, but more than that was the sense of relief. She knew what was in store for the three if they had not been rescued. Chong Ma had made clear that he had abandoned his plan to sell them. In the end, he had expressed no hesitation in putting a bullet through each young woman's head. Letty only wished now that she could find the Chinese girls who had been sold into sex slavery by Lyle and the triad gang in earlier years.

Victoria stayed at Letty's house that first night. Zhou came forward and slipped the jade amulet necklace into Victoria's hand. She smiled. "This was a gift from my grandmother. Guan Yin was supposed to keep me safe."

"And she did," said Jade.

"Yes, after some struggles, Guan Yin will see me home safely." Victoria turned to Esperanza and put the amulet necklace around Esperanza's neck. Esperanza smiled broadly and touched the jade amulet with her fingertips.

"Gracías," she said.

"Please tell Esperanza that I value knowing her," Victoria said, "and I hope to see her again. Please tell her that if she ever comes to Hong Kong, she and her angel will be my guests." Jade translated into Spanish.

Although Letty knew quite well that the young woman came from an affluent and influential Hong Kong family accustomed to elegant surroundings, Victoria gratefully accepted a place on Letty's couch. A representative of the Chinese Consulate in Los Angeles arrived early the next morning and took Victoria away, but only after a rather lengthy conversation with Zhou. The Consulate staffers would watch over her until she could be returned to her father in Hong Kong. One of them would accompany Victoria on her long flight home.

Eduardo and Esperanza didn't even wait until morning to return to the reservation. Eduardo took Letty into the kitchen where they could speak privately.

"We don't feel safe here in town, especially since Esperanza is undocumented. One traffic stop and she could be jailed and deported. I figure we'll be a lot less noticeable to the authorities out there on the reservation, and that means we'll be safer. I have to figure out what to do now."

"What do you mean?"

"I know this will seem crazy to you, but I'm planning on marrying Esperanza. I know what you're going to say. I'm really young, and she's even younger, and I've only known her a week. But that week was the best week of my life. I have this feeling that I was supposed to find her. Don't laugh, Letty. You know the old stories about Ban the Coyote? I think he led me to Esperanza."

"I won't laugh. Ban makes as much or more sense as anything I've ever heard. But it's not just how long you've known Esperanza. You'll have to support her. It's not like she can just go get a job. She's here illegally. She'll have to deal with ICE. If you are married, she can apply for an immigration visa. But she's not supposed to be living here even if she's married to you until she gets that visa. That will take time." The thought passed Letty's mind that Zhou and Jade would have to deal with the immigration issue, too.

"I know. I know. I can't help but worry. I think I'll probably seek out some legal advice on the visa so we do everything legally. Also it's time for me to get serious about making a living. I could get a job at the casino, and the Nation is hiring now. I saw jobs listed on the website for bus drivers and maintenance workers. Also, I was looking at the Tohono O'odham Community College classes. I could get training in a skill. I could become an electrician or a plumber and make a decent living. Actually Uncle Mando and I had a conversation once about bringing more solar energy to the reservation. I feel like I have some options.

"Yes, you do have options, Little Brother. Where will you live?"

"We'll live with Hu'ul. She's getting really old now, and she needs more help. She deserves a rest. Esperanza won't have to be alone when I'm working, and she can learn our ways from our grandmother. I know Hu'ul will love her, and she will love Hu'ul."

"Sounds like you have a plan. If you need help with tuition or an immigration lawyer or getting a more reliable vehicle to get to and from your job, I've got some extra cash these days. My client Mrs. Baird made that possible. If you need it, let me know."

"Thank you, Letty," Eduardo paused. "You know I can't remember much about my dad. We were pretty young when he died in that car wreck. Our mom …well, you know how she is. Hu'ul took us in and gave us a home and lots of love. Uncle Mando became a sort of dad to us and helped out a lot. And you, Letty. I want to thank you for being the world's best big sister and for helping us in the many ways you've helped us. Most of all, I want to thank you from the bottom of my heart for finding my Esperanza."

Tears came to Letty's eyes. "Thanks, Eduardo. Or should I start you calling Angelito?"

"Of course!"

They both laughed.

Zhou and Jade decided to go back to Jade's house. Victoria and Jade hugged each other with tears in their eyes.

"I say the same to you. You are my welcomed guest when you come to Hong Kong." Then Victoria whispered in Jade's ear. "I will come to your wedding." Jade smiled broadly and glanced at Zhou. Jade and Victoria laughed softly.

Will and Clarice decided to spend the night at Clarice's apartment "to give you some space, Big Sister," Will said. Letty couldn't help but laugh at that. Those two were so young and so obviously hormonal. She wondered how that first peck on the cheek from Clarice had transformed so quickly into "we can't keep our hands off each other." Then she remembered a week of rest and recreation that she and Chava spent together in Qatar. Most of the week had been spent in the hotel bed. She hoped that Clarice would make Will happy and help him stay on the right track. He had a soft heart and Letty feared it could be easily broken. And he was so easily distracted. Letty wanted him to study and do well in school. She hoped Clarice would help in that endeavor.

After everyone left, Letty was alone in her house for the first time in a long time. Not really alone. Millie was there on the couch again, waiting for her.

Letty sighed.

"It's okay, Millie. I bought that couch at Goodwill. No sense in being so protective of it. You are more important than the couch, right?"

Millie wagged her tail.

The next day around mid-afternoon Letty received a call at her office from the attorney Jessica Cameron.

"Whoo-hoo, Girlfriend," Jessica was clearly elated. "Those papers Zhou and Jade found are a real gold mine."

"Really? What have you found?"

"I put one of my paralegals on this immediately to study and decipher the numbers. You were right, Letty. The first group is made up of bank routing and account numbers. Preliminary findings suggest that several of these accounts are owned by Mr. Lyle and a couple of them by an unknown person with a Chinese name. We don't know yet who he is."

"The second set of numbers is indeed a listing of forms used in the purchase of guns. Looks like Mr. Lyle had quite a network going. He directly purchased some himself, and it appears that he arranged for the purchase through other individuals. His wife's name is listed as a gun buyer. His father, who lives in a facility for Alzheimer patients, purchased several guns. Obviously that was Lyle, too. Other names on the list will probably turn out to be people that Lyle paid to purchase guns for him, then he transferred ownership to himself. We suspect that the gun found at the crime scene will have the same registration number as one of the guns on the list. It will likely be one that was purchased by someone in Lyle's network of buyers. From what I know about Lyle so far, he strikes me as far greedier than intelligent. If we can prove that he shot and killed his wife with a gun that was purchased by one of his buyers, then he's a real dumbass."

"Anyway, when we saw what we had, we immediately requested that the court clerk issue subpoena forms so we can get subpoenas to take a much closer look at all these bank accounts and gun purchases. There seems to be one gun vendor in particular in north Tucson that sold Lyle a lot of guns. We want to see his records. Also Detective García has obtained a search warrant and will be looking at the Lyle home as well."

Jessica Cameron paused for full effect.

"And you'll be glad to know that José Gomez will be released from jail this afternoon. They just don't have enough evidence to keep him, especially in light of recent developments. Mrs. Baird asked me to convey her gratitude and tell you that she will be sending you a bonus for your hard work."

"That's good news, both about Gomez and a bonus!"

"Also, Letty, I've been looking for some time now for a private investigator to work with our firm on a regular basis. I'd like you to be that investigator. You did a stellar job on this investigation. Would you be interested?"

"Sure, if it means a steady stream of jobs. However, I'd like a break for a while from dealing with Chinese gangsters and their guns and their hatchets."

"I think we can give you a break from the triad gang. I have other cases for you, maybe not so exciting, but safer. So let's stay in touch."

Letty locked up her office and went home. All the loose ends with her family seemed to be tied up now. She wasn't so sure about Zhou and Jade. Letty stretched out on her couch and was immediately joined by an affectionate dog determined to lick her face.

"Okay, Millie. Let's take a nap now. We deserve it. And stop with the licking already!"

* * *

Zhou spent much of the day interacting with the Chinese Consulate staffer who had shown up to take Victoria home, and with other Consulate staffers by phone. He also had a phone call with his boss Yang in Beijing, and with his colleague Jean-Pierre Laurent at Interpol in Paris, France. Zhou took Jade to the doctor just to be safe. Jade's doctor pronounced her basically sound but suffering from bruises, a black eye, rope burns, and slight dehydration. He recommended liquids and rest.

Evening came and Jade cooked dinner for Zhou. He protested, saying that he would take her to a restaurant, but she refused.

"I like cooking for you, Zhou. And you like to eat my cooking.

"I do. Especially I like those baritas."

"You mean burritos?" Jade's smile had returned in full force.

After dinner Jade washed the dishes, then she leaned back against the kitchen counter. Zhou sat at her kitchen table.

"Zhou, what happens now?"

"I must return to China. My boss says I have to report."

"I don't want you to go."

Zhou fell silent.

"When will you leave?"

"Tomorrow."

Jade gasped. "Tomorrow? So soon?"

He nodded, frowning.

"Zhou," Jade's voice was small and on the edge of pleading. "Please don't go."

"I don't want to go. I want to stay with you," he said.

"Then do. Stay with me."

Zhou looked at her. Jade was beautiful and sweet and kind. She was everything he ever wanted. His greatest desire was to spend the rest of his life with her. He couldn't find the words to tell her how he felt. His heart was too full.

"Zhou, please." She looked at him with tear-filled eyes. "I'm afraid. If you go, I'm afraid I'll never see you again. Please don't go."

Zhou stood and stepped toward her. He grabbed her shoulders and pulled her roughly to him. He kissed Jade long and deeply, and she responded with her own pent-up ardor.

Holding her close, Zhou picked her up in his arms and carried Jade to her bedroom.

CHAPTER 20

THE months that followed the conclusion of Letty's investigation went fast. She had plenty of work. Lawyer Cameron turned out to be a reliable connection with some interesting cases. Letty liked working with her because of her no-nonsense approach. So far, the cases mostly involved white-collar crimes with a focus on fraud and stolen funds. No one had shot at her or threatened to kill her in six months, and for that, Letty was glad.

The triad smuggling business had imploded, thanks to Letty and Zhou's investigation and action. The Border Patrol and cooperating Mexican authorities found that the weapons smuggled across the border were divided evenly between the Sinaloa Cartel and the triad gang. The Chinese moved the guns to the port of Guaymas and shipped them to China, where they were sold for astronomical sums. Everyone involved believed that it would just be a matter of time before a new criminal gang would decide that purchasing guns in the U.S. and moving them across the southern border was a great idea. Vigilance continued.

When confronted with the fact that items from his personal laundry had gun residue on them, Fred Lyle broke during a police investigation interview. He admitted that he had shot and killed his wife. He blamed her for everything. She was selfish and demanding and expected to be taken care of like a princess, he whined. Yet when his business fell apart and he tried to generate income from another source, she couldn't accept the illegal nature of what he was doing. She threatened to go to the authorities and tell them that he was smuggling weapons. He couldn't allow her to destroy him like that. He would go to prison, and she would continue her life as before. So he decided to take advantage of the conflict between his son and José Gomez to blame the shooting on Gomez.

With his father in prison, and his mother dead, Travis Lyle was sent to live with a relative in North Dakota where he could finish high school. Letty laughed when she heard that. Travis had exploited young Chinese peasant girls for his sexual pleasure, and he had paid no price for his perfidy. So to go from sunny, 75-degree winter days in the Sonoran Desert to surviving a windy and freezing cold winter in the northern plains was small justice but better than nothing.

Letty's nights had become more tolerable. The violent dreams of exploding IEDs were fewer now. Those sudden, stabbing memories of Chava seemed to come less frequently, although Letty firmly believed that she would never get over his death. Often now when she remembered his face, Chava was smiling. It was a relief, and at the same time, a little sad. Letty didn't want to forget him. She wanted to honor his life and their love always. But she had to admit to herself that she was grateful for even the smallest respite from that pain she had carried for years.

What Letty didn't take into account was all the attention that the Chinese gangsters and the Lyle case would bring. The media were all over her for a few days. Newspaper and television outlets were fascinated that Chinese gangsters had been operating in southern Arizona. They wanted all the juicy details. Letty had to close her office for a couple of weeks just to avoid the media. She stopped giving interviews because she was saying the same thing over and over again, and she couldn't get any work done. She became worried that having her photo widely distributed was going to disrupt her work as a private investigator. After all, would she ever be able to do a stakeout again if everyone in southern Arizona recognized her on sight? So Letty went off the grid for a while until some new face and a new event grabbed the media's attention.

The upside was that Valdez Investigations became the go-to agency in Tucson. Between her new popularity and her relationship with Jessica Cameron, she had plenty of work. Letty considered bringing on a new employee but was unsure that she could afford to do that. A part-timer, a temporary worker available only for certain jobs would be better. If only Zhou were here, Letty thought. If only Zhou were here.

Meanwhile, she called on Marv Iverson about once a month. He grumbled as expected, but he always took the jobs she offered him. He actually liked stakeouts so she gave those to him. Despite his constant reminders to her that he was retired, Marv always seemed quite agreeable to taking on an occasional job with Valdez Investigations.

Eduardo found a job and started classes at the community college. Esperanza was welcomed warmly into the Ramone and Antone families. She found a once-a-week cleaning job on the reservation. She discovered the thrill of American thrift shops. She had already sent some money and used clothing back to her family. Progress was being made toward a wedding. She was still an undocumented worker, though, and it was going to take time and effort to make her legal. Eduardo was working on it.

Clarice and Will seemed more sober in their love than Letty ever imagined they would be. They bicycled together, they studied together, and they cooked together. They did everything together, and they seemed very happy. Much to Letty's approval, Will's grades went up.

And then there was Facebook and Millie. Will had posted a picture of himself with Millie several months before the Chinese triad incident. Someone copied the photo later and added the news story about how Millie had saved Will's life. The story went viral. Thousands of shares on Facebook, then on the Internet, made Millie the world's most famous pit bull. A new generation of female pit bull puppies received the name "Millie."

One day in May, Will received an email from someone named Jack Gilliam. He said he was from El Paso, Texas. He claimed he was a trainer of K-9 dogs used by law enforcement in Texas and nearby states. Many were drug sniffers, but they had other duties as well. Gilliam said he recognized "his" dog Ruby from the Facebook posts.

Will asked Letty what he should do. He was obviously worried.

Letty thought about it for a while, and then said to Will, "It would be nice to find out where Millie came from. So I'll check him out to see if he's legitimate. But he can't have Millie. She's ours."

Letty discovered that Gilliam was indeed a dog trainer, and a well-respected one in high demand among police and sheriff's departments in Texas, Arizona, and New Mexico. After more email exchanges, Gilliam was invited to visit Tucson to see Millie himself.

Gilliam said he was delivering a dog to Phoenix and asked if he could stop by on his way home. When he arrived, Letty let him in the side gate into the back yard. Gilliam saw Millie sitting next to Will on the back steps.

"Oh, man. She's had a rough time," Gilliam said when he first saw Millie.

"Yep. We think she was used as bait in a dog-fighting ring. I found her half-dead dumped out in the desert."

Millie lifted her head at the sound of his voice, and her ears went up. She ran to Gilliam happily wagging her tail.

"Hello, Ruby, girl." Gilliam rubbed her ears.

He then proceeded to tell Letty and Will all about "Ruby." Originally she was meant to be a companion for his children. She came to live with them when she was only three months old. The children were supposed to train "Ruby" in the proper ways of a family dog – basic commands like sit and stay, don't pee in the house, don't pester the family cat, that kind of thing. But Ruby had other ideas. She liked following Gilliam into the training area on his property where he worked with those dogs, mainly German Shepherds, that were destined to become police dogs.

"I guess she was really paying attention. I regularly teach dogs to attack on command when we see a criminal with a raised arm holding a gun. I guess Ruby…I mean Millie…learned how to do that just from watching the other dogs. She's pretty smart. But now you need to train her properly to attack only on command. Otherwise, she might think someone raising their hand for some innocent reason is attacking her alpha."

After a pleasant conversation, Gilliam announced that it was time for him to get home.

"You're not going to try to take Millie, are you?" Will asked.

"Nah. Of course not. She's your dog now. She's bonded to you. And obviously she thinks it's her job to keep you safe. Ruby is Millie now, and she lives in Tucson. You'll be glad to know that I got my kids another dog…actually two more since then. So they are not wanting for canine companionship."

"Thank you, Mr. Gilliam. We're really glad to know about Millie's first home and how she learned to protect those she loves. After all, Millie saved my brother's life," Letty added.

* * *

Everything seemed to have a happy ending except for Zhou and Jade. After that last night of emotional sharing and erotic pleasure, Zhou left very early the next morning.

Jade found a note on her kitchen table. "I will call you. I will return soon. I promise. Wo ai ni."

Through her tears, Jade looked up the words "wo ai ni" in an Internet Chinese-English dictionary. The words meant, "I love you."

Zhou called from the San Francisco airport. He called Jade again twenty hours later from Hong Kong. In the following three days, he called her twice more from Hong Kong. He also called Letty from Hong Kong.

"Letty, I have two topics to discuss with you. First, I learned that there is a …you call it ravine? Yes, a ravine about half a kilometer from the abandoned drop-off house on the reservation. I was told that triad gang dropped dead bodies there."

"What dead bodies?"

"When they were smuggling girls for sex trafficking, sometimes one would die. Her body was left there. I wonder if the bones of Carlos might be found there also."

"I will check it out."

"Second, I met with Ting and convinced her to leave us alone and to give up her smuggling efforts in southern Arizona. She wasn't happy with me. She said she lost a lot of money because of me. She told me that she had no interest in complying with my wishes. I was able to convince her otherwise."

"How on earth did you do that, Zhou?"

"What is it you say from that film? 'I make her an offer she cannot refuse.'"

"*The Godfather*," Letty said. "I look forward to hearing the details of your offer when you come home."

Zhou liked hearing the word "home" coming from Miss Letty.

* * *

After her call with Zhou, Letty asked Eduardo and Mando to see if they could find the ravine with human remains. The two men invited Mando's friend Johnny Chiago on his day off. The three went out on horseback. They found the ravine fairly quickly. Eduardo climbed down into the narrow top of the ravine.

"Uncle Mando, there are a lot of bones here. What should I do?"

Shadow Wolf Chiago responded, "Bring them up in groups that seem to be close together. We'll bag them."

Eduardo brought up several bones that he found in a small pile.

"Definitely human," said Chiago, shaking his head. "This one is a human femur – a leg bone. And this is from an arm."

"Looks like the coyotes had a go at them," Eduardo said.

"Yep, they gotta feed their pups," Chiago shrugged.

By this time, Mando was down in the ravine, too.

"Oh, my god. I found a skull," he called up to Chiago.

"Not surprised." This wasn't Chiago's first time to find bodies in the desert.

There were the remains of several human bodies, more than expected. The first estimates were six humans. They were taken to Pima County's medical examiner. After acquiring DNA samples, one set of bones was identified as belonging to Carlos Lopez. Another set belonged to Kevin Kwok, the Tucson businessman who had disappeared around the same time as Carlos. In the end, they found bones from seven bodies. One of the others was a male, probably one of the cartel smugglers or maybe an innocent migrant who got caught up in the smugglers' web. The other bones were from the bodies of four female Asians, the medical examiner told them. The ME said they were between the ages of fifteen and twenty-two.

Letty found it difficult to tell Jade about the bones, but she knew it had to be done. Jade cried and thanked Letty. "Now I can let him go," she said.

One month later, a memorial service was held for Carlos Lopez at San Augustine Cathedral. Hundreds of people came. Carlos was born and grew up in Tucson, and he had many friends and acquaintances. It seemed that they all came to his memorial, and several had kind words to say about him. Jade sat in stoic silence. A black lace mantilla covered her face. She thought about the years that she'd lived with Carlos. And she thought about a Chinese cop named Zhou who had disappeared just like Carlos had disappeared. Jade was numb with grief.

* * *

A few days after his call to Letty from Hong Kong telling her about the bodies in the ravine, Zhou called Jade from Nanjing. He told her he that he was visiting his family. He told her that he saw his mother, his aunties and uncles, and nieces and nephews.

A week later, his call came from Beijing. Zhou said he was going to see his boss and go over the details of the case.

Then the calls stopped.

Nothing.

Jade was frantic. She didn't know who to call. She tried his number again and again.

Nothing.

Then Letty got involved and tried to help. She contacted Interpol and after several conversations with Interpol agents, she eventually was connected with Zhou's colleague Jean-Pierre Laurent.

"Yes, I am aware of your working relationship with our colleague Mr. Zhou. You will not be happy to learn that he is in jail. That is why he is not calling."

"Jail! What the hell? Why is he in jail?"

"His superior Mr. Yang claims that Zhou is corrupt and that Zhou received bribes from a Hong Kong triad gang."

"That is *not* true!" Letty said vehemently. "Zhou is a very honest and ethical person."

"I agree with you, Mademoiselle Valdez. All of us here at Interpol agree with you. We are attempting now to prove Zhou's innocence. Mr. Wong is helping us. He is the father of Victoria, the girl you rescued. We have some preliminary proof that it was Mr. Yang who was, in fact, taking the bribes. He put Zhou in jail to cover up his own illegal activities."

"Zhou told me that there was a problem in Beijing that he needed to take care of."

"Yes, he told us that someone in the Ministry in Beijing was tipping off the triad gang. Rest assured, Mademoiselle Valdez. We are on Zhou's side. We have a high value for him and his efforts. We are working on this every day. I feel confident that we will achieve Zhou's release."

Letty told Jade this, and she burst into tears.

"At least you know he's not dead, and he didn't abandon you." Letty said.

"Yes," said Jade. "Thank you, Letty. At least he's not dead."

Weeks passed.

For Jade's sake, Letty called Monsieur Laurent every couple of weeks. He spoke English well but with a heavy French accent.

"We are making progress," Laurent told Letty. "We recently acquired surveillance video of a Hong Kong Red Pole giving Yang a packet of money."

"Was that Chong Ma?"

"Yes, Chong Ma. You know Chong Ma?"

"Yes. He's not a nice guy."

"No, not nice."

Another week passed and Laurent reported that Yang had been arrested. No word on Zhou.

June came to Tucson. This was the hottest and driest time of the year. June turned into July. The monsoon arrived, and afternoon storms, sometimes with heavy rain, became frequent. Then August came.

Zhou arrived in Tucson on an early flight from San Francisco by way of Shanghai. It was a sunny summer morning, but the humidity promised the possibility of a late afternoon monsoon storm.

He wanted to call ahead, but the time never seemed right. Also he didn't know what to say. He didn't want to promise Jade an arrival that might never come. After all, he could be picked up again by the authorities at any time. And he wasn't one hundred percent sure that the triad gang wouldn't try something, too, despite his agreement with Ting. He decided to wait until he was sure he would actually be able to arrive in Tucson again. When he was released from prison, he took the bullet train to Shanghai Pudong Airport rather than hang around Beijing even an hour longer. The flight across the Pacific Ocean from Shanghai to San Francisco seemed to last a lifetime. All he could think of was Jade and seeing her again.

Zhou rented a car at the Tucson airport and drove to Jade's house. The idea of surprising her was both thrilling and a little scary. He didn't know if she would still feel toward him as he felt toward her. But she wasn't home.

Then Zhou remembered. Sunday morning. Ladies' coffee. He found Maggie's home and knocked on the door.

Maggie answered. When she saw Zhou, her hand touched her heart. "Oh! How wonderful!" she whispered to him conspiratorially. "Leave your bags here and come with me."

Zhou stowed his luggage near the door and followed her into the dining room. Seated around the table were Seri, Letty, and his beloved Jade.

Letty grinned. "You! It's about time for you to show up!"

Jade cried out, "Zhou! Zhou!"

She struggled to her feet. Her pregnant belly was prominent at eight, almost nine months.

Zhou looked at her in amazement. His eyebrows went up and his mouth opened. "What happen to you?"

"*You* are what happened to me! Remember our last night together?" Jade said with a brilliant smile. "Come and meet your child. He – or she – is kicking right this minute."

Jade moved toward him and fell into his welcoming arms.

"I am going to be a father!" Zhou couldn't talk after that. He held Jade, his face buried in her red curls. Tears were in his eyes.

Zhou held Jade for a moment, then he pushed her away far enough to look into her eyes.

"You will marry me." This was a statement, not a question.

"Sí, Jefe!" Jade laughed.

"Yes, I am the Boss. You will marry me."

Zhou kissed Jade soundly, and the three women at the dining table cheered.

* * *

Letty went home soon after. Millie greeted her enthusiastically, and they sat together on the couch.

"Millie, I have some news for you. Will and Clarice want to move in with us in a couple of weeks. Her lease is about up. I think they think they are going to take care of me." She shook her head. "What do you think about that? Do you think I need someone to take care of me?"

Millie cocked her head. Her ears were up. Letty was speaking to her.

"Also I've been thinking maybe you need a friend to hang out with. When I'm working, you're here all by yourself. I bet you get lonely. So maybe a Lab or a Golden Retriever or a retired racing Greyhound? Or another pit bull? What do you think? Maybe we should just go to the animal shelter and bring home one of those Sonoran Purebreds. You know the Sonoran Purebred? Those are the dogs that are a little of this and a little of that – the Heinz 57 kind. Yeah, that's what we need – a Sonoran Purebred."

Millie wagged her tail and licked Letty's hand.

Thank you from the Author:

Hello Reader! Thank you for reading *Desert Jade,* the first Letty Valdez Mystery. I hope you enjoyed accompanying Letty on her private investigations. Please leave a review of this book on your favorite place to buy books (Amazon, Apple, Barnes and Noble, Kobo, etc.) and at Bookbub and Goodreads. By leaving a review for others to read, you can make it much easier for mystery readers everywhere to find this book. Thank you so much. Please sign up for my monthly newsletter all about art, books, and the natural world at

www.cjshane.com/contactnewsletter.html

C.J. Shane is a writer and visual artist based in Tucson, Arizona, U.S.A. She is the author of eight nonfiction books. Her first work of fiction, *Desert Jade: A Letty Valdez Mystery* (2017) was a finalist for Best Thriller Suspense, New Mexico-Arizona Book Awards. *Dragon's Revenge: A Letty Valdez Mystery* (2018) was a finalist for Best Mystery and Best Multicultural Work, NM-AZ Book Awards. The third Letty Valdez Mystery, *Daemon Waters*, was published late in 2019. Her first Cat Miranda Mystery, *Kissed* (2020), was a finalist for Best Cozy Mystery, NM-AZ Book Awards, 2021. See more at www.cjshane.com/writings.html